Dressed for Death
IN BURGUNDY

ALSO BY SUSAN C. SHEA

Love & Death in Burgundy

Dressed for Death IN BURGUNDY

SUSAN C. SHEA

MINOTAUR BOOKS
NEW YORK

DRESSED FOR DEATH IN BURGUNDY. Copyright © 2018 by Susan C. Shea. All rights reserved. Printed in the United States of America. For information, address St. Martin's Press, 175 Fifth Avenue, New York, N.Y. 10010.

www.minotaurbooks.com

Designed by Omar Chapa

The Library of Congress Cataloging-in-Publication Data is available upon request.

ISBN 978-1-250-11302-3 (hardcover)
ISBN 978-1-250-11303-0 (ebook)

Our books may be purchased in bulk for promotional, educational, or business use. Please contact your local bookseller or the Macmillan Corporate and Premium Sales Department at 1-800-221-7945, extension 5442, or by email at MacmillanSpecialMarkets@macmillan.com.

First Edition: May 2018

10 9 8 7 6 5 4 3 2 1

For my sons, Brian and Steve, and for Tim, always

ACKNOWLEDGMENTS

The Musée du Costume in Avallon is an extraordinary delight in the real town of Avallon. The charming woman who runs it looks something like my Mme Roussel, but that is not her name and there has not been a murder in her curated town house. However, the rest of Avallon has been reconfigured for my storytelling purposes. Avallon does indeed have a chocolate shop, a small store that specializes in local cheeses, a wonderful butcher/charcuterie, and a café at the crossroads. But I would not for a minute charge their proprietors with being the gossips that my invented characters are. My thanks again to early readers Steve Shea and Ceil Cleveland, to Isabelle Breton, to the great team— my editor, Alicia, and Shailyn, Sarah, and Susannah—at St. Martin's, to Kimberley Cameron, for setting me on this path, and to my dear friend Alice, for exploring Avallon with me in the dead of winter.

Dressed
for
Death
IN BURGUNDY

CHAPTER 1

Emile's new dog was barking again, a deep, rhythmic complaint that had as much to do with the presence of Katherine Goff's yellow cat sitting beyond the fence as it did with the dog's desire to be inside, away from the biting December wind. Katherine and Michael's two dogs, from the safety of their old stone house across the narrow road in Reigny-sur-Canne, deep in the Yonne region of Burgundy, had begun to bark in sympathy.

Katherine walked far enough along the driveway to confirm her suspicions. "Come on, cat," Katherine said, clapping her gloved hands together, "it's freezing out here, it's beginning to rain, and I have to get going."

Having considered the options, or perhaps because it was bored, the yellow cat allowed itself to be persuaded, and by the time Katherine opened the kitchen door, it was waiting, tail held high, to resume its rightful place on the threadbare upholstered chair in the corner of the living room.

For the thousandth time, Katherine argued in her head with Emile, the retired dentist, amateur musician, and *pétanque* court arbiter of Reigny-sur-Canne about his decision to buy a Rottweiler after last summer's tragedy. "Emile, it wasn't a crime wave."

But Emile was having none of it. He spoke darkly of the state of the world, of *la belle France,* of "foreigners," and of the resident family of thieves in Reigny, the latter a delicate topic with Katherine, who had taken one nimble-fingered member of the family under her wing. No, the only protection was to get a guard dog, one that would be loyal to his master's possessions and property at all times. Hence the arrival of a large, handsome, but unfriendly animal who had frightened Fideaux and Gracey so completely that they now resisted walking on leashes to the town's communal garbage collection corner since it went past Emile's newly fenced yard.

Katherine exchanged her damp parka for a heavier coat, pulled a knitted wool hat over her hair, and gave herself points for having taken the dogs out for a walk before it began to drizzle. She doled out breakfast for the animals, grabbed a slightly worn leather tote bag that had been a shockingly expensive twenty euros at a late-summer *vide-grenier,* one of the scores of town-wide attic sales that dotted the region in good weather, and locked the door as she left.

The old Citroën sat in the driveway but it was low on gas and she was afraid she'd run out if she used any getting over to Château de Bellegarde before she made it to the pump in Noyers. She couldn't seem to manage some of the simplest things on her own, embarrassing for a fifty-five-year-old woman who had been living in Los Angeles until three years ago. Fortunately, it was only a five-minute walk. Equally fortunate, her husband would be home in a few days from his recording session in Memphis. Just thinking about Michael finally getting his second chance at a music career warmed Katherine's heart, if not her nose.

December was not her favorite month, she thought as she walked up the road to the château. Christmas, still a few weeks away, was typically a pallid affair in Reigny, a few sad decorations in the run-down church, Mass offered by a different visiting priest every year, some ragged carol singing by the aged attendees, and then everyone off to a potluck dinner at the *mairie*. Spring was a distant hope, icy winds more likely than sun, and until Michael earned some royalties or concert tour money, the Goffs' budget would be too pinched for any expensive holiday presents.

She was still thinking about her husband's changing fortunes when a voice hailed her. "I say, Katherine, wait up," Pippa Hathaway called, holding the hood of a thin parka tight around her throat. Pippa was in her late twenties, close to six feet tall, and walked like a scarecrow, uncoordinated limbs moving to different rhythms. The spiky red hair that poked out around her head, as a result of a punk-inspired haircut she had recently gotten, only exaggerated the effect. Katherine wondered about the haircut. Was Pippa turning over a new leaf, coming out of her mousy shell?

"It's bloody freezing, excuse my French, and my anorak is leaking cold air. Whew." Pippa's loud exhale was visible in the air in front of her, but her voice was cheerful in spite of what looked like frozen fingers. "I left the good one at my dad's in London because I knew I was going home for the holidays, right? And wouldn't you know it's this cold and I'm frigid? Oh, by the bye, I ran into that darling Marie, the cheese maker. She's about to drop her baby, by the looks of her, and her mother's come down from Paris for good this time to wait for the birth."

The notion of new life in this hamlet of old people was cheering everyone up, although Katherine wondered what they expected a baby to do for Reigny's collective well-being. "I'll drop by and see if I can help, maybe do some basic *supermarché* shopping. I hope she lasts until after my lunch. You're coming, aren't you?"

"Righto. Wouldn't miss it. Shall I bring something, scones maybe?"

"Thanks, but I have a real French meal planned."

"Just as well. I'm a poor excuse as a baker, scones being about the best thing I do."

Katherine had thought hard before inviting a handful of women for a cozy get-together. The lunch she had hosted last July had turned into a memorable disaster. This time, she had spoken to Yves Saverin, the bookseller whose party crashing had launched the drama, and told him under no circumstances should he come even as far as the gate. And since it was winter, the party would be inside rather than under the pear tree, and she would put Gracey and Fideaux on guard duty at the door if necessary. The only man allowed to cross the threshold might be Marie's doting husband, he of the large ears, who seemed to believe his heavily pregnant wife could not move even a few feet without his watchful presence. Joseph and his Mary, she thought, and smiled.

"Where are you headed, Pippa? Why not stay in that snug little house in this rotten weather? I expect your cats are curled up inside."

"Oh, lord, yes, all six. Did you know I wound up with

another? A poor little stray that one of mine must have invited home. Black as the Death Star, all skin and bones he was, but he's fine now, eats like a bloody horse. As you say, curled up in front of the heater with the others. But I have to get into Avallon to pick up my car. I was hoping I might catch a ride with you if you're taking tourists in the Bellegarde van today?"

In fact, Katherine was headed to Château de Bellegarde to do precisely that. In the wake of her father's death and her assumption of his many business ventures, Adele's daughter Sophie Bellegarde had started a small tour company. It specialized, she explained to Katherine, in local sights, including her family's historic castle and the small shops in Chablis, Noyers-sur-Serein, or Avallon for wine tasting and to shop and stroll the cobbled streets. When Katherine suggested adding a stop at an art gallery, Sophie had brushed the suggestion aside. "They don't want serious things like that. Too expensive." Why, Katherine wondered silently, thinking of her stack of unsold paintings racked in the storage shed, was art relegated to the status less necessary than almost everything else money could buy?

A local farmer had been hired to drive the little van Sophie purchased for the tours, but he was in Spain for the month of December, and Sophie had begged Katherine to do the driving. "It's only this trip in December and they're all Americans. Even if he were here, Louis's English is fractured at best."

It was out of the question that her mother, Adele Bellegarde, elderly, a terrible driver, and a new widow in the bargain, could be pressed into service. Yves had resumed his role as Sophie's beau now that a wealthy American heiress had permanently removed herself from Reigny's small society. But he'd told Sophie he was much too busy to drive her tourists, although Katherine rarely saw a car outside the shop he kept in the downstairs of his house.

Since Katherine was at loose ends this week, she didn't mind some distraction. It was too cold to paint in her studio, there was no one to cook for with Michael in the States, and she had run through the stack of English-language books she had bought on her last trip to Paris. Chatting with the American visitors would be a break from trying to translate the lightning-speed French that everyone around her spoke.

Everyone but Pippa, of course. Pippa had no French beyond *baguette* and *fromage* and "please" and "good morning," which hadn't stopped her from coming up with a plot and characters for a murder mystery set in Reigny. To Katherine's surprise, Pippa had received some encouragement from a potential publisher in England, and she told anyone who would listen that she was on the verge of a major book deal. All she had to do now, she explained, was write the book.

"As long as there's room in the van, I'm sure Sophie won't mind if you hitch a ride. You know Jeannette has an after-school job at the museum, mostly sweeping up? She'll be riding back with one of the tour participants and me. Sophie's always been fine with that. What's wrong with your Fiat?"

"The brakes were making so much noise that people on the street were staring whenever I came to a stop," Pippa said. "Of course, people look at the car anyway. Do you know, I don't think I've seen another little Fiat around here?"

"It is distinctive," Katherine said. "It may be the color. Cherry red stands out." She didn't add that another reason might be the breathtaking speeds at which Pippa drove along the little roads that linked one small village to another and her habit of racing up to an intersection and slamming on the brakes so suddenly that people winced and feared for the cars or pedestrians in front of her. "What's all this you're carrying?"

"Oh, nothing, but you know I'm working on my novel and I have to be ready to photograph anything that might inspire me, and to take notes if someone says something important." Pippa held up a camera case and the kind of notebook students used in school.

"Do you expect to find much research material in Avallon today?" Katherine didn't know precisely how novel writing worked and wasn't entirely sure Pippa did either.

"One never knows, does one?" Pippa said, and the tone of her voice suggested this was a source of pleasure. "Will Michael be back in time for Christmas?"

"He'll be home in a week, plenty of time. Things have gone so much better than I dared hope. The album's close to being finished and there's a hint of a tour that he—we, actually—never thought could happen. And he's pleased with the songs he and Betty Lou have recorded with musicians J.B. rounded up in Memphis. She's fortunate to have a record producer for a husband. So, all is good."

"Brilliant."

Michael had hinted at more wonderful news when they talked last, but he wouldn't say what it was. Katherine was daydreaming about enough money to take the high-speed TGV train to Paris with enough left for a night or two at a hotel near the d'Orsay museum, or perhaps in the 5th arrondissement below the Panthéon somewhere. They had reached the tall doors of Château de Bellegarde before she returned to the moment and pulled on the thick rope that rang door chimes, a mash-up of old and new technologies that never ceased to irritate her. The oldest parts of the château had been in service before Joan of Arc had visited the area to drum up troops. Door chimes indeed!

They had to wait a few minutes for Adele's part-time housekeeper to open the door. Adele had introduced her new employee as the wife of a man who used to farm wheat and rapeseed but now sold tractors and other farming equipment, having sold his farmland to a distant relative. Now that she was alone much of the time, Adele Bellegarde had acceded to her daughter's insistence that she bring in someone to help with things.

"*Bonjour, Madame,*" Katherine said. The greeting was standard in France, she had come to realize soon after she and Michael moved to Reigny to begin their new life. You said it at the *boulangerie* when it was your turn to order bread. You said it at the stalls of every flea market venue. You began every conversation at the pharmacy and the art supply store and the charcuterie with a quick "good day" greeting to the woman or man in front of you.

"*Bonjour,* Madame Goff," the woman replied and waved at the foyer behind her as she stepped aside.

"Hullo," said Pippa in her friendliest voice as they came in and shut the door. "I don't think we've met. I'm Pippa Hathaway. I live on rue Benoit at the edge of town. Perhaps you've seen my cats?"

The housekeeper raised her eyebrows fractionally but said nothing.

"Madame lives in the other village in the commune," Katherine said to Pippa, then reverted to French to ask if Sophie was in the château.

"*Oui, Madame.* She is giving the tour and she asks if you can wait for her in the drawing room." The housekeeper turned and walked through a dark, cavernous space at least two stories high, its stone walls framing a polished wood staircase that branched in two at the landing. A pair of badly faded tapestries behind the stairs plus hand-pounded iron sconces set into the walls gave off enough atmosphere to impress tourists. It was a cold space even in summer. Today, it was so unwelcoming that Katherine all but trotted through it and into a more comfortable room furnished with upholstered furniture arranged in groups and a huge fireplace in which logs crackled and gave off a reassuring amount of heat.

"Brrr," said Pippa, heading over to stand in front of the fireplace, rubbing her chapped hands. "I wonder how they heat this place."

CHAPTER 2

"By burning twenty-euro bills," came a voice from the doorway. Sophie Bellegarde greeted both women with kisses, although Pippa, who had never gotten used to the traditional gesture, bobbed the wrong way and barely avoided knocking heads. The woman who smiled at her guests was so different from the timid creature of six months ago that Katherine was still getting used to her. As the successor to her late father's Paris firm, and with his instinct for deal making, she radiated confidence. And as the fiancée of Yves, she had found her proper place in Reigny-sur-Canne at last. Even Madame Pomfort, the stern arbiter of Reigny's social order, approved. Sophie had put on weight, Katherine noticed, which was a good thing, since she had been unappealingly waiflike before, and she now sported a sophisticated haircut and bright lipstick.

"The guests are freshening up and Madame Caron is giving them espresso and madeleines in the kitchen. After that, they'll be ready to go into Avallon. I can't thank you enough, Katherine, for helping out." Sophie always spoke English to Katherine, and her language skills were impeccable. "Next spring, I shall have figured out a permanent solution, but you are an angel."

"It will be pleasant to meet some Americans. Not that I'm not happy in Reigny," Katherine added quickly.

"I understand," Sophie said. "If I had moved to Cleveland, let's say, I'm sure I'd be lonesome for a bit of Burgundy."

Cleveland, Katherine thought. Yves must have been complaining about his former girlfriend's habit of comparing all things French against the high standards of her own American hometown.

"How is Adele?" she said. "I see her so rarely in this cold weather. She isn't walking, or at least not when I'm being dragged around by my two unruly beasts."

"She doesn't get out much, I'm afraid. Without my father's dog to make walks necessary, she stays in her sitting room a lot. Come over and visit, please." Sophie undoubtedly felt pulled in several directions now that she was effectively the head of the household, the owner of her late father's Paris business, and the fiancée of a man who needed a great deal of attention.

The medieval hall began to echo with excited voices and Sophie handed over the car keys before heading out, with Katherine and Pippa in her wake. She clapped her hands to get the attention of a small group of older people who were milling around putting on coats and hats and winding long scarves around their necks. In excellent English, she introduced Katherine as a prominent American artist who would be giving them a personal introduction to the lovely town of Avallon. "You are fortunate, ladies and gentlemen. Not only is Katherine well known as a painter"—Katherine thought that was a wildly overstated description of her situation after one exhibition in Burgundy—"but her husband is a famous rock-and-roll musician currently on tour in the United States." Another gross overstatement, Katherine observed silently, and one she'd probably have to back away from before this day was over. For now, she smiled modestly at the little cries of enthusiasm and jingled the car keys in the air. "And now," Sophie finished, "the van is ready. I hope you enjoy the balance of your visit to Burgundy. *Au revoir* and bon voyage."

In the courtyard, Katherine asked them to introduce themselves as they boarded. Mr. and Mrs. Harris from Pittsburgh, Ronnie and Marge from Houston, Della from "just about everywhere, I was in the army," and Catheryn from California.

"Lovely, another Katherine," Pippa said as she climbed into the front passenger seat and took her camera strap from around her neck.

"Spelled strangely, though. Call me Cat," the sixtyish woman said. "Everyone does."

"I'm Pippa Hathaway. I'm a Brit." She thrust a long arm back between the front seats to shake hands. "I'm currently writing a book about a murder in Reigny-sur-Canne."

Instantly, she had everyone's attention. "There was a murder here? Was it recent?" someone said. Katherine shot Pippa a look and the young writer hesitated.

"Well, yes and no, I mean, what I'm writing is fiction, you know? I'm a mystery writer." Her pleasure was slightly diminished when she had to admit to her audience that she wasn't quite published, so, no, they probably hadn't heard of her, well, undoubtedly hadn't. Yet.

The spotlight dimmed and Cat, the single woman traveler who had been to France before, stepped into the silence. "What's on the schedule for our visit to Avallon? Is it quiet in the winter, unlike Paris?"

Safely out of Reigny's narrow streets, Katherine was able to turn her attention to the group and begin talking about the market town. "No quieter in December than any other time of year. Avallon was a medieval town, a busy place by the twelfth century, although there are hints of Roman occupiers long before that. The old church supposedly contains remnants of its eleventh-century beginnings. If the weather were more hospitable, you could prowl the streets and see the old fortifications. But today, I think, is an inside day."

"You can say that again," said Ronnie from Houston, a small man with a permanently sunburned face and impressively large dentures.

His wife giggled. "Ronnie's always cold unless he's on a fishing boat in the Gulf of Mexico."

"I told her coming to France in the dead of winter didn't make a bit of sense, but you know women. Always have the last word. Say, what's this about your husband being a rocker?"

Katherine was torn. Michael was beginning a tour in a few months. Would he and Betty Lou be going to Houston? Should she try to promote ticket sales? Whatever she might have said was forgotten as the van left the cultivated fields behind and entered Avallon and her other passengers began to pepper her with questions. "Bellegarde's not the only castle around here, right? I think I saw a bigger one in a travel book."

"I think you might mean Chastellux," Katherine said,

slowing down as she neared the center of town where the traffic was dense. "It's a gorgeous property and, like Bellegarde, the owner is dedicated to restoring it." She didn't add that Sophie had no intention of adding a rival castle to the tour schedule.

Her destination was a closed-in, cobbled street with stingy parking places carved out of the space between the narrow sidewalk and the road. Katherine explained that she would walk with them to a few shops, then they would all go to the Musée du Costume, the entrance to which was behind the courtyard wall next to them. Mr. Harris, an older man who hadn't said a word during the trip, made a rumbling sound that might have been an objection to the museum visit, but Mrs. Harris was firm in her approval and said so. The other women were too, and Ronnie wasn't about to swim against the tide. Instead he asked if they could visit a bakery, a patisserie, he corrected himself. He'd love a croissant.

"Definitely. And you may see some other pastries that tempt you beyond the basic croissant—perhaps a penguin."

With that as a teaser, Katherine was able to get them moving, and, with umbrellas raised and sneakers squelching through what had become a steady downpour, Katherine led her troops onto the street of shops.

The chocolatier's shop was a little jewel box and smelled wonderful. Katherine's mouth watered. Next to her five o'clock glass of wine, there wasn't anything she looked forward to as much as French chocolate. Many of the boxes were wrapped in shiny gold paper or deep blue paper with wide silver bows for Christmas giving. Clear plastic boxes held perfect little rows of chocolates shaped like snails, and hard candies were offered in sparkling transparent cellophane wrappers, decorated with silver and gold streamers.

The ceiling lights splayed cleverly on all this shiny material and on a three-foot pyramid of blue boxes on the countertop behind which the store's owner stood, rubbing his hands together as the small crowd of tourists filed into his shop. It was a quiet day and his regular customers had not begun their own holiday shopping. The Bellegarde tour looked likely to fill a small hole in his retail budget, and he nodded his thanks to Katherine, whom he knew by sight if not by name. Katherine came in rarely, fancy chocolate being beyond her regular budget. But Michael had a weakness for the chocolate caramel molded snails, a specialty of this candy maker and, as she explained to her charges, a popular symbol of Burgundy.

"Oh, that's it," Mr. Harris said. "I told my wife I'd been seeing snails everywhere from the bakery to the cheese place. Remember, honey?"

His wife didn't respond. She didn't even appear to have heard him. Her attention was focused on a display of square chocolate tiles with what appeared to be minute paintings of flowers on their tops. "Stencils?" she said, squinting into the case.

"Ah, no, Madame," the salesperson said. "These are so ingenious, *non*? Little sheets that I must lay delicately onto the chocolate when it is not so hot but not completely cooled. *Très délicat*, you understand?"

Twenty minutes later, the small group swept out of the shop, buzzing about their purchases and the people back home who would receive authentic French treats for Christmas.

After sniffing the chocolate atmosphere, Katherine wasn't in the mood for sausages or pâté or the ham that the charcuterie case at the butcher shop displayed, but she ushered the Americans into the small store because she had a feeling they would be tongue-tied without a translator. They had been fine in the chocolatier's, mostly because he spoke charmingly accented English, but partly because the displays made it easy to point to little boxes while waving their credit cards and smiling.

Monsieur Sabine was not happy to see the small crowd of foreigners, doubtless understanding that the most they'd purchase would be bits they could snack on later since they didn't, presumably, have kitchens at their disposal with which to cook his stuffed pork roasts and elegant cuts of beef. His customary smile was forced and he merely nodded at Katherine as he said, *"Bonjour, Madame"* and wiped his hands on his spotless apron. Perhaps he had a cold. He didn't look well, pale with rheumy eyes.

The tourists had questions and asked Katherine to explain everything from the contents of the sausages to the origins of the ham. They wanted to know what was special and when Katherine translated, the butcher pointed to a delicate pink, rolled roast that had pride of place in the glass case and pronounced it *"feuilleté au lapin et piece de bœuf."*

"I think that means rabbit rolled inside beef," Katherine said, laughing. "It sounds more elegant in French, but I assure you it will be fantastic if it comes from Monsieur's charcuterie."

For a few minutes, Katherine indulged them. But when a stout woman carrying a woven basket entered and signaled her impatience, and the shop owner began looking nervously from the real shopper to Katherine and back, she suggested they head back to the museum. One of the men insisted on buying some ham slices and the woman with the same name as Katherine's pointed at a luscious pâté and ordered *"cent grams"* before Katherine could ask if she really meant to buy such a large slab. The store owner wrapped up the purchases hurriedly, gave them to the buyers without a smile, and seemed relieved when the last of the group passed through the narrow door and onto the street.

"He didn't seem happy for the business," Cat said to Katherine, tucking her package into the tote bag she had slung over her shoulder.

"I noticed his wife wasn't there. He was probably feeling overwhelmed. When the two of them are in the shop, it's a friendly place. He teases her and she laughs and shakes her head as she measures out the meats."

"The pâté looked and smelled too good to pass up. I expect I'll gorge myself on it in my hotel room tonight, assuming the traffic into Paris isn't too bad. I've tried my hand at making it but mine tastes alarmingly like meatloaf." Cat laughed.

Nibbling cone-shaped "penguin" cakes covered with black and white icing that suggested their name, the tourists made their way back to the van, all except Cat, who had promised to be right along. Her French was better than the others' and she was determined to find out how real pâtés were made. "I'm sure I can get tips from the butcher, even if he is a little snappish."

"I think it's his wife who makes it, but go ahead and ask. He'll be flattered," Katherine said.

The rain had tapered off and Katherine instructed

everyone to leave their wet umbrellas in the van. "I won't spoil the surprise of this hidden gem. The curator speaks not a word of English, so I'll translate what you don't understand. But it's really the objects themselves that are the story, that and the fact that Madame Roussel is at least ninety years old and has collected and maintained this treasure trove with the help of her daughters for decades. Wait 'til you see what she has to show us."

Katherine rang the bell. The visitors heard the sound of locks being undone, one after the other, and then the tall wooden door swung open and a woman barely five feet tall stood beaming at them, her white hair gathered loosely into a bun that made her seem at least an inch taller than she was.

"*Entrez, entrez, mesdames et monsieurs,*" she called cheerfully in a thin, sweet voice, bobbing her head and gesturing with one arm. The hall they crowded into was so small that the visitors hardly had room to turn around. The miniscule floor space was hemmed in by chunky nineteenth-century chairs, and the curator, with repeated cries of "*Excusez-moi, s'il vous plaît,*" darted around the space, squeezing herself behind a rickety table where she dispensed hand-stamped tickets in return for a few euros each. Having accomplished that, she set about fixing all the locks again.

"Ladies and gentlemen, please meet Madame Roussel. Madame, we expect one more person, who should be coming in a moment," Katherine said. Laughing gaily, the woman undid her work at the door, clapped her hands together, and began her explanation of the collection in rapid-fire French that Katherine tried gamely to keep up with. Fifty years of collecting, mostly French but all European, silks and brocades not made anymore, don't overlook the furniture, and the objects in the glass cases. . . .

She paused for breath and looked her question at Katherine, who said, "I don't know what has kept our other guest. Perhaps you could take these people up to the next floor and I'll keep watch at the door?"

"*Pas possible, Madame,*" the curator said, shrugging her shoulders. She couldn't leave the front door unlocked, she never did that.

Just then, there was a knock, and to Katherine's relief, Cat entered, shaking her umbrella off in the doorway without seeing Madame's distressed expression at the puddle it threatened in her hallway. Order finally restored, the curator tended to her locks, waved her arms over her head like a soldier leading a charge, and headed up steep stairs at the end of the dark hallway, pointing out objects on the walls and in the cases at every step.

"Did you say she collected all this herself?" Mrs. Harris said. "It's unbelievable. Look—an ebony fan, and those blue kidskin gloves, and look at that silk mask. I wonder what it was for?"

Katherine was already stammering as she tried to translate the women's questions and Madame's answers, which were far too detailed for her to follow exactly. When the group reached the first room on the *premier étage,* which in France meant the second floor, there were gasps of delight. A salon, its tall windows covered in heavy red velvet drapes, lit with a chandelier that dripped crystals, and decorated with ornate furniture, was the backdrop for seven or eight mannequins posed languidly on chairs, leaning against the mantel, and standing with arms delicately raised to show off their evening wear. "The time between the world wars," Madame explained in French. Twinkling at the group and standing on tiptoe, she sang out, *"Vive les américains,"* and clasped her hands over her heart before turning to Katherine and beginning a rapid-fire explanation of why Americans would always be heroes to her after the Second World War. The tour group caught on and accepted the compliments as their due, Mr. Harris even bowing slightly.

GI's with their chocolate bars and chewing gum probably had no idea of the impact they were making in 1945, Katherine thought, but the unadulterated happiness on Mme Roussel's face was genuine, and touching. *Vive les* GI's, Katherine thought.

Checking her watch, she realized this museum visit was going to take longer than Sophie's schedule allowed. It would be straight to the train station for most of them, although Cat would be transported back to Bellegarde, where she had left her car.

The men in the group brought up the rear as the tour progressed and spent their time in murmured conversation about the American stock market. The women were completely taken by the silver-backed hairbrushes and spider-seamed stockings, the silhouette cutouts of hoop-skirted dancers, and the tableaus in each room.

Katherine had stopped to look at a delicate pair of earrings in a case opposite the final tableau in a room on the museum's top floor and didn't hear the first sounds that signaled something out of place. It sounded like more exclamations of pleasure. But when Madame began screaming in her high-pitched voice, and Mrs. Harris started saying, "Oh lord, oh lord, oh lord," Katherine spun around and pushed to the velvet rope that cordoned off the display.

Madame was holding on to the rope's stanchion, and turned to give Katherine a wild stare. Her face was a pale greenish gray and she looked like she was going to faint, so Katherine grabbed her in a hug. The woman turned and buried herself in Katherine's arms, beginning to sob.

Mr. Harris and Ronnie had both caught up, the stock market forgotten as their wives kept moaning.

"What the hell?" Ronnie said, trying to see what was causing the upset.

"Probably a rat," Mr. Harris whispered in Katherine's ear as he moved up next to her at the entrance to the room.

But it wasn't. By this time, Katherine had picked out the reason for the women's horror. Draped along the chaise longue at the center of the room, one arm over the back of the sofa and another resting on the floor, was a woman in costume. The costume, Katherine noted with one part of her brain, wasn't fitting her as well as their outfits did the rest of the mannequins. And no wonder. It was no blandly smiling figurine that looked glassily out at the visitors. It was a middle-aged woman and she was very, very dead.

CHAPTER 3

Pippa's first thought when she finally understood what was in front of her was that she was twenty-nine and had never seen a dead body. Well, her mum's in the coffin, of course, but she had been made pretty, hadn't she, by then?

She didn't have more time to think because the sweet old lady who ran the museum slid to the floor, looking quite pasty. Katherine dropped to her knees trying to revive her, and the noisy Americans were all yelling at once.

"Pippa," Katherine called over the confusion. "Run to the gendarmerie for help."

"Yes, yes," she began, and ran a few steps toward the stairs before wheeling back. "I don't speak French. What will I say?" She hated never knowing how to talk to people, but couldn't seem to keep the French words in her head, much less the order of the words. And now, she'd be too panicky. She looked around for help. The two older women were sitting on chairs as far away from the open doorway to the room as possible and neither looked good. The suntanned man was patting his wife on the back but she seemed to be in shock. The other American man was standing in the middle of the space poking at his cell phone. Good. Maybe he was calling the police. But he swore loudly.

"I can't get any reception in here even when I turn on roaming, at never mind the cost," he said to anyone who would listen. No one but herself was listening, she could have told him.

The American woman nicknamed Cat went over to Katherine, who was looking, Pippa had to say, as if she might scream at any second, and bent down to take the hand of the old woman. "I'm a nurse, let me tend to her while you take care of this mob."

Katherine nodded and started to hoist herself off her knees when Pippa saw the old French woman reach out a hand and tug on Katherine's arm, pulling her close. Pippa saw the woman whisper something to Katherine, and saw the surprise on her friend's face. Katherine's head turned sharply to look back at the corpse on the sofa. Then, she nodded gravely at the museum curator, who was struggling to sit up.

"What did she say?" Pippa asked when Katherine came over to her. Katherine whispered, "She recognized Mme Sabine. You know? The butcher's wife?"

"I'm going to get the police. You stay here. No one can go into the room, understand? And no one can leave."

Katherine really could be a bit bossy at times. Of course Pippa knew the rules of a crime scene, for heaven's sake. She had been doing a bit of research in the form of reading British crime fiction recently. "Absolutely. You can count on me," she said. The thought flashed through her head that it was a shame she had left the camera and her notebook in the van. She wasn't altogether sure the police would let her take pictures of the scene of the crime later. Perhaps if she explained that she was a professional of sorts too?

Katherine was speaking in a loud voice, telling the tourists that she would be right back, and then she disappeared down the stairs.

"Right then," Pippa said in what she hoped was a suitably official voice, "please stay where you are and try not to touch—I say, sir, no one's allowed in there."

The man with the phone had his hand out to move the velvet rope stanchion when Cat's voice cut in. "Do. Not. Touch. That," she said in a voice so forceful that everyone stopped talking and looked at her, and then at the man. He backed away. Bully for her, but he might have paid attention to me in the first place, Pippa thought.

She steeled herself to peek again at the woman on the chaise. She reminded herself she had a duty to her craft to take in what details she could. Actually, it was rather repellant. The woman's body was turned away from the doorway, but Pippa could still see part of the purple face and one bulging eye that seemed to be looking at a small stuffed dog nearby in the scene. Her tongue, which Pippa hadn't noticed before, was not entirely in her mouth and was too ugly to look at for long. Quickly, she moved her gaze to the woman's body, which was mostly covered by a black, beaded dress wrinkled below her knees. The arms were bare, and her hand that touched the floor was curled. Other than that, she looked, well, almost normal. Not that, precisely, Pippa chided herself. Not really normal. More as though she had been resting comfortably when something quite un-normal surprised her.

In the distance, the doorbell rang twice and even though

the sound was softened up here by all the stone and velvet, Madame heard it and struggled to her feet. Voices from below made their way faintly up the stairwell and then they all heard footsteps jogging up. Katherine climbed into view, huffing a little from the exertion. "Thank goodness. That was Jeannette at the door, coming for her after-school job. I've sent her for the police. *Vous pouvez rester calme, Madame.*"

Katherine had spoken in English except for that last bit, but whatever it was, Madame clearly didn't agree. She rattled out a stream of what Pippa guessed were questions aimed at Katherine in a ragged, breathy voice. Pippa thought the woman should be grateful, but she only looked upset. She made a move to go to the stairs, but Katherine stepped in front of her.

"She's weak," the American nurse said to Katherine. "Her pulse is slow, and I think she might faint again. We need to get her water at least."

"I'll take her downstairs. Jeannette told me her apartment is behind the foyer. Right now," Katherine said, "she's upset because I've left the front door unlocked. But the police have to be able to come in."

"Wait a minute," the man with the phone said. "How do you know the killer isn't still in the building? He might sneak out while we're hanging around up here."

Pippa hadn't thought of that. As someone with some experience of crime, she ought to volunteer to go down and guard the door. But what if the American tourist was right and there was a killer in the museum with them and what if he rushed the door while she was trying to guard it?

"That's a terrible possibility, but I suppose you're right," Katherine said. "Let's all go down."

Pippa's thoughts were a jumble. Think how it might look if there was a killer and she and this stranger foiled his getaway? Wouldn't that do a lot for her reputation in the crime world? She took a deep breath. "I'll go with him."

CHAPTER 4

The next half hour was pure hell. Katherine had a headache. She had to be polite to six unhappy Americans who wanted everything translated and who were worried about missed trains and meals. At least a dozen policemen crammed the space, first the municipal police, whose offices were around the corner, then the gendarmerie, who had been called as soon as the local cops realized this wasn't a heart attack. They kept coming and going, running up- and downstairs, calling loudly to each other and demanding answers at every turn. By now, everyone was crowded in the small entrance hall except Mme Roussel, who was semireclining on a daybed in her little apartment, the door to the foyer open so she could see and hear everything and could keep a sharp eye on the open door to the museum.

Pippa was no help. She had apparently decided it was her job to photograph everything and everyone, to the irritation of a score of busy people. She pleaded with Katherine to explain her unusual status as a crime author to the captain in charge. Katherine had refused, telling Pippa it wasn't the right time, and she knew she had sounded short. But, really.

The only truly useful person was Jeannette, who fetched the Avallon police quickly, and who was now out buying madeleines for the visitors with euros Katherine had pressed on her. The gendarmes let the teenager leave because she had come in after the body was discovered and had never been up the stairs. But the rest of the group had to stay, a uniformed gendarme said, until they could get statements from all of them. He was obviously unhappy to hear they were—all but Cat—determined to catch the evening train to Paris.

The sun had set, this being December, and the museum was chilly. Cat had insisted Madame wrap herself in a blanket and turn on the space heater that appeared to be the only source of warmth in her apartment, indeed the whole building. She was sipping a tisane that Cat had made for her and loaded with sugar, and there was some color returning to her wizened apple cheeks, but she still looked distraught.

Katherine pulled aside the head policeman, a captain in the gendarmerie, early on to tell him what Madame had whispered to her, that she recognized the dead woman as the wife of Avallon's butcher, the very man Katherine had led her visitors in to see earlier in the day. The captain had spent some time after that with Madame, presumably to ask her how the woman got into the museum. Katherine wondered that also, especially since the proprietor was so obsessive about keeping the big wooden entrance door locked. But she couldn't very well ask, not now at least.

"No one wants to help more than me," Mrs. Harris said, coming up to Katherine. "But my husband and I have to get to the train. I don't mind the extra expense of a taxi, even though transportation to the train was part of the cost." She gave Katherine a look that suggested this was an act of grace that should be commented on, but Katherine's head ached too much to do more than nod unhappily. "We cannot stay any longer. Please tell these policemen we must leave. When Mr. Harris attempted to do that, the young officer appeared not to understand a word he said." This time, her raised eyebrows suggested that she, for one, didn't believe that for a minute.

Overhearing her, which was unavoidable since they were in such close proximity, Ronnie with the tan chimed in. "That goes for us too. We have one night in Gay Paree and then it's home to Houston. No time to lose."

It might not be relevant to the occasion, but Katherine could have smacked Ronnie from Houston with the cookie Jeannette had thrust in her hand for the stupid "Paree" business. Jeannette was already soaking up every ounce of the drama, no doubt ready to entertain her school friends tomorrow, and Katherine bit her tongue. Calling forth the last bit of energy she had, she waylaid the captain, not the same man as the lieutenant who had investigated the unfortunate death in Reigny last year, alas, and begged him for a moment's time.

"Sir, these people are worried about missing the train and their flights home. I can assure you they were in Mme Sophie Bellegarde's charge from early this morning when they got off the train in Montbard until I brought them here, and that they were in a group Madame was leading on the tour of the *musée* when we came upon the unfortunate scene. They're not from here and they've never been in

Avallon before. Do you think you could release them and let me drive them to the train station? I could do that and come right back if you wish to talk with me again."

He looked at her, at the ceiling, and again at her. Mrs. Harris's voice rose in complaint from a few feet away and Ronnie chimed in. Mr. Harris edged up to Katherine and began, "Listen, Mrs. Goff, you need to tell this guy—"

"*Oui, Madame*," barked Captain Borde. "*Vous les prenez.*" And as Harris made to continue, the policeman turned abruptly, spoke to one of his underlings, and vanished up the staircase.

The younger cop asked Katherine to have everyone write down addresses and contact information and give the information to Katherine before they got on the train. So grateful she could have wept, she told him she absolutely guaranteed it and would be back in a short while.

"You're good to go," she called out. "The man in charge said I can take you now." With rushed words of relief, the Americans hurried out of the house and through the courtyard gate. Katherine, right behind them, was startled to find a small group of people clustered there in the dark, coats pulled closely around their necks, curiosity bathing their faces.

A couple of teenage boys were using the van's fender to try and climb the courtyard wall. "Vamoose," she said, unlocking the van's doors and wondering if the word was French. The boys jumped away. They may not have known the word, but they understood the tone of her voice. They looked to be Jeannette's age and Katherine wondered if her young neighbor had already begun to tell her version of the crime story. Fleetingly, she wondered if fifteen-year-old

Jeannette and Pippa might be natural allies in creating tall tales from real-life beginnings. Pippa would have to learn some French first, unless Jeannette wanted to practice more English.

There were four or five official-looking vehicles parked half on and half off the street at the *musée* when she got back, having safely dispatched everyone except Cat, who had stayed with Madame. Wrapped up to her nose in a puffy quilted jacket, Jeannette was hunched on a hard-back chair inside the front door watching the action and chewing on a fingernail. A policewoman was crouched down next to the daybed in Madame's little living room and Madame, who appeared to have recovered, was talking to her rapidly, with many arm gestures, and bright pink cheeks.

"I found a little brandy after she drank the tea, and it seems to have helped tremendously," Cat said in Katherine's ear, the hint of a smile in her voice. "Her pulse is normal and I think she'll be fine now. A few minutes ago, a woman showed up who said she was a daughter. She's gone out to buy some food."

The teenager looked up from her observation post and said something about being hungry, and having to get home to feed her brothers.

"Jeannette, *chérie,* I'll check with the captain and see if we're all free to go now. It looks as though they have plenty to do, judging by all the vans in the street." A few minutes later, Katherine had permission and, having given someone the details on where to find her, the women filed to the door of the curator's room to say their goodbyes. Mme Roussel asked Jeannette if she could come tomorrow to dust and clean up and the girl shrugged her agreement. Katherine felt a little tug of wistfulness for the ebullient girl-child of six months ago who had skipped and pranced her way into Katherine's life with a child's openness. Adolescence had tapped her with its wand and Jeannette had learned that speaking more than was necessary to adults was not cool. Still, she was a good girl, and Katherine could still draw a laugh and a confidence from her when they were alone.

Pippa, deposited at the auto repair shop, waved Katherine off with a nod to say her car was ready. The van was warm once the heater and fan got going, and Cat seemed to want to chat in the coziness of the dark car. "Was the dead woman someone you recognized?" she said, looking over at Katherine.

"I'm afraid her condition was so shocking I didn't notice at first, but Madame told me and I guess it isn't a secret. She was Bertholde Sabine, the wife of the sausage maker we visited this afternoon."

"No," Cat said. "I'm shocked. He was so distracted when I tried to talk about his pâtés. He said his wife was the one who made them, but that she was in Beaune today. Do you think the police have told him by now?"

"*Mais oui,*" came Jeannette's voice from the backseat. "I was going to the patisserie for you, Katherine, and I saw two flics looking in his window." Katherine translated for Cat, who explained her French was pretty good. "The shop lights were off, so they went to the next door and knocked. I think the Sabines live upstairs and the police were going to his apartment to find him." Jeannette leaned forward to share this detail, and Katherine saw the animation in her face. Nothing like a scandal to entertain people.

"Odd that M. Sabine thought she was away." Katherine was thinking out loud. "It's a pretty long trip. Unless she drove, he would have taken her to the train. Makes me wonder how long she had been in that room." Involuntarily, Katherine shuddered at the remembered sight. Fortunately, Jeannette had not been allowed upstairs or the child would have had nightmares. Or, Katherine thought, glancing at the girl, who was now sitting forward, all ears, maybe she would have had a gruesome story with which to impress the other teens in school tomorrow.

Cat said, "I keep coming back to the impossibility of sneaking a body past that sweet old guardian of the door. But if that wasn't possible, was the butcher's wife alive when she entered, and how did her killer escape?"

Jeannette jumped into the conversation again, speaking in English. "But, yes, she was there for the special lunch."

"What lunch, *ma chérie*?" said Katherine, while Cat looked over her shoulder at the girl.

"Madame told me about it because she said I would have to take out the extra bag to the *poubelle* today."

"The trash bin," Katherine added for Cat's benefit.

Jeannette seemed to realize the tale might lose some color if Katherine had to translate and switched to English. "The ladies who take care of the church, you understand, making it nice for Mass and the special lectures, they come—came—to the museum for a special tour to see the rosaries and the jewelry with pictures of Mary."

"I had no idea there was such a collection," Katherine said.

"It is on the highest floor, at the end of the hallway, in an old *vitrine*, uh, a case with the glass?"

"The highest floor? That's where the woman was found," Cat said to Katherine.

"*Oui, exactement,*" Jeannette said, forgetting her English and wiggling even closer to the front seats.

Katherine thought the girl was becoming entirely too thrilled by the idea of murder and was glad when she reached Jean's untidy courtyard on the main street in Reigny-sur-Canne, filled, as always, with used tires, farm implements, and curious dogs only partly visible in the light from a bare bulb over the front door. "Okay, Jeannette, here you are. If your father needs any explanation as to why you're late, let me know. Thank you for being such a help today."

The girl reached over the seats for the traditional double kiss on the cheeks before jumping out with her school backpack and opening the gate. The dogs began to bark, one of her brothers opened the house door and began shouting something to her, and Jeannette was already calling out that she had a scary experience to tell them all about before Katherine pulled away with a shake of her head and a chuckle. "That girl somehow makes her life work, although I'm never sure how she does it," she said to Cat as she steered up to the big driveway, the gravel circle, and the tourist's parked car near the entrance to Château de Bellegarde. "Thank you for helping with Madame. I hope the rest of your stay in France is much calmer and happier than today."

Cat opened the door, smiled at Katherine, but hesitated a moment before saying, "I'm still a bit puzzled. M. Sabine was not himself before any of us knew his wife had been strangled. Oh, she was strangled," she said as Katherine looked at her in surprise. "The poor woman showed all the signs of having been choked to death somehow, while she was in that position, or close to it. I'm a nurse, remember? The police are sure to have seen it immediately. I wonder if the Sabines had had an argument, or something, before. And I wonder how long she was in Beaune."

Cat shrugged. "Maybe I've seen too many TV shows, but it would be interesting to know if the police are interviewing the husband." She leaned back into the car. "Thank you, Katherine. It's been a pleasure to meet you. I'm only sorry I didn't get to see your studio, or hear about that fascinating husband of yours. I'm half-tempted to come back after my meetings in Paris. *Au revoir,* then." She closed the door and a moment later had started her car, turned on the headlights, and wound her way down the driveway.

The château was dark except for the back wing where Katherine suspected Adele and Sophie were eating dinner. She decided to drive the van back to her house and return it tomorrow. Her headache had abated somewhat, but her mind was a tangle of random thoughts, not the least of which were related to what Cat had said. Over a large glass of red wine, or maybe two glasses since she surely deserved them today, and the leftover *lapin moutarde,* stewed rabbit with mustard sauce that was frozen from when she had cooked it for Michael, she would try to make sense of all the suspicions floating around in her head.

CHAPTER 5

The next day, the local newspaper had the story. After dropping the van off at the château, Katherine walked downhill to the little café, Reigny's only commercial enterprise, for an Americano and a peek at the newspaper. There was no doubt: Bertholde Sabine, the butcher's wife, was dead, apparently strangled and hidden in the costume museum. René, her husband, had collapsed when the gendarmes informed him and was said to be prostrate with grief. Neighbors and customers said they were a close and loving couple married almost forty years, and had plans to retire to the south of France in a few years. "Ç'est tragique," more than one person said to the paper's reporter. Poor M. Sabine was much to be pitied. His wife was also his partner in the shop, and the more practical among his neighbors wondered if he would be able to keep the business going without her.

Sophie Bellegarde, with Yves trailing behind her, came in as Katherine finished reading, unwinding thick scarves as the warmth of the café hit them. Sophie immediately came over to Katherine's table and looked down at her.

"Good morning, Katherine. You must be in a state of shock. I cannot believe what I read. But tell me," she said, dropping into a chair opposite Katherine, "how did my tourists take it? Did they make their trains all right?"

"Yes, although not by much. Luckily the Avallon station had one late train and I was able to help the Harrises arrange a transfer to get to Paris, although much later than they had planned."

"You are wonderful. *Merci beaucoup.* I wonder," the younger woman said, looking appraisingly at the artist, "could I ask you one more favor?"

Katherine looked down at her cup so Sophie wouldn't see the slight flare of irritation. The new Sophie was so much bolder than the scared rabbit of six months ago, and there were times Katherine rather wished for the former person.

"They are Americans, and I hardly know how to talk with them so that they will be—how do I say it?—settled, and will speak well of Tour Bellegarde to their friends. If you wrote them a note, I feel confident you could make them realize how sorry we are at what happened." She looked inquiringly at Katherine, who knew she'd agree. She always said yes. It was part of her need to be liked, she realized, and to feel needed and, dammit, important, her Achilles' heel since childhood.

She gulped the last of her coffee, folded the paper back to the way she'd found it on the shelf, and said, "Tell me what you want me to say and I'll do my best. I'm sure they don't blame you though. How could they?"

"It was undoubtedly the highlight of their freezing day in our neighborhood," Yves said, having joined them with two little espresso cups, which he plunked down on the table without asking if they might join Katherine. "It's almost as cold inside my house as it is out of doors."

"That is because you never turn on the heaters, *chéri.*" Sophie looked at her fiancé with a combination of affection and mild annoyance.

"And that, my dear girl, is because I cannot afford heat. I am but a poor bookman stuck in a backward village where no one appreciates books."

"Then you must broaden your business. I have given you several good ideas already. I do not know why you resist."

There was an increase in the quality of annoyance in this exchange, Katherine noticed. She put down a euro and a fifty centimes piece and pushed her chair back. "I must stop by and see how Marie is getting along. She is due any day, you know? The visiting maternity nurses have been keeping a close eye on her, but that darling husband of hers is a nervous wreck."

"There's no cheese making at this time of year. The cows won't produce again for a few months. It's too cold for *pétanque* and he doesn't have anything to distract him," Yves said. "Poor guy."

"You could ask him to help you fix that rotting corner in the bookshop," Sophie said. "You really must get to it, Yves. There is a smell, you know?"

Yves upended his espresso cup to drain it and placed it back on the table with a small but meaningful thump. "I must go, ladies. So much to do, as my darling fiancée reminds me daily. I will see you"—he nodded at Sophie—"for dinner, my love. I may be slightly late." He kissed Katherine's cheeks and then Sophie's, and hurried out, winding his handsome new scarf twice around the neck of his tweed jacket.

"Yves is looking very debonair," Katherine said.

Sophie looked at Yves's retreating back as if calculating the relative truth of her friend's remark. "Perhaps," she said after a pause. "He is definitely improving now that he has stopped trying to fit in with that gauche American."

By whom you mean Penny, Katherine said, but not out loud. Penny of the Cleveland family money and sensibilities, whom you replaced in Yves's affections, or perhaps in his vision of his fortunes now that you have taken over your father's successful business empire. She reminded herself that she had vowed not to get caught up in other people's dramas ever again. Anyway, Penny was, according to her emails, happily settled in Rome. "It's fabulous here and I've met so many Americans. I'm seeing this handsome man, Sean, who teaches history at the Rome International School. He's writing a novel. You'd love him. You and Michael must come and visit."

As she walked toward Marie and Raoul's farmhouse, Katherine wondered if she and Michael would ever get to Rome. The dream of more money, enough to indulge in at least a few small luxuries, was entangled in her head with Michael's musical success, and Katherine scolded herself for those moments the financial possibilities overshadowed the artistic importance. It wasn't loyal and it wasn't loving. What if he and Betty Lou had great moments onstage—cheering audiences and wonderful reviews—and it didn't translate into sales of streaming songs or more tours? Would she be as thrilled for him? If not, she chided herself as she approached the cheese makers' door, then shame, shame on her. Michael deserved better.

Perhaps she had a frown on her face from her mental reproaches when the door opened, but the lovely woman who stood there looked momentarily taken aback before she recognized her visitor, and exclaimed her welcome, pulling Katherine in and closing the door.

"It is so cold today. *Bonjour,* Mme Goff, we are delighted to see you. Did you come to visit my daughter? Marie is sitting in the kitchen, where it is warmer. Raoul is in there too. Come, come." Marie's mother, Helene, was a professor in Paris. Marie and Raoul's baby would be the first grandchild and she was almost as excited as her son-in-law and a lot less nervous.

"Bonjour, Madame," the soon-to-be parents said in unison as Katherine came into the overly warm kitchen, pulling off her hat. Raoul jumped up to bring a chair from the kitchen table closer to the stove. She could hardly refuse the kindness but shrugged off her coat as quickly as possible. Marie struggled to get up, but Raoul murmured for her not to stir. He would get a coffee for Katherine.

"No, no," Katherine said. "I just came from the café. I wanted to see if you'll still be able to come to lunch? It's only a few women in the neighborhood—Madame Pomfort and Madame Robilier, of course, and Pippa, our English friend. Jeannette won't be there because it's a school day. Very informal, since we'll be crammed into my little house. But I know everyone wants to wish you well and to meet your mother."

Helene, Marie's mother, beamed her thanks. "This weather, it keeps us in too much and I cannot meet my children's neighbors as I should like to."

"How are you feeling, Marie?"

"She's tired when she stands and the nurse says the baby will come any day," Raoul answered before Marie could speak. He was so earnest that she had to smile, and his jug ears only enhanced the look of a puppy determined to please.

Marie looked at him with amusement before turning to grin at Katherine. Her eyes twinkled. "If Raoul could have this baby for me, he would. I keep telling him *ç'est normale*, but he does worry so. Even Maman can't convince him to go back to his work in the barn." She turned to Raoul and said in mock seriousness, "You must think of the baby cows, *chéri*. How will those *mamans* feel if their little ones are born in a dirty stall with leaks from the roof, eh?"

Katherine remembered that she had seen a calf in the frosted pasture the other day, clearly newborn, its coat not yet licked and still stumbling. "I was worried, Raoul, that it might freeze."

He laughed. "Not at all, but I went looking since I knew she was in labor before dawn and she and the little one had a day in the barn. It's a little heifer. Maybe we'll give it the same name as the baby."

"No, no," Marie said quickly. "We don't yet know what we will do with it." She shivered and looked up at Katherine in appeal. "What if it must be slaughtered next year?"

"Oh, don't say that," Katherine said. "I can't reconcile my love of beef stew with the beautiful animals I walk past every day." She laughed, but felt her face color. Really, she was a silly woman, not like these sturdy farmers.

"That's how I'm feeling right now," Marie said, her mouth turned down, "probably because I'm pregnant."

Helene stepped in to change the topic. She explained that Marie really was due any day and so it was hard to make plans. "We had the visiting nurse, the lactation specialist, and the veterinarian for one of Marie's beautiful cows all in the same day." Her peals of laughter set the others off.

"Have you met Reigny's newest resident?" Katherine said. "I have invited her too, now that we've met formally. She's moved in part-time to take care of her grandfather, old M. Lacrois, who lives in the mustard-colored stucco house near the church. He's been failing for years, and Emile told me she's come to be with him in his last days."

"And to take over the house?" Helene said, still smiling. "That's the way, you know? A paid-for home in the country, no matter how modest, that can stay in the family for at least another generation."

"Like this one," Raoul said.

"Yes, *chéri*, but you paid your old uncle handsomely for it," Helene said soothingly, "and that helped him considerably. He was grateful that you stepped forward, and even more grateful that you and Marie wanted to keep the cattle and the farm."

"I've only met Lacrois's granddaughter once, briefly, but she's quite chic," Katherine said. "Her name is Josephine, with the same surname as her grandfather. I doubt she will want to revive the *tabac* that the old man operated in his house after the war. The women who've lived in Reigny forever tell me it was never much of a success and now the building's in bad repair. All that's left as a reminder of its commercial past is that faded sign on the side wall."

Marie, who had been listening while gently rubbing her immense belly, said, "Jeannette told me Mme Lacrois is from Beaune. Such a wealthy, tourist-centered place. I wonder what she can find to do in Reigny or why she'd be interested in taking over that old place."

"Maybe she will sell it after all," Katherine said, "or fix it up to let out during the summer as a *gîte*."

Marie nodded. "Jeannette, who can, you know, be quite candid, says the woman talks constantly about how lovely Beaune is and how shabby Reigny is. Jeannette does not like her much."

Marie's comment surprised Katherine. It was good, though, that the teenager was reaching out to someone a bit closer to her own age. Katherine had admitted after last summer's problems that she felt maternal toward Jeannette, but she wasn't sure how that should work, not having had children herself. Maybe she could teach the girl tap dancing, her secret vice. No, perhaps painting lessons would be more to the point. "Jeannette is the most opinionated person in this town—well, perhaps excepting Madame Pomfort—and a great gossip. Does she visit you, Marie?"

"Yes, I think she is curious about the baby making, you know. But she will be an excellent babysitter and I like her. She's a good girl underneath the posing."

"Yes, she is," Katherine said, pleased at Marie's understanding of the girl. Jeannette was dear to her, a motherless waif quickly growing into awkward teenager, but, as Marie said, a good girl.

Ten minutes later, Katherine reluctantly left the warmth of the cheese makers' house and walked back home. The dogs were sleeping in front of the cold hearth, the yellow cat had retreated upstairs to Katherine's unmade bed, and nothing in the refrigerator looked interesting for lunch. Briefly she considered practicing her tap dancing in front of the full-length mirror in her bedroom, but even that sounded dreary. If she weren't careful, she would fall into self-pity and a glass of wine in lieu of lunch. No, she would sketch for a new painting even if she couldn't work in the freezing studio. But first, she would make a fire. That would perk up the animals too. She missed Michael and would have called him except she couldn't ever figure out the time difference and it was probably the middle of the night in Memphis. How would she react when he was gone for much more than a week when the tour started? She'd think about that later. For right now, a crackling fire and perhaps a piece of the mushroom quiche she'd bought in Noyers.

CHAPTER 6

Pippa woke up while it was still dark. She was freezing underneath her pile of blankets. Most of the time, she managed to avoid feeling lonely, a spinster in the making. On a morning like this, though, it would be lovely to have someone to cuddle with. Even thick socks and the presence of a couple of cats nestled up close to her legs couldn't make up for December's damp cold, which seeped in the old window frames and through the stone outer walls. The wooden shutters didn't do much except make her cottage darker in the winter light.

Her father had warned her that the old heater in the house was dodgy. He had intended to fix it when he and Mum took up residence, before her cancer diagnosis and quick death. Now, he had no interest and she had no money. Maybe when she went home for Christmas she could hint at it, always assuming she could get his attention. Telly and take-out Punjabi food seemed to occupy all of his time now. He hadn't been terribly supportive on her visit in October when she told him she was writing a mystery novel. "Well, pet," he had said, looking up from an old BBC comedy to smile absently at her, "your mother always said you were a bright one."

Pippa had already shopped for Dad, tinned chocolate biscuits that were softer than the ones she'd grown up with in London, and the little chocolate snails every candy store in Burgundy featured. Snails were some kind of symbol here, or maybe a mascot, although she couldn't think of anything to be less proud of, much less to eat, smothered in garlic and oil. Disgusting buggers, snails, but the French had strange tastes, didn't they?

Take that sausage maker, the new widower she was going to investigate today. As she dished out cat food into a half dozen bowls and put the kettle on for tea, she remembered going into the shop several times after she first arrived in Burgundy. She had tried a few of his sausages and found most of them too strong tasting. Give her a good banger and mash any day. She wondered if he had poisoned his wife, the woman they found in the costume museum, with something disguised in the sausages.

She shivered, as much from the memory of what she'd seen as from the cold. The heater had begun to thump its news that warm air was fighting its way into the pipes. She opened the door and six furry bodies sauntered past her into the yard to spend the morning looking for a bit of sun on the rock wall and tracking the movements of everyone who walked, biked, or drove past this last house in the village.

Pippa looked speculatively at the feline squad before closing the door to keep such heat as there was inside. Their behavior reminded her that she needed to be watchful too, not only for her book research but to see if she could help solve this crime. The newspapers at home always reported that the police first suspected the husband or boyfriend when a woman was killed. She didn't know if the French thinking was the same, but that was a good enough place to start. Did Mme Sabine have a boyfriend? she wondered. Her recollection was of a slightly plump, middle-aged woman who seemed generally comfortable but maybe a bit prissy. Rather old to have a boyfriend, surely, and hardly the type to go raging off into an affair.

She had her car back now and could keep a bit of a watch on the butcher. Surely, if he had strangled his own wife, he would give it away, behave strangely, maybe have a breakdown or say something he shouldn't. She would go in to the shop and buy a couple of the plainest sausages or some pâté and strike up a conversation. Yes, she decided, buttering some toast and pouring a fresh cup of tea, that would be her plan for today. That and talking to Jeannette, who might have seen something while she was working at the museum, emptying the bins and dusting, something she didn't even realize was important but that she, Pippa, would understand was a clue.

It was a bit of luck that she met the teenager a half hour later coming out of the café, a bulky coat seeming to weigh her down, but her golden hair still floating around her head like a bright sun. She held a half-eaten brioche roll in one hand, a paper bag and a bottle of soda in the other. "Hullo there. I hope that's not breakfast," Pippa said, and regretted it immediately. Jeannette wore a sullen look around the village these days except when Katherine or Mme Pomfort were around. Those two had become Jeannette's protectors last summer in that rather bizarre drama that gave Pippa the idea for her current novel, and they still treated her like a pet fawn. But for the rest, the girl's attitude toward adults reminded Pippa of her classmates in the upper form at school, scornful of teachers, dismissive of their parents, derisive of everyone outside of their clique. Pippa had been an outsider, always too tall, too shy, too uncoordinated at sports. The same girls who had focused their mocking behavior on adults turned on her too. Not that she had wanted to be part of their gang. She wanted to read, and write stories, and go to the cinema. Her mum wanted her to go out and get fresh air all the time, but her dad usually stuck up for her. "Leave the girl alone, Mary. She'll get plenty of fresh air when we retire and spend our winters in Spain." He'd wink at Pippa when he said it, knowing it would set Mum off about how, at this rate, they'd never get out of King's Cross.

Mentally shaking her head to let go of sad memories and concentrate on this potential witness to a present crime, Pippa said, "Just kidding about the breakfast, you know. I was hoping to run into you. About the other day at the museum—"

"I was not there then, when they found her."

"I understand. I was, you know. I was wondering if you had been there, oh, say, a day or so before?"

"I told *les flics* I am there on Mondays, when the museum is closed. Mondays and Thursdays I go, only then unless Madame makes a special ask." She darted a quick look at the Englishwoman's spiky hairdo, took a bite of her brioche, and made to circle around Pippa.

"But, I say, are you quite sure? I mean, did you go into that room on Tuesday?" Pippa took a step so she was partially blocking the girl. Detectives had to be aggressive, she was sure.

Jeannette took a large swallow of soda, and shrugged in that particular way the French had, a long lift of the shoulders, almost to the ears, the chin pushing forward.

"*Mais, non,*" Jeanette said. "On Monday, but not the next day. Tuesday was the lunch with the ladies and their guests, the husbands, you know? I had to come a special time on Tuesday after school was over to clean up. *Il était un nuisance.* The *poubelle*—how do you say—the garbage box— was full."

"So you didn't go upstairs to that room on Tuesday, then?"

Jeannette shook her head and said something that Pippa took to mean why would she since she had dusted Monday? Only "le premier etagé et le foyer," where, apparently, the small crowd of special visitors had left church pamphlets and muddy bootprints. The ladies had eaten lunch on the balcony overlooking the grand salon, on the second—or was it the first?—floor display. It was a fractured conversation— English, French, and adolescent jumbled together. Pippa wasn't sure what else she could ask until she had thought about it further. Smiling again to show she was grateful, Pippa moved around the girl to open the café door and Jeannette slipped away up the path toward her house.

They had milk but there wasn't another brioche in the paper-lined basket on the counter. "*Désolé, Madame,*" the owner said, not looking sorry at all, pausing in his swiping of the bar surface with a wet cloth. Well, no harm, really. She had accomplished her major task by interviewing Jeannette. She added pastries to her list for the *supermarché.*

She was looking forward to ten days in London with Dad, although she wondered what he'd say about her new hairdo. Actually, she knew what he'd say. He'd be upset. On the positive side, she had plans to bring an empty suitcase to London so she could stock up on scones, tinned shepherd's pie, and crumpets to bring back through the Chunnel. But before she left, she promised herself she would figure out what had happened to the butcher's wife, or at least come up with some clues she could share with the police in Avallon. If nothing else, it would sharpen her skills as a mystery writer.

CHAPTER 7

The writing wasn't going well. Somehow, writing about exciting events wasn't as interesting as observing them. Pippa slammed the lid of her laptop down a bit too hard and got up. She had promised herself a strict hour or two of work before heading in to the butcher shop, but it was only one o'clock and her mind was drifting. The cats were sleeping, some inside, some on the steps, and it was so quiet she had almost dozed off staring at the computer screen. The sun was making a brave effort and it was time for a brisk walk. That would refresh her and lead to a breakthrough.

She set out along a path that went directly from her backyard through a stand of trees that met the road. A run-down set of train tracks provided a walking route. Katherine had told her that the line was an offshoot of the local web of rail service that existed when the alternative was mostly carts and horses. Used by Nazis ferrying the provisions they commandeered from the locals, it was only a ghost now, grown over with wildflowers in the summer and decaying weeds in December.

Something was nagging at her. Losing her train of thought happened a lot, but this had something to do with the murder at the museum. She resolved to concentrate on remembering, but she had reached the road and walked less than a kilometer when the two-tone sound of gendarmes' sirens grew loud. In a few moments, she turned to see three cars, their blue lights flashing, heading toward and then past her at high speed. Toward L'Isle-sur-Serein, perhaps? Two more police vehicles zoomed past, one an unmarked car but with a blue light, and the other an ambulance. What could it mean?

There was only one way to know. She turned and ran back to her cottage, grabbed her bag and her camera, and, honking to make sure the cats were safely away from the car, she backed out of the driveway and headed for the nearby town at top speed.

The Serein was visible off to the left, a small river that gleamed dully beyond the leafless trees that lined its low banks. It curved away and then swerved back closer to the road, leading the way from one farmhouse to the next. Pippa took the road over a small bridge and into the center of the town, where she had to slam on her brakes as she approached what, in these country towns, constituted a traffic jam. A small crowd had gathered near a ragged line of stopped police cars, their blue lights still flashing. Men in thick sweaters and knit caps, women in print dresses paired with socks and sturdy shoes, a few toddlers trying to wrest themselves free of restraining hands, and a half dozen uniformed policemen were all leaning over the low wall that held the water back from the street and the stone buildings across from it. There was a lot of shouting, alas all in French. Pippa decided parking rules were suspended, and simply stopped behind the last police car in the street, as did the driver of a mud-spattered truck right behind her.

"*Quel est la?*" she said to a woman standing on tiptoes to see over the crowd. "What is it? What's happening?"

The woman, who carried a straw basket from which protruded bunches of green leaves, looked up suspiciously into Pippa's face, her pursed lips suggesting either the question or the questioner was out of line. She shook her head. "*Qui sait? Un corps dans l'eau, vous comprenez?*"

Pippa did comprehend, at least the body and the water part. Another murder? Was it possible? The only thing to do was get closer. Edging toward the policemen who were pointing and calling to someone, she could see that two other officers had gone around to the other side of the riverbank and were scrambling down the bank from the shrubbery that dipped into the slowly flowing water. They waded under some branches, intent on getting to something they could see. The crowd noises increased as everyone, it seemed, shouted at the two men. Pippa had no idea if they were getting instructions, warnings, or encouragement, but she knew what she wanted to get. She pulled her camera out of her bag and started clicking. The waders, the watchers, the thing entangled in the branches.

Suddenly she pulled the camera away from her eyes and gasped. It was a body, the flesh of an arm bobbing in the water, tangled in a thicket of wet leaves. As she turned away in horror, her stomach tightened and she saw pricks of light in front of her eyes. She couldn't faint. Steady on, girl, remember you're a writer and this is your job, she scolded herself. Buck up. Swallowing hard, she peeked, in time to see a hand, the fingers still graceful as it floated toward an officer.

She dropped her head to fiddle with the camera and take what she hoped was a steadying breath. She was disoriented when a loud cry went up from the onlookers, followed by gales of raucous laughter. Laughter? She whipped her head around and saw one of the men in the water tugging hard at the corpse while his partner was grinning. How could that be?

"Makeen, makeen," someone shouted above the general noise. Then others took up the cry, but Pippa couldn't understand what they were saying. Damn this language thing.

"I beg your pardon," she said to the man next to her, a swarthy fellow with a three-day beard and a missing front tooth. "What is everyone saying?" He looked at her blankly. Taking a deep breath, she managed, slowly, *"Quel est la?"*

He grinned broadly at her and put his hand on her shoulder to turn her toward the scene. *"Un mannequin, d'accord? Dans un magasin?* A doll, yes?"

"Bloody hell, a store dummy, you mean?"

"Oui, oui," he said, scratching his chin and nodding to her as he melted away. Around her the crowd relaxed. It was a joke, not a tragedy, something to gossip about over a *café crème,* not to send you to bed afraid of nightmares. The police were still working, those in the water tugging the thing free and those on the near bank opening up a bag they might have put a body in so as to take this curious bit of flotsam away. Pippa looked around to see the ambulance back out of the crowded space and make for the bridge and out of town, followed by a couple of police cars that had been in the original caravan. Women closed their cardigans

tighter around their torsos and headed back to the warmth of their houses or shops. Children pleaded in vain for more time outdoors, however cold it was, and were dragged off under protest. A man in a jacket that sported the name of a soccer team chatted with a man in a jacket that advertised a car company. The energy of the crowd fizzled.

Pippa wished for a warmer jumper, and was about to put her camera away when she noticed something odd. The policemen had hoisted the mannequin over their heads and across the narrow channel to their waiting colleagues, who leaned far over the wall to grab it. Only then did Pippa see that the dummy was bald. She took pictures as fast as she could, then went over to a small knot of gendarmes standing near their cars and smoking.

"Excuse me. I say, are you from Avallon by any chance?"

They looked at her as if she were speaking a foreign language. Well, she guessed she was but this was important and surely one of these people had some English. She was definitely not up to explaining this in French.

"Did you need something, Madame?" a young woman said in heavily accented English, dropping her cigarette and stepping closer to Pippa.

"Not exactly, I mean, *oui*. Look, I'm sorry I don't speak French, but this is important. That store dummy? Do you think it came from the costume museum in Avallon?"

The young woman's face showed nothing. She looked from Pippa to the thing lying stiffly on the pavement. Dripping wet and half-covered in debris from its time in the river, it was grotesque in its similarity to a human body as it rested on hard cobblestones, face turned unseeingly to the sky. "Do you work at the *musée*, Madame?"

"Of course not. That's not my point. It's the same kind of store dummy they use. I wondered if one was missing from the museum. It could be evidence of a crime, don't you see?" The young policewoman looked at her uncomprehendingly. "Oh dear, I can't manage this in French, I'm so sorry. Is there someone . . . ?"

"Philippe," the policewoman called over her shoulder, and spoke rapidly to a young man who ambled over to her.

Pippa realized she was holding her breath. Black hair, a lock of which fell forward as he smiled at her. Dark blue eyes like deep water, a discreet cleft in his chin. And, he was taller than she was. Without thinking, she stood up straighter.

"I speak English, Madame. Please tell me what it is you want us to know. Do you recognize the doll?" His voice was charming, she thought, and his accented English was adorable. And here was a coincidence—he had the same name as she did.

"Madame?" he repeated, and Pippa woke from her daydream with a start.

"No, well, perhaps yes. You see, I think it was in the Musée du Costume—you know it?—in Avallon. Are you with the Avallon police?"

"Yes, we are from the Avallon brigade of gendarmes. You must be referring to the dead woman discovered in the salon there, yes?"

"Yes, that's it, precisely." Finally, someone who understood. "You see, the body was substituted for one of the mannequins. So, don't you think this must be connected to that murder?" Pippa waited, hoping she hadn't spoken too quickly or, more importantly, that she didn't appear to be some kind of nutter.

The handsome cop nodded and smiled as if he approved. Maybe he'd ask for her name and phone number so he could follow up, said an unbidden voice in her head. The police-woman's face had changed from impassivity to open suspi-cion. "And who are you, Madame?" she said, whipping a small notebook from her jacket pocket.

Pippa fell back to earth. Why hadn't Philippe of the blue eyes and cleft chin asked for her address instead of this of-ficious policewoman who made her feel like a criminal? She opened her mouth to explain she had been there when the body was found, but had sudden misgivings. What if they thought she was like one of those criminals she had read about who show up at the site of investigations? Would she get home before Christmas if she were locked up in a French jail? The woman was waiting, pencil held up, notebook at the ready, and the handsome one was still standing there, looking at her encouragingly. Oh dear, why had she spoken anyway?

"Will you give me—us—your name, Madame?" he fi-nally asked, perhaps thinking his fellow officer's bad English had been too hard for her to understand.

She found she was stammering. "I'm Philippa Hathaway, you see, I live in Reigny-sur-Canne, on rue Benoit, near the edge of the town, near the road you came here on. Not that that's important." Oh dear, I am making rather a mess of this, she thought. I have to stop staring into his eyes. He really will think I'm mental. "I was with my neighbor, who was driving some tourists to the museum. I needed to pick up my car, so I hitched a ride. And then, all of that happened and . . . I was an innocent bystander," she finished, knowing she sounded like a fool. "But, I write murder mysteries—"

Bad move. "Murder?" The woman's pencil was poised, almost quivering at the possibilities.

"Well, I'm working on my first novel, but it's made-up, you know, not the real thing." Pippa tried to laugh. "What you'd see on the telly, those dramas, you know."

The young woman sighed, but he of the blue eyes nodded again to show he understood. "You think that the dummy is a signal that this incident relates to that most serious crime. Both happened in the same area and near the same time and you wanted to make sure we realized it."

The policewoman snapped closed her notebook, gave Pippa what looked like a pitying smile, and turned back to her colleagues. Philippe reached into his shirt pocket and leaned toward her as he handed her a business card. "If you need to reach us again." He gave her another almost intimate smile, bowed slightly, and rejoined the group of officers, who had finished their cigarette break and were nodding at instructions being given by an older man in a jacket and tie. How lovely it would be to meet him for coffee, she thought while looking at the card, perhaps even for dinner in that cozy café she had passed by so many times because it always seemed to be occupied by couples.

The small group of officials laughed all together and Pippa's face burned. They had probably been told about her comment. Pippa felt daft. Of course the police had put two and two together. Who wouldn't see that if they knew about the dead woman on their pitch? She tripped over a cobblestone and almost lost her bag as she tromped back to her car, and hoped the handsome cop hadn't seen her clumsiness. They would probably be able to figure out who killed the poor woman from this find in the river. And here she had almost thrown up when she saw the thing floating around.

Stupid, stupid, she said to herself as she unlocked the car and ducked in, her head as always grazing the edge of the roof. She sat there for a few minutes, trying to push away the dark mood. I'm a novelist, no one expects me to be a real investigator, she told herself. But, wait, didn't that show that she was getting this business of clues right? It would help her write her book.

She dared to glance back at where the knot of policemen had been, but they weren't in sight. She shook herself and turned the key in the ignition. She had to drive forward, along the now-empty road edging the river and its low wall. She turned to look once more at the scene, wondering how it could have taken her so long to see that it wasn't a real person. The figure had been loaded in a van and taken off. The police must have finished here and walked to the ad-joining street, probably looking for anyone who'd seen the dummy dropped in, if this was where it happened.

From this angle, as she drove cautiously forward, some-thing small gleamed at the edge of a puddle near the wall that kept the Serein at bay. Curious, she put the car into neutral next to the water and got out to see what the object was. Probably a small euro coin, but still. She fished it out of a depression made by someone else's tire.

It was a slender gold cross on an even more slender gold chain that was twisted and crushed. There was a flat charm attached to the chain too. Perhaps someone standing here had lost it during the crowded moments. She should turn it in, but a stubborn voice in her head cautioned her that the police might laugh at her again. It could be a clue. If she gave it to the police, she'd never know. If she held on to it for a little while, maybe she could learn something. Clearly, the coppers weren't interested in sharing information.

She'd take it home, examine it, and if it didn't seem important, she'd bring it back to the town and hand it over to someone. They had a mayor, most likely. Every little town had someone who was available to deal with local problems. Maybe Katherine would come back with her and explain where she found it. Then, if the mayor thought it was important, let him bring it to that arrogant policewoman himself. Yes, tomorrow would be soon enough. She jammed it in the pocket of her anorak and drove out of town and back toward Reigny.

She felt guilty enough about taking it that she half-believed the policewoman's car would come barreling along the narrow road behind her, lights flashing. But nothing happened and she arrived at her house with no more excitement than several of the cats waiting impatiently to be let in out of the cold. They brushed by her as soon as the door was open far enough to squeeze through, rude creatures, and demanded milk before she'd even taken off her coat. "Really, now," Pippa said, "you'd best be more polite than that when I'm gone or Madame Robilier will just leave you without your afternoon snacks."

She looked at the old clock on the wall. Too late to drive to Avallon and back. Her investigation of the butcher would have to wait. For now, she had a significant clue to examine.

Fifteen minutes later, a mug of strong black tea in hand

and the rest of the cats in and draped everywhere in the room, she fished the cross from the coat pocket and dropped it on her desk. "All right, thing. If you're a clue, prove it." Two of the thin rings of the chain were open wide, and one was clearly too short to be whole. Elsewhere, the chain had doubled back on itself and been crushed into a tangle that wouldn't come unstuck. Unless a lot of pieces were missing where the links had opened, Pippa thought it had been a short necklace, and would have been visible at a woman's neck. Definitely not a man's, much too delicate.

The cross wasn't damaged. Other than an almost un-readable gold mark, there was nothing unusual. It didn't look old or handmade or in a shape that might indicate a particular culture. The charm had some kind of design engraved on it, but no writing, and the design didn't look familiar.

Pippa sat, tapping her front teeth with the rim of the small magnifying glass she had pulled from her mug of pens, pencils, and letter openers. What now? The digital camera was still in her bag and she fished it out and started tapping through the images. The backs of heads in the crowd, the wet street, the police cars fanned out at the bot-tom of the road, the river, brownish and clotted here and there with debris from the trees and bushes that hung over it. A policeman up to his waist, leaning toward a protrud-ing foot. A series of quick shots as he tried to grab a leg, an arm, his face contorted with concentration. Then, a shot of the dummy, now clearly unreal in its rigidity, rising up as the policeman yanked on a false limb, its blank face turned up to the sky, mouth slightly open.

Pippa closed her eyes and pictured the mannequins in

Madame's museum, the same vacant expressions as they gazed through the visitors, graceful hands turned out, palms up, as if in welcome or explanation, jewelry around their necks and dangling from their ears, bands across their foreheads or feathers in their hair, feet clad in heels. Stop, she told herself, think. Something . . . hair, that was it. The dummy in the water had no hair. Where was the wig? Wasn't it glued on or something? Would it come off in the water? Maybe it came off in the car of whoever brought the mannequin to the river, which would be a clue, wouldn't it?

CHAPTER 8

Katherine had snapped at the yellow cat for getting under-foot and been harsh in commanding Gracey to get off the chaise longue. The dog had looked up at her in surprise through a frizzy mop of hair before staggering off to the cor-ner of the threadbare Persian rug. The animals didn't under-stand this dark mood, but Katherine knew it was because Michael, in his call last night, had told her he had to stay in Memphis a couple more days.

"I hate it too, sweetheart, but we're so close to nailing this last number and J.B. needs a couple of new vocal tracks from me. He wants to lay them over the bridge."

Whatever. Katherine's knowledge of the structure of music was about even with Michael's ability to see the dif-ferences among eight tubes of red paint when they went into an art supply store. What she understood too clearly was that she was on her own for more than the scheduled two weeks, what he had promised when she drove him to the train.

"Don't let it drag out any longer, please. The dogs miss you. I miss you. And it will be Christmas soon, Michael."

"I promise, word of honor. What do you want me to bring back from the States, Kay? Anything. You name it."

"How about a day in Malibu, complete with mojitos and guacamole and a reason to wear sunglasses?"

He laughed. "How about a Memphis skyline refrigerator magnet and a bobblehead Elvis?"

"Don't you dare." But she had laughed and reminded him that she loved him before they said goodnight, well, goodnight from her since it was full daytime in Tennessee.

Now, on a quiet Sunday morning with a weak sun breaking through the clouds as she drank her *café crème* and nibbled at the end of yesterday's baguette smeared with fresh-made butter from the farmers' market, Katherine wondered what to do with her day. No more tourists to drive. After the horror of the last trip, Katherine would have been reluctant to take on a new group in any case. She was too restless to paint and couldn't face the small washing machine that was also a clothes dryer if you didn't mind that the clothes took hours to dry. Her plan had been to start a fresh cassoulet or perhaps a long-simmering stew flavored with a half bottle of red wine to celebrate her husband's return, but now she'd poke around in the refrigerator for something simple and eat on the chaise while reading a Balzac novel *en français*, a slog but good mental exercise.

To distract herself, she thought again about the scene in the museum, wondering so many things. Why poor Mme Sabine, who had always seemed so cheerful, if more religious than most of the French people Katherine came in contact with, always adding a *"Dieu vous garde"*—God bless you—as she handed over wrapped packets of pâté? Why in the museum, a magical place guarded almost obsessively by an old lady who never quarreled with anyone as far as Katherine could see, and who, everyone knew, kept the doors locked at all times? Then, of course, the tactical questions: How could the killer get in, and if Mme Sabine was actually killed on that chaise, how did she get there in what must surely have been after hours?

"You, cat, you look like you know everything, so tell me, please, whiskered detective?" She put down a saucer of milk by way of apology for her earlier impoliteness and the yellow cat bent to lap it up without answering Katherine's question.

There was a quick knock on the kitchen door and Katherine glanced at her watch. She could hardly say a visitor was interrupting her, and it might be the pregnant Marie's mother. When she opened it, there was Pippa, too tall to come in without ducking her head, stumbling over the raised doorway, and talking nonstop.

"Oh, I say, I am glad you're home, Katherine. May I come in? Thanks ever so. I need your help. Yes, thanks, I'd love a cup of tea if you're having. I'll put my anorak here, shall I?"

The young woman, pretty with her flushed cheeks, but so gawky and unaware of her surroundings, was like a tornado, Katherine thought. She tried to make a path for her guest through the dogs, who had jumped up at the first noise, thrilled to have something interesting to investigate, and the cat, who jogged underfoot and away up the stairs. Pippa plopped down on the chaise, absently reached under her to pull out the book Katherine had left open, closing it with a snap so Katherine's place was lost, ran her fingers through her hair, and looked up.

"There's been a development," she announced.

"A what?"

"In the murder case, of course. Didn't you hear the sirens?"

"Sirens?" Katherine said from the kitchen, where she was filling the teapot with leaves and hot water. "When was that?"

"Yesterday. They were on the way to L'Isle-sur-Serein. It's related to the murder at the museum."

"Wait, slow down," Katherine said, parking the tray of tea things on a table she cleared by pushing piles of paper off to one side. "You're going to have to start at the beginning."

"Herbal?" Pippa said, disappointment in her voice. But she accepted the steaming mug without further comment, and even sipped from it while Katherine pulled the ancient armchair closer and sat.

"Now, what's going on?" Whatever it was, Katherine admitted to herself, it was a lot better than laundry or trying to make a bad sketch morph into a good study for a painting.

Pippa described the drama, the detective's instincts that drove her to follow the sirens, the discovery that turned out to be only peculiar and not tragic, the clue she had found on the road, and the clue she had deduced from what they didn't find. She ended on a note of triumph. "We're making progress, wouldn't you say?"

Katherine wouldn't say that at all. A bunch of objects found or unfound that Pippa had presented like a box of Legos ready to be fitted together neatly into what?

"I spent all last evening making notes and trying out ideas," Pippa said by way of explanation. "We know Madame Roussel and the killer had to be in the museum at the same time, right, since she lives below stairs, or rather behind them? So the old dear, who we know keeps the doors locked at all times, must have some idea who did it, mustn't she? Or at least who could have done it."

"I'm sure if she had any ideas, she told the police right away. They may already have arrested someone for all we know."

"Oh." Pippa looked as if she hadn't considered that. "Well, perhaps you could call them and find out?"

"Hardly. Think about it, Pippa. The police would have no reason to confide in me and I'm not bold enough to try them, to tell the truth. Why do you think you need to try and solve this anyway?"

The young woman didn't answer right away, but sipped her tea and stared at the painting Katherine had hung on the wall opposite, a half-finished one in which Jeannette, posed in eighteenth-century costume, leaned on a stone wall and gazed at a vineyard on a distant hill. Katherine had put it there so she could see what wasn't working yet in the composition.

When the Englishwoman finally spoke, she sounded much less sure of herself. "Maybe I'm being stupid. I suppose part of it is feeling isolated most of the time, not understanding things. This is something that began right in front of me and is still happening that way too. I feel more involved in things. And I'd like to be of use. No one should die that way, being left on view for strangers to find."

Katherine heard the wistfulness in Pippa's voice and looked at her, seeing another side of her neighbor. Sometimes she forgot that the writer was young, single, living alone in a strange country with only her dream of being a writer to sustain her. Katherine didn't know that she would have had the courage to do the same, although she realized she had made a dramatic jump. It was less daunting since she had Michael and more years of experience than Pippa had.

"I agree that we all want to help her and her husband, who must be deep in grief. If you think the cross you found could belong to his wife, I think you should give it to the gendarmes in Avallon right away. We can't know what if anything it means, but they can make sense of it. Do you want me to go with you to translate?"

Pippa said, "I think I can manage that much at least. I met one of them who speaks English and I even have his card."

"Good. Now, about the wig, isn't it likely it's in the river, torn off by the current or a branch from a bush near the bank? The murderer can hardly have been so stupid as to hang on to it, and why would he, assuming it's a he, of course?"

"Yes, but it's missing and that bothers me. The gendarmes would surely have searched hard for anything else while they were in Serein."

"The museum has been searched from top to bottom for clues, I bet," Katherine said. "Maybe they did find it. Why not ask your policeman?"

Pippa blushed. "Not my policeman. His name is Philippe, a coincidence."

Katherine studied the woman, wondering if Pippa's tenaciousness about the cross and the wig might be inspired, at least in part, by the chance to see a policeman named Philippe. "Right. I think a trip to Avallon is called for. Let me know how it turns out."

"Actually, I had planned to go in yesterday. I want to observe the butcher. You know it's most likely the husband in cases like this." She looked so sure of herself, but Katherine thought the writer was on the wrong track.

"It'll be closed today, his charcuterie, I mean. It's Sunday. Given the tragedy, I'd be surprised if it's open on Tuesday. Monday everything's closed, remember."

"Oh, I say, I hadn't thought of that. Tuesday, then, for my visit to the shop." Pippa gathered her things, came close to tripping over Fideaux, whose small size in comparison to Gracey sometimes fooled people into thinking there was only one dog in the house. She backed out of the kitchen door, promising to let Katherine know what happened.

The weather was improving, the wind gone for now and the sun strong enough to warm the patio. Katherine decided to move an easel outside and paint, if only to take her mind off murder and Michael's absence. At times like this, her motivation was weak. There was no upcoming exhibition to be preparing for, even though she had sold a few large oil paintings at the gallery six months ago in Vézelay. She wasn't being shown in any other galleries, and the August weekend in which locals and visitors toured artists' studios had not brought even one potential art patron to her house even though she and Michael had put out hand-painted signs at the crossroads, and she had worn her most dramatic clothing, treasures uncovered at the outdoor flea markets, the *vide-greniers*, that every village in the Yonne *département* of Burgundy held once a season.

Emile's dog, which had been quiet for at least an hour, started barking, and, unless Katherine's ears were playing tricks on her, he was coming closer. She glanced at the driveway gate, which was closed, good thing, she thought. Then, a neon-red ski cap bobbed at the gate.

" 'Allo, 'allo, Katherine." It was her neighbor, being pulled along by his watchdog, which had stretched the leather leash to its absolute maximum and had its gaze fixed on Katherine. "I would come in to say a proper hello," Emile shouted over the dog's noise, "but Napoleon would want to play with your animals."

I'll bet he would, Katherine thought, as in rip off their limbs one at a time. "I understand. He's quite a handful, isn't he?"

"He is really friendly, you should come see."

Now or never, Katherine decided, and she walked slowly the length of the driveway, Napoleon becoming more agitated the closer she got. "Emile, I have to say, he doesn't look pleased to see me, and he most certainly doesn't look like he wants to be friends."

"But no, he is only gruff when he is protecting my house. Look, his tail is wagging."

And in truth it was, frantically. Safe on her side of the metal fence, Katherine permitted herself a soothing greeting but kept her hands in her pockets. Napoleon looked intently at her, his deep brown eyes assessing her, whether as a target or a new friend Katherine wasn't sure. At least he had stopped barking and was only whining now. "I haven't seen a dog other than ours this big since Albert's big one— Michael used to call him 'the German dog'—died. Do you let him come in on these cold nights?"

Emile looked sheepish. "Well, sometimes, even though the man who sold him to me insists these dogs want to be outside all the time. There's an old blanket in the kitchen next to the wall heater, and he sleeps there. But," he added, "if a thief comes, voilà, Napoleon is next to the door, growling, I can assure you."

"And barking," Katherine said, making a small face to

hint that barking was, in Napoleon's case, not to be encouraged further.

Emile hastily changed the subject. "Where is Michael? Is he on tour yet?"

Katherine described Michael's recording work in Memphis and the hopes for an American tour in the spring. Emile grinned and bobbed his head the whole time, even throwing his free arm in the air in a fist at one point.

"I said so the day he arrived. Here, I said, is a famous musician come to stay with us in Reigny. What an honor for us. I think next year, there will be time for him to play with me at the fête. It was too busy this year, but we shall plan and rehearse, yes?"

Katherine laughed. "This has been a wonderful surprise, although Michael has been writing songs for the past few years. Fingers crossed, Emile, that the album is a hit and the tour goes well. Then you may say a country rock star lives next door." She didn't respond to his suggestion that he and Michael play together. She knew Michael would never agree to it. He was laid-back in most things, but where music was concerned, she knew he'd resist playing with someone who had no musical talent and a weakness for accordions and amplified guitar chords.

Emile would have talked longer, but Napoleon noticed a long-eared rabbit move in the field across the way and began barking and yanking on the leash. Emile barely had time to wave and wish her a good day before he was loping along behind his hound.

Katherine went back to the easel she had set up, rubbed her chilly hands, and began the painting by mixing two reds and a drop of black on her palette, which was already thick with dried oils. She squared her shoulders and faced a canvas on which she had sketched a dancing trio of women. She raised her brush at the same moment a familiar voice called out.

"Katherine, *bonjour,* can I come up?"

Katherine decided that painting was not in her immediate future and called, *"D'accord,"* loud enough to be heard at the bottom of the garden. Remembering that Jeannette was on a mission to improve her English, she amended it to "Yes, please come up."

The teenager bounded into view, came over to her favorite adult, and kissed her enthusiastically on both cheeks and then a third time, the signal of special affection. She smiled, something she did so rarely these days that it delighted Katherine, and put a small paper bag on the table. *"Un croissant.* It was the last one they had in the basket. I got it before the Englishwoman could. She was probably angry." If Jeannette was sorry, it didn't show.

"Thank you, thank you. Yesterday's baguette was stale."

Jeannette darted a glance at Katherine, and grinned. "This is—how do you say—stale too, then, because I bought it yesterday."

Katherine laughed. "I will enjoy it anyway. Did you pass Emile and his guard dog?"

"Silly thing. It sounds so mean, but all it wanted was to lick my hand. I think it might have wanted the roll, but I told it absolutely not."

"Really? You have a way with animals, I guess. Would you like some coffee with cream?" It was hard to stick with English when some of the French food names were so international, but if Jeannette wanted to visit America, a dream she had confided to Katherine only recently, she would have to learn. If she went to New York, L.A., or other cosmopolitan cities, they might call it *café crème* too, but she'd best be ready for more conventional American terminology.

Jeannette settled in for a visit and Katherine decided she would sketch the girl's face quickly and add it to the canvas later. By now, she could have painted it from memory, but then she would have missed the expressions that passed over the teenager's features, a glossary of emotions that came and went with a measure of high drama.

Jeannette had been a twelve-year-old, otherworldly creature of beauty and innocence—if you discounted her magpie-like habit of stealing teaspoons—when Katherine first started drawing her, with golden hair as beautiful as any Renaissance angel's. This last year had been tough on her emotionally, not only because of last summer's scare, but because she had hit her midteens and had been obliged by peer dictates to take on the bored, silent postures of her school friends. Katherine had a hunch it was more of an act than a personality change, and that it was necessary in order to be accepted. Since being accepted was her own keenest desire, Katherine was in no position to quibble with the girl's newfound sulkiness. Only with Katherine, pregnant Marie, and for some reason old Mme Pomfort was she the same girl Katherine had begun to mentor.

"So, how are things in school?"

"*Comme si* . . . as usual, I think. Marie-Françoise told me she has had the sex with her boyfriend. She said it was nothing special, but he wants to do it again."

"I'll bet. Did they use a condom?"

Jeannette looked shocked. "I would not know. That is too private."

"Well, it won't be private for long if she swells up like a balloon."

"A baby? No, that is for old people like Marie and Raoul. Did you know they will have me to take care of the baby sometimes? They will pay me. I am saving for a moto . . . What is the word?"

"A motorbike? Aren't you a bit young for that?"

Jeannette made a face, then shrugged. "I will not be young by the time I have saved the euros. *Zut,* even a used bike is very expensive."

Thank heaven for that, Katherine thought. "You don't have a boyfriend yet, I hope, not if boys in your class want sex."

"No. Lucien, her boyfriend, is older. He will finish with school this year. The boys in my class are all *stupide,* like little boys always hanging around and making the comments."

"Ah." Just wait, Katherine thought, busy with her oil sketch. "Did I see you with some of them at the bus stop last week?"

"Mmmm," the girl said by way of choosing not to answer, retreating into silence and picking at a withered hollyhock stem. "Did you know the gendarmes spoke to everyone who came to the *musée* for weeks and weeks, trying to find out what happened and why the butcher's wife was murdered?"

"Yes, I expect they would. That means they talked to you again, I'll bet. I hope you weren't harassed by them."

"What means, I mean, what is the word?"

"Did they push you hard to say something you didn't think is true, or make you feel scared?"

Jeannette laughed. "Scared of *les flics*? *Jamais,* never. My papa told me never to say anything except if they ask it. They didn't ask me much except if I knew how to work the locks, which I don't because Madame always does that, except on the little door to the *poubelle,* but that's not even a whole door, and no one even sees it from the street."

Katherine was having a devil of a time catching Jeannette's smile. The girl lifted her head and cocked it in a certain way that made her smile an entire body pose. But she moved so swiftly that Katherine couldn't capture it and she knew if she asked Jeannette to pose, it would be artificial. She gave up for the moment, put her brush down, and sat on a metal chair that held on to the cold and damp too well.

"Are you still working for Madame Roussel? How is she? The poor woman was distraught the last time I saw her."

"She is fussy, as usual, and won't go upstairs to the room where it happened. She did not want me to go, but it is a mess after *les gendarmes* so I told her I will have to clean it up and straighten the mannequins' clothing next time I am there. She has asked me to do other days until things are *normal* again."

"I expect she's happy to have you there to help."

"Oh yes. I am to go tomorrow, in fact, because the *musée* is closed until the new year. She wants me to give the rooms and the frames in the hallways a polishing and to clean out some old boxes that need to go into recycling. Of course, Madame Josée helps too, but I like the extra work because I can make more money."

"For the motorbike."

"*Mais non,* for Christmas presents for my brothers and Papa. My sister is not coming home. It is too far from where she works and she has little time off." Jeannette stuck out her lower lip, which only made her look more charming. "I have not seen Angelique for three Christmases. Papa doesn't care and the little ones hardly remember her, but she is my only sister."

"I've forgotten where she lives, but perhaps you can visit her next summer."

"*Mais non.* She is married and her husband does not like visitors, she told me. Anyway, it is too far. She lives in a village near Lille."

"That *is* far away. Why there?"

"He drives a truck for a company there, so that is where they had to go."

Katherine massaged the muscles in her back, which had begun to tighten, working out here. "Well, *ma petite,* I must clean up and do my chores too. I will be in Avallon tomorrow to see the dentist. Would you like a ride home after you've finished school and done your work at Madame's?"

Jeannette's eyes lit up. The public bus that made the circuit from village to village in a big loop took forever, Katherine knew. They agreed on a time and place and Katherine accepted the girl's goodbye kisses and waved her away down the garden steps. The gate squealed when Jeannette closed it and Katherine reminded herself to oil it. But perhaps she'd leave that for Michael, who had been having a vacation while she labored here alone. Yes, she would leave it for him.

CHAPTER 9

Katherine found herself almost an hour early for her dentist appointment the next day. Driving into the center of town and deciding at the last instant to swerve into the parking lot that might once have been an urban park before cars were so common, she had squeezed into a narrow, angled spot under the bare branches of one of the trees that still adorned the space. The veterinarian's office was across the street in a line of old stone town houses. She and Michael had brought Gracey in only last month when she stepped on some broken glass in the overgrown lot behind Reigny's common garbage collection spot. The vet's assistant had suggested with a straight face that they carry the dog into the examining room at the top of the stairs, unfazed by Gracey's similarity to a brown bear.

She walked in the opposite direction to the main shopping street, waving to a white-coated pharmacist who was holding the door open for an elderly woman. *"Bonjour, Luc, comment ça va?"*

The young man waved back, and Katherine thought how handsome he looked in his perennial shirt and tie, his raven-black hair slicked back over a high forehead. When she needed shampoo or toothpaste, he or one of the women who worked there with him treated her purchase as serious business and were unfailingly solicitous, a far cry from the vast, understaffed drugstores of her past in Los Angeles. It made her sad to see the *supermarchés* taking away some of the business of the traditional French pharmacies. Progress wasn't, always.

She was walking in the direction of the shop that sold wool hats and scarves when she realized that the gendarmerie, the police headquarters, was off to the left, across the street and on one roughly parallel to the main street. There were white and blue police cars pulled up on the narrow sidewalk in front of the building. Pippa's plea for information came back to her and, she had to admit, her own curiosity with it. She angled across the cobblestone pavement, inhaling to give herself courage, and walked into the building. Finding herself boxed in by interior walls and closed doors, she almost turned and left. But a voice stopped her. *"Oui, Madame, avez-vous besoin d'aide?"*

Did she need help? Was it enough to be curious? Was that mere nosiness? Could she say no and back out the door? You got yourself into this, she scolded herself, now deal with it.

"Are you here to see someone?" the voice continued in French. Katherine turned to find the source of the speaker and there he was, visible inside a window that was only open at its bottom half. Since he was apparently either seated or extremely short, she had to bend down to look at him straight on. Pippa would have had to get on her knees.

From this awkward position, which didn't seem unusual to the gray-haired gendarme, Katherine tried to explain that she was hoping there had been some resolution of the murder of poor Mme Sabine. "I was there at the time so the shock was intense. I'd like to know the killer has been captured." Even to her it sounded thin. To the policeman, it was clearly none of her business.

"I have no information," or that's what she thought he said. She wasn't sure how to prolong the conversation.

"You would know if someone had been arrested, a suspect?" Her French was rapidly deserting her. She was much better ordering sausages or tomatoes, or asking if it was the correct train. The vocabulary words around killing and suspects went beyond what she had learned in classes and by immersion in Reigny's daily life.

"*Désolé*," was his only reply, and then the outer door opened and two young women wrapped to the ears in printed scarves came in chattering and laughing, and made further delicate probing impossible. Their laughter followed her onto the street, where the sun was losing its battle to incoming clouds and the temperature was dropping.

She needed to buy small gifts of candy for her neighbors and some for Michael. Well, for herself too. But maybe after, not before, her time in the dentist's chair. It would hardly do to show up with a bag full of candy. The dentist, a charming woman who lived above her clinic, would give her a stern lecture, and Katherine hated to be lectured to.

As she settled into a plastic chair in the dentist's reception room to wait her turn, Katherine realized the assistant was talking with the patient who was leaving. "Poor man. Did they have money troubles?" the woman asked, leaning forward over her desk.

"Hardly. He talked altogether too much about the place . . . retired, somewhere in Provence, not here."

Katherine caught only part of the conversation as she pretended to be reading *Le Monde*.

"Pricey, isn't it? But they were . . . so long ago."

"Yes, and . . . every penny. Certainly, their sausages are too expensive, although I will say they are the best unless you go to Beaune, and no one . . . for a sausage."

The assistant smiled. "Certainly not, at least not for sausages, eh? Mme Sabine . . . What will happen to the business, I wonder?"

". . . a shame, and right before Christmas," the client said, winding a bright green knitted scarf around her neck. "She went away every week? Well, we shall never know. . . . I'm sure she will go to the sky."

The sky? Just when she thought she was making progress in the language, Katherine was brought up short by the lapses in her vocabulary or in her ability to eavesdrop on other people's conversations in rapid French. What was this about Provence, about Beaune, about money?

Twenty minutes later, as the dentist, a brisk woman in her early forties wearing a formfitting wool dress, gold hoop earrings, and knee-high boots, began to examine her teeth, Katherine realized all was not lost. Docteur Lafarge hardly waited for Katherine to settle into the reclining chair before she pulled a white cotton coat over her dress and began to dissect the mystery. Katherine had only to raise her eyebrows or make an inarticulate questioning sound to keep a steady flow of fact, speculation, and civic concern coming. Fortunately, the dentist spoke excellent English, having spent a year in New York City as a nanny before coming back to France to begin her baccalaureate studies.

"I heard, my dear Mme Goff, that it was you who found the body?"

"Urghhh."

"Ah yes, I understand, not you alone. Poor old Madame had to see it, and see it in her exquisite salon, such a blow for someone so old and frail. The butcher is devastated, you know? Taken to his bed, I hear, and unable to speak. And the police, merciful heaven, are looking at him as a suspect. Spit please."

"But why would they suspect him?" Katherine managed before being instructed to open wide again.

"Scandalous, I agree. The Sabines were as close to turtle-doves as one could imagine, always together at the store, smiling and joking back and forth. They were both patients of mine, you understand? He talked always about the little house in the south that they would buy when they retired, ideal for two older people in a tidy village near Aix. He had pictures. It belonged to a friend who had agreed to sell it to him in a few years. Can you imagine the sorrow?"

Given a chance to speak as one tool was removed from her mouth and before the next one was inserted, Katherine said, "Do the police have any evidence to suspect him?".

"Open, if you will. Nothing other than that one assumes some kind of crime of passion between spouses, although if you ask me they are too old for that. *Comprenez*?" The dentist winked.

Katherine understood. "What do you think?" she said.

"Me, I suspect some nasty piece of work from outside

the area. There are no murderers here. Why?" she said as Katherine signaled the question with her eyebrows. "Perhaps a robbery gone wrong although I must admit I don't see that the *musée* has much that would sell on the black market. Old jewelry, perhaps? Or perhaps the villain violated the woman. God forbid." She stopped to cross herself. "The gendarmes must do more to protect us all instead of standing around outside their headquarters smoking, *n'est-ce pas?*"

Having gargled, been declared cavity-free, and released from the chair, Katherine asked if the dentist had any theories as to why the victim might have been in the museum.

"Ah," she said as she ushered Katherine out into the waiting room, where a young man with a pained expression and a swollen cheek sat reading the same *Le Monde* Katherine had abandoned thirty minutes before, "that is easy because I was there also. Yes," she said as Katherine made a noise of surprise, "two days before they found her. It was the annual gathering of the ladies of the church group. We take care of the altar and make arrangements for the priest to do baptisms and funerals when he visits us on his rounds. Once a year we do something special together as a little reward. This year, it was lunch at the *musée* and a tour of the new exhibit. My husband and M. Sabine even stopped by for dessert and coffee. No, it was nothing, *ce n'était rien,*" she added as Katherine gasped. "The gendarmes already know about it. My husband had to open his office and M. Sabine must have left even before that. The exhibit was wonderful, as it always is. Madame has a gift. It was late when the rest of us left."

Katherine would have liked to ask her more—this was a new piece of information—but the young man jumped up, clutching his jaw. The dentist glanced at him and gave her American patient a farewell wave that morphed into beckoning the suffering man into her examining room, and the door closed with a firm click. As she fished out euros to pay her bill, Katherine wondered how these new pieces fit into the puzzle. She also wondered if the dentist had shared everything with the police?

"My boss, she is too kind," the assistant said with a snort as she handed Katherine the receipt. She was young, and had a sharp nose that seemed to twitch in anticipation of scandal.

Katherine was startled at the open admission the receptionist had been eavesdropping. "Why do you say that?"

"She and Mme Sabine were both involved in the church group, so she does not like to think badly of her." The woman looked up at Katherine with an indignant expression. She spoke in French and English combined, and seemed prepared to say more as there were no other patients in the waiting room.

"You think there's something else to consider?" Katherine said, feeling her way.

"Think about this, Mme Goff. Every Thursday, Mme Sabine took the train and spent all day away from the shop. Yes, ask anyone, she dressed nicely, drove to the station and left. Must have come home after the shops closed because no one saw her. The next day, there she would be in her apron, smiling and acting *normal*, you know, and her husband none the wiser."

"But what's so strange about that? I'm sure he knew she had gone somewhere. Perhaps she went shopping, or tended to an old relative. . . ." Katherine let her sentence die away seeing the almost scornful look on the young woman's face.

"Ask my sister, who works at the chocolatier across the street from them. She heard it the other day from someone. Madame was having an affair. Someone in Lyon, perhaps, or Beaune. Dressing up? Every Thursday? No wonder her husband was seized with passion and strangled her." She finished on a note of triumph.

Katherine didn't know what to say. It sounded ludicrous. "Do they have family? I heard he is grieving deeply. Will anyone be coming to help the widower run the shop?"

The assistant shrugged. "I think she has a brother somewhere, although maybe it's he who has a brother, and I know she has a sister, although she lives in Belgium and has health problems. I expect my boss's lady friends from the church group will lend a hand. But you watch." She gave Katherine a meaningful nod as the door opened and a woman entered, half-dragging a boy of six or seven, who was wailing.

She wasn't sure who she felt sorriest for, the scared little boy or the dentist who would have the job of reassuring him that the long arm with the point on the end of it wasn't a tool of torture but of salvation.

CHAPTER 10

She told herself she wasn't pursuing gossip but getting ready for *Bonne Noël* as she opened the door and the tinkling of bells announced her. After all, she had been planning to buy chocolate.

The shop was busy. Two women in front of her were waiting for help, holding the small boxes Katherine's American tourists had snapped up. There were foil-wrapped balls in a large glass bowl, and rows of miniature marzipan fruits and vegetables on trays under the glass counter, cleverly designed leeks and cabbages and cucumbers alongside doll-sized oranges and strawberries. The customers were chatting with each other and with the chocolate maker and his two helpers. The shop smelled of chocolate, sugar, and almonds.

Katherine thought how Christmasy it was. The holiday spirit in France, she thought, how lovely. And then she heard one woman say *"meurtre"* in a darker voice and the good feeling passed. "Murder" in French combined with the tone of voice in which the speaker uttered it made the meaning clear.

The speaker was talking to the *maître chocolatier,* who had moved to one side while his assistants continued to take people's euros. Katherine eased in his direction while glancing around for small presents for Mme Pomfort, Marie and Raoul, Emile, Jeannette and her brothers, and her other neighbors. She was determined to maintain the goodwill last summer's work on the fête had generated. Mme Pomfort still ruled Reigny with a firm hand, and, even though they had become allies, Katherine wasn't entirely sure Madame wouldn't pounce if she felt even the slightest bit offended by a lack of special attention from the new American in her town. The candy box for Mme Pomfort had to be bigger than the others.

She was still trying to figure out how to join the conversation when there was a lull in business. The gossiping woman looked at her watch and gasped. She explained that she was to have met her sister at the new bookstore ten minutes ago. The other customers had departed and the helpers' bodies relaxed into signs of weariness. The owner made a shooing motion with one hand and said, *"Allez, allez,"* which Katherine took to mean they should take a break.

He turned to Katherine. "Mme Goff, always so good to see you. I hope your American tourists enjoyed their visit? And have you come in for your own selection of *les petits cadeaux,* the little presents? We have been working day and night and, as you see, there is much to choose from."

"Oui, Monsieur, merci. Yes, thank you, I am shopping. Everything is so beautiful here." He bowed. "I overheard one of your customers talking about poor Mme Sabine, and I have to ask, is there any news? I was at the museum, you

see, when her body was discovered and I feel somehow connected." She hoped that didn't sound ridiculous.

"*Tragique*," he said in a theatrically sorrowful tone of voice. "But what can you expect in a situation like that?"

Like that? Katherine's confusion showed plainly.

"M. Sabine must have heard the rumors and investigated. Madame was having an affair. Everyone suspected as much." He nodded, the extra flesh under his jawbone becoming more prominent. "My dear wife, who is an invalid, a great pity, spends a good deal of time sitting in the window upstairs. She knits." He pointed at the ceiling. "She told Antoinette, my assistant in the kitchen, and Antoinette told her daughter, who works behind the counter, and only then did I hear because my wife is no gossip."

Obviously not, Katherine thought. Even the dentist's assistant had heard. "But why would someone think she was having an affair? They always seemed to be such a close couple, laughing and teasing each other."

"Women can tell, *n'est-ce pas*? My wife saw her hurrying to the station on Thursday mornings, all dressed up, her hair freshly washed. And then"—the chocolatier leaned in closer to Katherine and dropped his voice to a whisper—"at the end of the day, she would come home and my wife said she looked satisfied." He nodded slowly, looking sideways at Katherine.

Good lord, Katherine thought. Is it possible we women are being scrutinized to determine if we've had sex recently? She'd have to devise a shopping route that avoided passing under the chocolatier's window from now on, or at least after Michael got back.

"So you think M. Sabine killed his wife because he found out she was seeing someone else?"

"Mais non." He looked affronted. "It should be obvious. The lover followed her back here and found out she was a married woman. Undoubtedly *un crime passionel.* I can tell you, I am not the only one who thinks so. I heard it from a gentleman who was visiting from Beaune. He saw the news in our paper, and her photo. Yes, yes, he told me he saw her on the street there with a man more than once and they were holding hands like lovers."

"Where did you hear this?"

"I was at the café. I only allow myself one aperitif after the shop closes. I must come home to my wife, you understand. She is so isolated, poor dear. But this man was talking to Remy behind the bar. I couldn't help but overhear."

I'll bet you couldn't, Katherine thought, but reminded herself that eavesdropping was not a sin and she had no right to think ill of the chocolatier. "I hope you told the police. They need to know." Of course, it could have been innocent, Katherine reminded herself, or a mistaken identification.

"As I understand it, they think it was a random event, a deranged man passing through who saw an opportunity. This is a happy town and we do not have murders, Madame. This is the first one in more than ten years and the last one was, voilà, a crime of passion like this. I still remember. A vintner whose wife left him to take up with an Australian picker she met during the grape harvest."

He looked ready to launch into a detailed account of that old crime, but Katherine wasn't interested. "Have the police spoken with your wife?"

"Ah, the gendarmes, they are determined not to under-stand. Of course, they haven't bothered to speak to my wife. If they did, they would understand. But *non*, even after I told them she sees everything from that upstairs window."

Katherine admitted to herself that the police might not have seen any reason to interview a woman whose only contact with the victim was glimpses from a distance, and whose impressions were so negative. She was tempted to angle for a visit to the invalid herself, but quashed the idea. This was not her job, and she had other chores she needed to tackle instead of standing here listening to gossip. She chose a half dozen small boxes of candy for the neighbors, a selection of truffles for Mme Pomfort, and a box of molded chocolate snails for Michael, and put her purchases on the *carte bancaire* credit card Michael had given her before he left. She banished Michael's reminder that the credit card did not signify money in the bank, only an obligation to produce it at the end of the month. She'd worry about how to pay for her largesse later, after the holiday. Maybe her husband would come back with the news that they didn't have to worry about every euro now. He had said he had great news to tell her.

CHAPTER 11

On the sidewalk, she hesitated. There were no more errands to do in town and Jeannette would not be ready to head back to Reigny. She was restless and hesitant to abandon the town in which this crime had taken place without knowing more facts not gossip, however. She ducked into the bistro near the indoor farmers' market and treated herself to a big bowl of onion soup and a glass of red wine. Warmed by both, she buttoned up her coat, scooped up her shopping bags, and went back onto the street. A blast of cold air seemed to push her in the direction of the museum. Yes, she would stop by and see how the old lady was doing, perhaps give her one of the boxes of candy. After all, there was daylight left and nothing special to do at home. The animals would all be sleeping, almost hibernating, and it would be quiet, too quiet.

As she hurried along the narrow sidewalk, she collided with the umbrella of a man who was passing. *"Pardon,"* she said, juggling her bags. He had been holding his umbrella down so it almost grazed his head, Katherine thought, so it was no wonder it hit her even though she was short. He lifted the umbrella briefly and glanced down at her, frowning to suggest—or so she thought—that it was her fault. He was good-looking, with dark blond, wavy hair and a bit of a cleft chin in an angular face.

"*Rien*," he said half under his breath, and brushed past her, his jacket, with some sports logo on it, too short to keep his pants from being obviously damp. All the rain and chill was making people grouchy, she decided. Annoyed at his rudeness rather than her carelessness, she rang the museum's bellpull at the same instant a gust of cold air blew stinging raindrops in her face. She was relieved when Madame's daughter opened the door.

"We are closed, *désolée*," the woman said, peering out, sounding not at all desolated, but impatient. When she looked harder at Katherine, she stepped back inside, and gestured for Katherine to follow her. "I didn't recognize you, sorry," she said, her voice friendlier. "You're Mme Goff, from Reigny? You bring visitors to the museum sometimes?"

"Yes, on Mme Bellegarde's behalf, as part of her tours. I wanted to find out how your mother is. You're Josée, aren't you, Madame's daughter? Jeannette has told me about you. I am concerned about the shock your mother has had."

"Thank you, Madame, I am coping." The curator, looking older than she had a week ago, joined them, pushing aside the heavy velvet drapery over the doorway to her private apartment, the same type and vintage of the ones that covered the windows in all of the display rooms. She reached up to bestow polite kisses on Katherine's cheeks. "It was a tragedy, absolutely, and I am not sure the museum will ever be the same to me."

"I tried to rearrange the salon," her daughter said, patting her mother's hand before perching on one of the wooden chairs in the entry room, "but the gendarmes would not let us touch anything anywhere in the museum while they looked for clues, you understand."

"Did they find anything?" Katherine said.

"Who knows?" Josée said. "They don't say anything, they make a mess—"

"They leave the door unlocked," her mother chimed in.

"Have they finished now? I wonder if I could see the room? It was so chaotic and I didn't get much of an impression." Katherine wasn't sure how to explain why she wanted to go upstairs. She wasn't even sure herself. But, somehow, it was important, not that the police would have missed something, but so that she would at least have a clear picture of the space in which Mme Sabine had been lying when the members of the tour group saw her. Mother and daughter didn't seem to find her request strange.

"If you'll permit me, I won't join you," the curator said. "I'm still fatigued and, truthfully, I don't much like going to that salon. But Josée doesn't mind, do you, dear?"

"Of course not. When I am here, I am Maman's second set of hands," Josée said, "and feet, on these steep stairs." She sounded tired, Katherine thought. The two of them labored up the three flights of narrow stairs in the dim light. The velvet rope at the entry to the salon had been moved to one side, as had the mannequins, who were now clustered in a far corner staring vacantly at each other and the walls.

"It is still a mess, you can see. There are pieces of the décor that have been left on tables, under the chairs. I can't imagine what they thought they would find, but unless it was an ant, I am sure they scooped it up," Josée said. "The gendarme captain said he would come later today to talk to us, and after that Jeannette can help me clean the room and I may reconstruct the scene as my mother designed it. But Maman doesn't want the chaise where the poor woman died to remain in the house, so I will have Jeannette and one of her schoolmates help me carry it down to the alley."

Katherine asked her about the costume Mme Sabine was wearing and Josée said the gendarmes took it away.

"So often your creative mother also includes period shoes, patterned stockings, dress gloves, and other beautiful touches."

"They took everything on the chaise or lying loose on the floor. You know the dead woman was not wearing any of that, though, only the dress, a beaded gown I myself found in a *brocante* in Nice years ago? Much too small for Madame. The poor thing began to unravel from being handled so carelessly."

It took an instant for Katherine to realize the "poor thing" in question was the gown, not the dead woman.

"You heard about the mannequin being found in the Serein?" Katherine asked as they stood in the doorway of the salon staring in.

"They want me to come to the gendarmerie to identify it. Who else's would it be? Of course it is ours, but I'm sure it is beyond repair." She snorted. "This has all been so hard on my mother, and terrible for the museum she has given her life to."

Seeing Pippa in her mind, Katherine had to ask the next question. "Was the mannequin's wig in the mess?"

Josée shook her head. "No, I don't think so. It wasn't on

the list of things they took, which I had to sign. At least, I don't remember it. You understand, this whole business has been so upsetting. Nothing like it has ever happened at the museum."

"I am so sorry," Katherine said. "The ruined costume was on the mannequin before the, um, the incident, wasn't it? I have always wondered where the costumes that aren't on display at one time are kept."

Josée said that as there were no closets in an eighteenth-century house the materials were stored in armoires in every room, and a specially built cedar storage room in the *sous-sol*, the basement. "One of the gendarmes whispered to me that he guessed Madame's body was stored in an armoire for at least an hour or two before being outfitted and laid on the chaise, but I doubt it. The armoires all have horizontal shelves and the storage room is very small and filled with garment bags and shelves, also."

"I wonder if that means she wasn't killed here. I hadn't thought of that." Katherine filed away the information to share with Pippa, although it hardly solved the crime. Katherine was about to ask if there was anything she might do to comfort the curator when the unmistakable sound of the bell interrupted them.

"Excuse me a moment," Josée said, "Mother doesn't want to answer the door. I must go down." She lowered her voice. "Do not tell Maman, but when I am on duty, I do not do up all the locks every time. *Mon Dieu,* it is too much."

As the woman's steps faded, Katherine argued with herself. The police were finished with their investigation of the room. How much could it hurt to walk in? It was testimony to the forcefulness of the curator's personality that Katherine felt a frisson of guilt as she stepped into the salon and even looked quickly behind her in case Madame had decided to supervise her visitor. Immediately, she understood Josée's disapproval of police tactics. A single black satin shoe lay on its side under the chaise, a pair of gray kidskin evening gloves, looking as soft as silk, were crumpled, tossed at the edge of a side table, and the drapes over the high window were pulled open crookedly, one side bunched at the bottom and the other still partially closed from midpoint to the top.

The chaise had been moved so it faced completely away from the doorway. It had to have been angled toward the doorway before or no one would have seen the figure sprawled on it. She noticed the massive armoire set against the window wall. It was open and its top-to-bottom shelves were stacked fully with folded evening clothing, set off by a row of charming feathered caps hung like laundry from a ribbon that stretched between the armoire's interior walls. She itched to investigate. What she could do in a painting if she had even one of those frothy hats. But she was here to see if anything jumped out at her, some detail the police wouldn't think to notice. For a moment, she wished Pippa were with her. For all her excess of imagination, the writer did have the kind of curiosity that would come in handy right now.

She crossed to the window and looked down. How had the killer gotten in and out again? Definitely not by the front door, or Mme Roussel would have seen her. Unless Madame had been in her apartment for some reason, the sound of locks would be muffled by those extraordinarily thick drapes. Jeannette had mentioned a half door through which she brought the trash and recycling outside. There was an alley that went all along the backs of the houses that she could see from up here, but there was no obvious way to reach it from the solid back wall of the museum's tiny garden, now a dull mass of winter-frosted weeds. Did Jeannette carry the trash can around the block to the alley?

She fingered the drapery, old velvet, lined with something even heavier, fringed with long tassels and weighted further by a deep bottom hem. The sloppy way they had been left bothered her and she shook out one and straightened it from top to bottom, leaving some space for looking out. Katherine pulled the drape so that its folds were even and squatted down to straighten the hem. As she groped in the thick fabric, she felt something more fragile, a piece of paper.

She stood up, hearing someone climbing up the stairs and marching purposefully into the hallway behind her. A voice from across the room said, "Madame, what are you doing here?"

She turned and smiled at the florid face of the captain she had met the day Mme Sabine's body was found. "It's only me, Madame Goff, trying to make this place a little less disordered for when our dear Madame can bring herself to come up and begin to re-create her tableau."

Katherine stood, the piece of paper instinctively crumpled in her fist, and her fist hidden at her side. Why, she didn't know, but Pippa's voice came to her: "A clue." She had to get a grip or Michael would start scolding her for getting involved where she wasn't needed. He wasn't back yet, however, and as she made a space for the policeman to join her at the window, she smiled at him again to reassure him she was harmless. Depositing the scrap of paper in her pocket, she held out her hand. "I was the tour guide for the Americans that day."

He stared at her, nodded abruptly, and said, "You aren't here with another tour, I think?"

"No. The Bellegarde tours are over for the season and the museum is closed. I was helping because their normal driver is away on holiday. I'm a neighbor of theirs and I'm American so it was easy for me. Well, it would have been easy except for this." She shuddered.

The policeman grunted and switched to English. "We do not have murders in our town. This ruthless killer will be caught, I assure you, Madame."

It was touching, really, that at least some of the people of Avallon believed there could not be a terrible criminal residing alongside them. But the chocolatier's gossip and the dentist assistant's eagerness to add to the minority view was an alert that crime could happen anywhere and be committed by one's neighbor.

"Are you able to share any news? I only ask because the people I've spoken to in some of the shops are nervous. What if it's someone who might kill again?"

The policeman looked out the window, but didn't say anything. As Katherine was about to give up and leave, he spoke. "We are looking at everyone who knew her. We are asking for information on any strangers who were here the few days before her death. We may not know who did this at this moment, but we will find the guilty person, definitely, *bien sûr*."

Katherine opened her mouth to mention the stranger that the man in the candy store had told her about at the same moment he uttered an exclamation. Curious, she looked out the window. A garbage truck was backing slowly along the alley. It stopped at the building next to the museum, the two properties being separated by a stone wall, and a young man in a reflective vest came around the back of the truck to disappear through a gate into the next little yard, which was paved over. Seconds later, he was back with a small trash can that he put on a lift to be upended into the truck. He let the empty can bang on the concrete as he returned it, then he came over to the side wall of the museum and, to Katherine's surprise and, apparently, the policeman's, since he uttered another exclamation, ducked into a short door in the wall that Katherine hadn't seen from the angle of the window and disappeared from their sight. A door banged and there he was with a different trash can, ducking back through the adjoining side wall and headed to the neighbor's alley gate.

The policeman muttered, *"Merde,"* and hurried out of the salon. Katherine heard him crashing down the stairs and stayed where she was. Okay, this was important, but why? The truck was backing along the alley. Did that mean there was only one way to access it? But the gendarmes' station was only a couple of streets away and surely they figured that out already. They already knew the trash was picked up by the municipal service. They had talked to Jeannette, who explained she put it out on Tuesday while she was cleaning up.

Filing the incident away to share with Pippa, who would undoubtedly seize on it and add some kind of outlandish interpretation, Katherine turned away from the window. She remembered the flimsy piece of paper she had jammed in her pocket, the one that was caught in the hem of the droopy velvet drape. Pulling it out, she smoothed it enough to read it. It had an unusual medieval-style cross underneath which was, she guessed, a prayer or a piece of scripture. The announcement of a "special Mass" with a time but not a date. Written in an elegant, swooping hand diagonally across the page was a message. *"Dieu t'aime,"* God loves you. Interesting, the "you" was the familiar "tu" form that made the message seem more personal. A religious tract, perhaps?

Katherine stuffed the paper back in her pocket, not sure it meant anything. What she needed right now was a warm café and a hot chocolate. Maybe she could persuade Madame to come with her. The dear woman badly needed some cheering up.

CHAPTER 12

The officer in charge of the investigation was standing inside the locked museum door, quizzing Madame, who was sitting on one of the large chairs, looking like a schoolgirl called before the principal. He seemed confused and asked her to say again how she took out the trash. Did she go around the block to deposit it outside the wall? Madame looked up at him and asked why she would do that?

"There is no back door to the alley," he said, waving toward her apartment.

"Of course not. We go, or at least the schoolgirl who helps me twice a week goes, through the old half door in the below stairs."

"But the trash goes through a neighbor's yard, yes? Why didn't you tell my men?"

"I don't recall them asking me. But what difference can it make?" Madame asked. "The trash goes out once a week unless there has been some special event. And no one but us and the man who owns that yard knows about the door, and he doesn't live there anymore. The house has been empty for almost a year."

"The trash collectors know. Anyone who saw them picking up your trash would know."

"*Mais non, Monsieur*. Not necessarily. If you think about it, all they see from the alley is the collector coming in and out of the neighbor's door in the wall. It gives me much peace of mind, I assure you, especially since the wooden door frame downstairs in the *sous-sol* is warped and the lock doesn't fit quite right."

The man made a growling noise in his throat, told her he would send two gendarmes back to check the back exit and the neighbor's back patio for evidence, and turned to leave, at which point Madame began the cumbersome process of unlocking the door. The policeman shifted his weight from one foot to the other and left without the customary goodbye as soon as she swung the door open.

"What was that about?" Katherine asked.

"Only he knows, I am sure," the old lady said, shaking her head. "But it means we shall have more gendarmes in the museum and I had to tell Josée and Jeannette just now to put off getting into that room to clean it still longer, I fear. Are you ready to leave also?"

Katherine realized Madame was holding on to the doorknob, ever the guardian of her private realm. She asked Madame if she would like to go out for something warm to eat, "something to cheer you up a little?" but Madame declined the offer. Her daughter would stop at the market and bring her some soup and a little sweet and she would be fine, thank you. Perhaps another day? "Please say *au revoir* to Josée for me," Katherine said, bending down to exchange kisses.

The rain was steadier now, and cold. Katherine wanted

only to get back to her house, turn on the electric heat, and maybe indulge in a hot bath if the balky hot-water heater would cooperate. She ducked her head and began to circle back down the main street toward the lot where the car was parked. The street was almost deserted. Even the optimistic shoppers had given up. Only a couple dashing toward the parking lot under the trees and a solitary person, maybe the man she bumped into, standing in the shelter at the bus stop. He was just handsome enough to remember.

As she passed the Sabines' shop, she glanced into the window. The store was dark, as she would have guessed, and there was a notice taped to the glass from inside. A blurry copy of a snapshot of a smiling Mme Sabine and the notice of a memorial service at the church in Avallon. She made a mental note of the time. She could hardly say she was a friend of the deceased, but she was a steady customer, and the Sabines recognized her when she went in to buy the *boudin blanc* sausages Michael insisted on eating at least once a week. She turned back to the sidewalk and had taken a few steps when she bumped into someone in a long black overcoat. *"Pardonnez moi,"* she said. She needed to watch where she walked. Twice in one day was too much.

"Rien," the man muttered in a cracked voice, it's nothing. The voice sounded familiar. Katherine was startled to see it was the widower himself, turning away from the door of the apartment above the shop. His collar was up and he was wearing the kind of billed cap Katherine usually associated with tweedy golfers. He looked different only because she had never seen him except in a dress shirt with a bow

tie and the sleeves rolled up, and a white apron tied around his waist. His face today was ravaged, pasty, the shadow of an unshaved beard and dark circles under his eyes making him look unkempt, ill.

She wondered if she should say anything to him, offer condolences. Surely, he had heard more than enough of those, and if some of the gossip was right, he was under at least a degree of suspicion as the spouse of the victim. He didn't look like a killer, more like a depressed and preoccupied—and already wet—man trying to get somewhere. Still, she ought to say something. Lifting her arm toward the poster in the window, she said, "I am so glad to know about this. I'm sure many of her friends and customers will want to be there."

He nodded, made a sound that might have meant agreement or thanks, and walked away down the street in the same direction she was walking, but faster. Katherine shrugged. Of course he didn't want to stand in the cold rain and chat with a casual customer.

Looking past the hurrying figure, Katherine saw a cluster of young people at the next intersection. They were laughing and chattering loudly, perhaps waiting for the bus, some shivering, some with their chins buried in the collars of the insubstantial jackets that, like those of young people everywhere, telegraphed their complete disdain for inclement weather. They all wore backpacks, no one had an umbrella, and they were soaked. The gold-blonde curls cascading from a thick, red knit scarf wound high around one girl's neck had to be Jeannette's. The girl had gotten to the bus stop early since the museum job had been put off.

Her back was turned to Katherine. M. Sabine had paused to use an ATM behind the clot of teenagers, who seemed to all be talking at the same time.

Katherine glanced at her watch. If the kids were waiting for the bus, it would be another fifteen minutes. She had time to finish her last errand and she could still give Jeannette a ride back to Reigny. People who had no other option complained all the time about the lumbering bus that took forever, stopping at every small crossroads between Avallon and Reigny.

After darting into the patisserie and waiting in a short line to buy two pistachio *macarons* she silently promised the dentist would be followed immediately by a vigorous toothbrushing, Katherine headed downhill toward the group of teens, who were looking at Jeannette at the moment. She was telling a story and her back was to the bank and its ATM. She probably didn't realize M. Sabine was there, finishing up his transaction and taking a phone from his coat pocket. He looked distracted and Katherine hoped Jeannette wasn't telling her friends about the body at the museum, although she had an unpleasant feeling that was the topic.

Confirming her suspicions as she got closer, a boy facing Jeannette suddenly kicked her in the shin and jerked his head toward M. Sabine. Jeannette turned and saw the man and when she faced the group again, her mouth was open in an exaggerated O. The kids got quiet, signaling whatever it was that teenagers meant with their various gestures and body moves, then parted into groups of twos and threes, hitching up their backpacks and studiously not looking in the butcher's direction. Jeannette and another girl ducked into the flimsy protection of the bus stop roof. The man who had been sitting there looking at his phone screen absently got up and wandered out, sticking his phone in his pocket and opening up his umbrella. Katherine didn't know everyone in Avallon, but something about this man made her sure he didn't live here. Odd place to visit in the depths of winter, she thought, and then Jeannette turned and, pushing her mane of hair away from her face, came to meet her.

"You still want a ride home?" Katherine asked after giving and receiving kisses.

"*Merci. Je suis trempé comme une soupe.*" She laughed as she complained about being soaked to the skin, and held up one arm to show Katherine that the rain had penetrated the fabric of her coat.

Jeannette chattered as Katherine drove slowly through the downpour, the car's heater blasting and windshield wipers laboring noisily back and forth. School was boring. The teachers were forever leaving the classroom to chat with each other during class. Romain, the boy in her history class, was handsome but never talked to her.

"So you aren't happy?"

"Oh, *oui*, I like being with my friends, you know? Especially after school."

As they got closer to the entrance to Reigny where Pippa lived, Jeannette was apparently reminded of the Englishwoman because she began to tell Katherine about Pippa's cornering her and asking questions about her work at the costume museum.

"She ask me about the *toupee*, you know, the hairpiece, on the mannequin, and if it was in the salon, and I say I cannot get into the salon yet. I clean—cleaned—on Monday and the dead woman did not turn up there until Thursday. Today, again the flics are saying to leave everything alone." She held up her hands in an exaggerated, palms and shoulders up, expression of confusion. "On Monday, the displays in that salon were as they should be, *comme il faut*, yes?"

Katherine pulled up in front of Jeannette's house, the motor running, and, replaying the reactions of the police officer, said, "But you did a special cleanup before Mme Sabine was found, didn't you?"

"I had to straighten up after the tour the church women took, but it wasn't hard, paper napkins and plates, and wineglasses on the mezzanine. Some empty wine bottles. Nothing on the level where Madame was murdered."

"About the cleaning up," Katherine said, thinking about the policeman's surprise when they stood at the window watching the garbage collector at work, "I'm not sure how you get the trash out. Is there any way to the yard through Madame's apartment?"

"No, not at all. You'd have to climb through a window, yes? The basement is only a small place I get to by going through the hallway, and it has a funny door that I duck down to get through. The trash can is just inside the door to the yard. It is a nuisance to get outside at times, I tell you." She made a face.

"I was looking at the yard from the salon upstairs today. There doesn't seem to be a gate to the alley. Where do the trash collectors pick it up? I saw a side entrance from the next house."

"*Mais oui*, I don't throw it over the back wall." She giggled and looked at Katherine.

Katherine hesitated. She knew Pippa annoyed people

with her pestering sometimes and Katherine didn't want to do that. She still felt she was on probation as a member in good standing of Reigny's community. Hers was a fragile acceptance in a small town with so many sensitivities. Still, she had a piece of paper in her coat pocket that demanded some explanation. Probably it was nothing, but Mme Sabine deserved at least a small measure of support in death. "When you cleaned up the day before the body was found, what did you actually do? Can you remember? It's only because I'm so concerned that nothing is overlooked in bringing this horrible murderer to justice, you see?"

Jeannette picked up her backpack from the floor in front of her. Her lower lip stuck out as if she thought she would be criticized for a lack of attention to her work. "Nothing in that room, only sweeping in the hallway in front of it, where they had grouped to look at the rosary collection, and below, where they had set up a food table. In the other tableaus, I do the regular thing—sweep the carpet, dust the tops of the furniture, use a cloth on the small things sitting on the tables. Since no one goes into the rooms, there's not much to do except look for cobwebs. I told the flics all this when they asked."

"And all was as it should be?"

"I think so. It is hard to remember. It was ordinary, you know?"

"Listen, Jeannette. I know it seems like Pippa Hathaway and I are asking a lot of questions, but we were both there and it still concerns us." Jeannette nodded and glanced over at Katherine, her face relaxing a bit. "I'm going to say something that shouldn't frighten you, but I think is impor-tant. I don't think it's wise to talk about what you know, what you saw, or even that you were there with anyone else, well, anyone but the police when they ask. It's best that no one else hear about you and how close you were to the murder site, okay?"

"Okay," the girl said, with no apparent worry in her voice. *"D'accord,* only my friends already know."

"I realize that. But I think it's best you don't spread the information any further."

At that moment, the door to the stonecutter's house burst open and what seemed like a herd of small boys rushed out into the courtyard, calling for their big sister. " 'Nette, come in, come in, we're hungry. What's for dinner, 'Nette?" Their hair getting plastered to their heads in the downpour, the boys, in good spirits, banged on the Citroën's passenger-side door, rapped small knuckles on the closed window, and peered in.

Jeannette opened the door. *"Ta gueule,"* she shouted, shut up, a term Katherine had heard kids in groups use on their way to or from school or soccer games, always in high spirits. It had the same effect now, that is, none. It wasn't until the girl got out, leaned her head back into the car, and thanked Katherine for the ride that the boys seemed to realize they were getting drenched, and raced back into the house.

"Is there enough food in the refrigerator to feed that horde?" Katherine said, laughing.

"There is never enough for them."

"Tell you what. Send one of them over to my house in fifteen minutes. I bought a lot of sausages thinking Michael would be home tonight, but he won't get back for a few more days and the sausages won't keep. I had to buy them at the supermarket since M. Sabine is closed for now. There are way too many in the package."

Jeannette smiled her thanks and slammed the car door. In the open doorway of the house, two boys and a puppy clustered, watching her with interest and waiting for her attention. It was too much for a fifteen-year-old girl, Katherine thought, as she drove up the hill, got out to open the stiff gate, and parked as close to the house as she could, but what choice did she have? Jean was either out doing whatever brought in a few euros at a time, or sitting at the café, striking up conversation with neighbors who couldn't avoid him and who rarely offered to buy him the glass of wine he hoped to snag.

Tomorrow, she would have her small lunch party, hope that the weather was better, and only after that would she sit quietly and try to make sense of the odds and ends, the clues as Pippa would call them, that were piling up about Mme Sabine's last hours and her grotesque death.

CHAPTER 13

Entertaining at the little stone house Michael had bought for her when she wished for a place in France was more complicated in the winter, when it had to be indoors. The misshapen rattan chairs that sat under the pear tree from the moment its tiny green leaves sprouted until the last yellow ones curled and fell were stacked haphazardly in the storage shed now. The long table stayed outside, but was draped in a plastic tarp to minimize water damage. At this time of year, when they were by themselves, Katherine and Michael ate off a rickety table that sometimes held a telephone and other times a stack of art books. But six guests required some creativity. Katherine hoped that by standing her paintings around the edges of the living room and plunking a small, stone Virgin on a bed of straw in the center of two tables pushed together, the women she was hosting would be less likely to notice that none of the chairs matched and a few were of odd heights off the floor. She would reserve the one with the lowest seat for herself even though that would make her look like a small, gray-haired child allowed this once to sit with the grown-ups.

It would be awkward, she told herself as she sniffed the bubbling coq au vin, made with an Irancy red wine that the *cave* owner assured her was eminently drinkable, especially if cooked. At least that's what Katherine thought he said, although after she had purchased it and was walking back to the car, she wondered if that could have been right. Perhaps he had been joking. The dish was a favorite in this part of Burgundy and a bit risky since everyone coming to lunch would doubtless have more authentic recipes than hers.

However well or poorly the resulting meal turned out, today's gathering would be more successful than last summer's. No more Albert Bellegarde to break a plate over Yves's head. Yves, undoubtedly warned by Sophie not to come near the Goffs without an invitation, certainly would not drop in and set a major drama in motion. The invading Americans, Penny and Betty Lou, were long gone and not missed by the denizens of Reigny-sur-Canne. Instead, it would be an intimate group of women united in their good wishes for pregnant Marie as Christmas and her due date approached. The only wild card, if you could call her that, was the old man Lacrois's daughter, Josephine, and since she said she intended to stay and take care of him in his waning months, Katherine thought the other women in the village should welcome her.

She sliced bread, barely noticing Gracey and Fideaux, whose heads swiveled in unison following her motions as she put each cut slice in the basket. The winter salad was made and resting in the refrigerator and two bottles of ruby red wine had been opened to let them breathe at the recommendation of the owner of the small wine cellar in Noyers who had talked her into a vintage slightly more costly than those she regularly bought from the five-euro bin. The cheese course was resting on the highest shelf in the kitchen to avoid tempting the dogs, who loved the creamy Brillat-Savarin as much as she did.

She was pleased to have today's party to keep her from missing Michael quite so much while she waited for his return, and to distract her from the murder scene at the museum. That setting had come back to her in a nightmare last night. Poor Mme Sabine had stood up from the divan, unwrapped a ligature from her neck, and smiled ghoulishly at everyone while shouting *"Dieu vous garde"* at the top of her lungs. Remembering the image, Katherine shivered. She looked at her watch. Good, enough time to change into the maroon vintage heels that complemented her 1930-ish dress only partially obscured by a warm sweater, and bribe the dogs up to the bedroom with the crusty ends of the baguette.

Josephine Lacrois was holding forth on some aspect of Beaune's entirely superior cultural life, the fourth or fifth she had described in great detail while gesturing with polished nails and ring-covered fingers. Mme Robilier, whose nature was to soothe and admire, perhaps the result of caring for a husband with dementia, was listening with a rapt expression. Her hands twisted and clutched each other in her lap, however, a hint that she was not as relaxed as her smile indicated. The reason for her nervousness was undoubtedly her neighbor and sometime rival, the widow Mme Pomfort, Reigny's leading citizen. Mme Pomfort was not so enthusiastic about the out-of-town guest. She had been interrupted by Mme Lacrois every time she tried to counter Beaune's charms with those of the ancient and historically important town in which she lived and ruled. Marie sat smiling absently, rubbing her distended belly and sipping a cup of warm water. Marie's mother, Helene, turned sparkling eyes on the dueling women, clearly enjoying it as much as she might a good tennis match. Pippa was alternately shredding and nibbling a piece of bread as she stared into the middle distance and gnawed her lower lip, missing everything that wasn't translated for her by Katherine.

"Do you know who attended last year's wine auctions?" Josephine said. She rattled off a list of celebrity names that Katherine vaguely recognized. "The most famous wine district in France, you know, the Côte-d'Or. And the tour buses coming to us like magnets. They all want to see the old Hospices and the van der Weyden altarpiece. You have seen it, I'm sure? The most beautiful painting in all of France, to be sure."

Katherine had enjoyed Beaune and the altarpiece very much, but surely it wasn't the most beautiful painting in France. What about the Monet water lilies and the Mona Lisa and the . . . She snapped back to attention as Mme Pomfort raised her voice in protest.

"I never did care for it. Too religious, if you ask me. And the old hospital struck me as rather grim." In an effort to be charitable, she added, "But I did have a wonderful lunch nearby, the best chocolate mousse I have ever eaten."

Marie made a happy noise as if the mere mention pleased her taste buds. Hastily, Katherine passed the small plate of chocolates, part of her purchase in exchange for gossip the day before, to the pregnant woman. Marie smiled beatifically at her as she popped one in her mouth.

"Isn't part of that hospital complex, the building that

isn't a museum now, still in use, for poor people and or-phans?" Helene looked around the room.

"Oh, indeed," Josephine said, "it is, run by the nuns, of course. They do such charitable work every day, centuries after the Hospices was founded."

"Nuns, is it?" Pippa said after Katherine translated.

"Yes, such godly women, and they also raise money to help pay for the services, they and the people in the local Catholic parish. I, myself, have often made small contribu-tions. There is a saintly man who arranges for collections, you know, for Beaune and for other important charitable works in Africa. Beaune is fortunate to have such generous Christians in its midst."

"Oh, indeed," Mme Robilier said. In Reigny, the bat-tered little church was hardly more than a refuge against sudden downpours when it was even open, a forlorn rem-nant in a town with little use for religion except among a few old people and the occasional family wanting a baptism or funeral. Even then, the ceremony had to wait until a priest could be rounded up from somewhere else, frequently one who made a circuit once or twice a year.

"In fact, I have some lovely news," Josephine said, swiv-eling her head around the room to make sure everyone was listening. "I have asked the priest in Beaune if he can come to Reigny to say a special mass during the Christmas holi-day. Of course, we will have to clean the church and bring in candles and little heaters and flowers." She beamed.

There was a brief silence. Marie's mother smiled po-litely, Marie looked puzzled, and Reigny's two grand dames looked discomfited.

To fill the silence, Katherine jumped in. "I'm happy to

help make the church presentable. We need to do that anyway for the Christmas gathering. I don't suppose your priest could come then?"

Josephine laughed. "Oh no. There's a large congregation in Avallon that would be shocked if he weren't there on Christmas day. I myself will be there with a gentleman friend." A slight flush rose on her neck, and she patted her hair. "But I think if the good father sees an enthusiastic parish here, he might encourage other priests to include Reigny in their visits more regularly."

"Madame," Mme Pomfort said, "this is something the residents of Reigny-sur-Canne must discuss among themselves. I'm not sure there is what you describe as an enthusiastic parish to be had. We mostly go about our business on our own."

Katherine thought Madame might be thinking of the church garden, wishing to avoid any attention to her current possession of it. Mme Robilier looked at her clan's garden foe thoughtfully before nodding. She might have the same reasons for wishing to keep the Reigny property disputes within the family, so to speak. It was one thing to wage internecine war over whose ancestors were given title to the valuable space next to the church, and quite another to think of taking on Church or State for rights to the pretty square of arable land at the center of town.

Of course the French state had, after the revolution, seized all the churches and their property, and the government in Burgundy had given this building to the two towns in the commune. Since the other town had withered to nothing, it belonged to Reigny. The garden, well, that was another matter. Was it originally Church ground and therefore the *mairie*'s to rule? Or were Mme Pomfort's claims by distant relationship to a branch of the Bonaparte family—and Mme Robilier's grandparents' equally valid assertion of a long-ago deed to the land—legitimate? The feud, supported by periodic coups that kept the two families alert for decades, might never be settled. At the moment, there was a truce, for which Katherine was grateful. She didn't want to be asked to take sides in the delicate balance that was residency in Reigny.

Josephine had found her voice and begun to speak when Pippa interrupted. "I say, Katherine," Pippa said in a loud voice that stopped Josephine in midsentence, "didn't you say Michael has wonderful news? Can you tell us?"

"I'm not sure what it is yet," Katherine said after translating the question for her other guests. "It has something to do with the tour and a phone call he got the other day. I think he wants to surprise me."

Helene raised her eyebrows in a question and Katherine had to take a moment to explain to her and to Josephine that Michael was a musician whose truncated career had recently gotten a boost from some visiting Americans with big ambitions and the apparent ability to achieve them.

"He's finishing an album with Betty Lou Holliday that will be sold as a CD and streamed, not that I understand any of the technology, only that one can make money from it, and the songs can be the centerpiece of a tour next year."

"Hallyday? Is she related to Johnny?" Josephine said, her eyes lighting up at the reference to France's longtime pop idol.

"No, she's American, and it's a different spelling," Katherine hastened to say. Josephine's face fell.

"Will they come to Burgundy?" Marie said. "If they do, we can all go see him."

"I doubt anywhere in Europe. But Betty Lou is a famous American country music personality and that's why her husband, their producer, thinks all of this will be successful."

"Michael must be chuffed," Pippa said.

"I think so, if that means excited," Katherine said, and laughed. It was hard enough translating to French for the other guests and then to English for Pippa. Adding slang spun her head.

Into a short pause, Josephine leaned forward. "But none of you has mentioned the big news, your murder."

Katherine thought that was because it would spoil the mood and, from the expressions on Marie's and Mme Robilier's faces at least, she felt sure she was right. Mme Pomfort, however, sat up straighter and opened her mouth as if to say something. However, her eyes sparkling, Mme Lacrois beat her to it.

"I knew her, of course. Yes," to a few murmurs, "perhaps better than you did even though you shopped with her. Dear Mme Sabine was as dedicated to the mission fund in Beaune as I was."

"Really?" Katherine spoke aloud before she could stop herself.

"Oh yes, I saw the newspaper and immediately said a prayer for her soul. She was a good woman, *je vous assure.*"

Mme Pomfort's lips had snapped closed at this bombshell, this superior hand the newcomer had displayed. Momentarily silent, she eyed her new rival for dominance, her lips pursed and her expression hostile. From where she sat, Katherine recognized the look she had been treated to for so long, and briefly sympathized with old man Lacrois's granddaughter. But not for long. Katherine realized the woman was relishing her announcement and intended to make the most of it.

Josephine Lacrois made no mention of lovers or other illicit encounters her friend might have had and, indeed, was eloquent in praise of Mme Sabine's commitment and generosity, her Christian sympathy with the less fortunate, and her admiration for the priest who came from his missionary work to speak with the support group both women belonged to. A woman of great virtue, all in all, quite like herself, Mme Lacrois implied.

"This will interest Pippa," Katherine said, nodding in the direction of the writer, whose attention was drifting among all the French chatter. "She's a mystery writer," she added. "She is sure she will be able to solve the crime herself, as a creative exercise only, of course."

Mme Pomfort made a sound that might have been disgust, or perhaps incredulity, and Katherine made a mental note to fill Pippa in later since the young woman had clearly missed the gist of the discussion.

"Ç'est vrai?" Josephine said, looking at Pippa with considerably more interest than she had during lunch. "She intends to do the police work, then?"

"Not exactly. But Pippa is good at figuring things out, and it's rare that we, or rather, she, has the chance to be so close to a real crime."

"And she has ideas, yes?"

"I'd better not try to speak for her. I will probably misstate something. Pippa," Katherine said, switching to English, "Mme Lacrois is interested in what you're learning about the murder of Mme Sabine."

Pippa brightened. "Tell her not much yet, but I will do more research tomorrow. I'm sure it will become clear soon." She beamed at the Frenchwoman as Katherine translated.

"Ah, admirable. If your English friend wants to talk with me about dear Bertholde, I would be pleased to meet her for an aperitif some afternoon." Josephine looked at Pippa as she spoke, an exaggerated smile miming her enthusiasm. "I would love to hear more about this investigation."

Pippa nodded enthusiastically, although Katherine wondered how the young woman would manage, given that Pippa and Josephine could only conduct this much of a conversation through her, and she was getting tired. Translating accurately wasn't easy.

The luncheon wound down shortly after that. Marie apologized for leaving first, her mother in tow, but said she had to lie down after such a good meal. Mme Pomfort reminded Katherine that she had offered to touch up the Reigny church's faded painting of Virgin and Child, which Katherine privately thought should be erased, being an amateurish nineteenth-century imitation of a medieval-style fresco and not worth restoring. Having been slow to earn them, however, she had to stay in Madame's good graces, and so she promised to come and inspect the work in a day or so and to have it ready for *réveillon*, Christmas Eve. There would be music, a bit of singing, and reading of the scriptures by a few residents the next day. No Mass, but a community meal in the community room at the *mairie* afterward.

Josephine was effusive in her thanks to Katherine as she

pulled up the collar of her fur coat. "You are *trop gentil*, too kind, Mme Goff. I shall see you in church. Until then, let us hope they capture the madman who killed Bertholde Sabine. *Dieu vous garde.*"

In the midst of her goodbyes Katherine suppressed a shudder as the phrase brought back her nightmare. Another godly woman like the murdered Mme Sabine. Maybe the holiday season was encouraging people to feel more religious?

CHAPTER 14

The house was quiet, the dishes were washed, and Katherine sat on the divan with Gracey at her feet, nibbling at the last of the open box of chocolates and trying to read Emile Zola's *La Débâcle*, which seemed to her a long and tedious chronicle of a long and tedious war. She was only doing it because Yves had assured her it would be good for her understanding of both French language and French history. Katherine suspected he had also been trying to make a sale. Setting up a shop that dealt in rare books in a tiny hamlet like Reigny was a dubious recipe for success. Perhaps that's why he had offered her a discount on the price, the only way she could have afforded the little, leather-bound edition with the thin paper and the pen and ink illustrations. Maybe she should ask Michael to bring back an English translation since she was still mired in the early chapters and had to admit to herself she had no solid idea of what was happening in the story. The Avallon murder was more intriguing, although the instant she thought that, she apologized mentally to the victim. Murder as entertainment? She had looked away from the victim as quickly as she could once she understood what had happened. But Madame's face had burned itself into her memory.

Was Pippa right in saying the gendarmes would think first of the husband as the killer? Working side by side every day, the couple could have built up resentments that their customers never saw. And then there was that snoop's salacious speculation that the woman was off having an affair. The mannequin in the river was a complete puzzle. Why? And Pippa had it in her head that a missing wig and a cross dropped in a puddle were clues. Katherine was about to get up for a cup of herbal tea before bedtime when the cell phone next to her rang. The best news, the caller was her husband.

"Hello, darling," she said. "I've been hoping you would call. What time is it there?"

"Hi, Kay. Noon here, and I'm happy to say, I'll be on a plane soon. We finished everything last night, listened to it this morning, and we're done. No looking back. This is it."

"I'm thrilled, not only for you and Betty Lou, but selfishly for me. I've missed you so much."

"Want to hear the title of the CD?"

"I think so unless it's Holliday and Goff, which sounds like a sleazy law firm."

" 'Looking Back, Looking Forward.' What do you think? See, it hints at the new version of 'Raging Love' and both of our former styles, but also says we're going somewhere new."

"I like it, although I'm still nervous about Eric's reaction when he hears that you're singing that song."

"Here's the big, big news. I was going to wait to tell you, but I can put your worries to rest, Kay."

She waited, holding her breath.

"J.B.'s lawyers talked to Crazy Leopards's lawyers, who said using the song was fine. Then—can you believe this—Eric called J.B. and asked to meet with us?"

Katherine's stomach fluttered and she swallowed hard. "He did? And?"

"He not only is fine with us doing a new arrangement but he wants us to open for the Leopards on their next tour, which happens to be next spring, when we want to schedule ours."

"I'm stunned. What's the catch?"

"Yeah, I fished around for that too. We had dinner with J.B. and Betty Lou, then Eric suggested he and I go out for a beer. I think he feels guilty for all the crap, for the way they cut me out of the band and tried to copyright my songs without sharing the copyright."

"He said that?"

"Not exactly, but he did say the band got a lot of bad advice back then and that they changed managers three or four years ago. Remember, that's when they offered to settle about the copyrighted material?"

Katherine was happy for Michael, but her protective instincts were aroused. If Eric was scamming her husband a second time . . . well, she didn't know what she'd do but she would be livid. "I think this will be great for you and Betty Lou, and I imagine J.B. and his lawyers will make sure it's all spelled out in an unbreakable contract before you bank on it."

Michael laughed. "You don't have to warn me, sweetie. I've been burned before. Yes, J.B. is all over it. I have to say he's also so happy he acts like someone who's taken a few too many snorts."

She was silent again. Michael had never been into drugs, but was Memphis and the high from this news tempting him?

He laughed again. "Your silence speaks volumes, Kay, and no, I'm excited but sober. Sober and, I swear, cautious. But you have to agree, this is potentially the biggest boost we could have dreamed of. The Leopards fill huge stadiums and sell millions of songs. There isn't anything that could be a bigger push for Betty Lou and me, and, of course, J.B., who's having a hard time waiting for the lawyers to get the contracts in order so he can start telling the world."

"It's the best news, darling, or almost. Knowing you'll be here soon is the best. When do you leave Memphis?"

"Day after tomorrow. I'll be home Friday. Can you pick me up at the train station?"

"Can I? I'll be the one jumping up and down and waving like mad from the parking lot. Will you be bringing the music so I can hear it right here?"

"Absolutely. That and your Elvis bobblehead doll."

Katherine was too wary of Eric's double dealing from the past to be completely ready to relax, but if—*if*—it were true, Michael was finally going to be doing what he loved the most, after a long time existing at the margins of the music world he had loved. If audiences liked what they heard, it would change their lives in ways she couldn't see yet.

Money, for sure, and in her heart of hearts that was a

big deal. She was tired of being broke, of having to weigh every purchase against the danger of overstepping their budget. She liked their little stone house, but simple things like a reliable water heater and a roof that didn't leak would be heaven. Bones every week for the dogs, a new winter coat. She stopped herself. This was precisely what she couldn't allow herself to do.

Jumping up so quickly that Gracey snapped out of a sound sleep and struggled to her feet, Katherine told herself the dogs needed their last, short walk, and then time to lock up and go to bed. With Michael coming home Friday, she had to shop, plan a good dinner for him, and do whatever detective work the crumpled paper required. Michael would try to talk her out of getting involved, she knew. The yellow cat, who had found a warm spot next to Katherine's thigh, seemed to be standing in for Michael. It looked up at her with eyes full of disapproval at her plans, and stalked off on stiff legs.

Wednesday passed in a flurry of preparations for Michael's return. Katherine had tried to fill the void left by his absence with activity. But the moment there was a specific day set for his arrival, the hours until the evening train was due threatened to stretch into something untenable. So, she looked around her and found a thousand ways to distract herself. The cobwebs festooning the dried herbs hanging over the doorway between the kitchen and the living room were unappetizing. The layer of dust along the top of the bookcase was thick enough to write in. The ordeal of cramming sheets into the peculiar French washing and drying machine could not be put off another day. She hadn't trudged up to the *poubelle* with the bag full of trash after the ladies' lunch because it had been so cold. She worked in a storm of determination to fill the time productively. By Wednesday evening, she was too exhausted to do anything but let the dogs out into the yard instead of a last walk, and to make herself an omelet.

She needed to go to Avallon tomorrow to lay in food, fill the gas tank, and see if the religious tract in the drapery had come from the local church and what it might mean. It hardly seemed like a clue to anything, more likely a discarded scrap from the meeting of the church ladies that had drifted to the window during the confusion after the discovery of Mme Sabine's body. Katherine ignored the little voice that asked her if she really believed that.

Before it was completely dark, a flurry of raps on the door and a familiar voice calling "*Ç'est moi*" brought Jeannette into the kitchen. "*Bonsoir*, Katherine," she said as Katherine closed the door behind her.

"English, please," Katherine said in mock seriousness. "You want to practice, right?"

"Yes, thank you." The girl's English was improving and, although Katherine was not going to say so, her accent and choice of words were going to make some American boy fall hard for her when and if she made it to the States for the visit she dreamed of. "I will stay later than the bus comes to Reigny to do my work after school at the museum because Madame tells me Thursday—"

"Told me," Katherine said.

"—told me that the police may be with her for a while. If you will be in Avallon in the afternoon, is it possible that I come in your car, please?"

Katherine told herself she could time her chores in town so she could give Jeannette a lift. Why not? Maybe she could even sketch in the studio early in the day if the weather stayed as clear as it seemed tonight. "Absolutely, that is, yes." With a kiss and a grin, Jeannette ducked out into the night and Katherine heard the gate squeak as she headed back down the hill. These days, Katherine thought as she closed the door, it wasn't necessary to count the silver or see if the little objects picked up at flea markets were still in their places on tables and bookshelf tops after the daughter of Reigny's resident petty thief had left. She smiled and felt a small surge of pride in Jeannette.

CHAPTER 15

Thursday morning, the wind and rain had returned. Instead of sketching, she settled on the chaise with a book about French costumes through time. It had been a flea market find for ten euros after some bargaining, only slightly foxed, its page edges yellowing and its binding slightly loose, but rich with color illustrations. Rococo ladies in beribboned gowns, men wearing powdered wigs and vests with ruffled shirts. Not that she'd use them for inspiration, really. Her favorite historical period was earlier, and her chosen models were Burgundy's hardworking peasants, even if they were idealized.

After a lunch of cheese and bread, she put on boots that could stand up to the wet, a sweater at least two sizes too large that draped almost to her knees, and the old black coat that was not waterproof but had a collar she could turn all the way up to her nose if necessary. She was hesitant for an instant when she saw her reflection, definitely that of a witch, although not so bad for a fifty-five-year-old, as she pulled on her black wool cap and reached for her tote bag.

Funny how foreigners thought "France" and pictured Provence on a sunny day with lavender and van Gogh's irises and sunflowers. Truth was, if Reigny didn't get a sunny day soon, she would scream.

The longtime population showed little sign of the siege mentality that gripped Katherine. People walked briskly but seemingly cheerfully in Avallon, stopping to speak to acquaintances, tipping their umbrellas to fend off blowing rain, ducking into shops to look at everything from lingerie to hardware. It was less than two weeks before Christmas and there was a sense of happy purpose everywhere. Katherine eyed a hand-knitted sweater for Michael, but it was shockingly expensive. A tweedy cap with a short bill like the one the butcher had been wearing the other day looked useful, although even small luxuries like that would have to wait until she was sure his good fortune was not going to go up in smoke. He never wore a hat other than his Stetson, anyway, the real thing and good in any weather, he told her every time she doubted.

Before she was loaded down with groceries, she decided to visit the church. Maybe a table in the foyer would have flyers like the one she'd found on the floor at the museum. The big wooden doors weren't locked, but it was as chilly inside as only cold stone could get when she pulled one open and stepped in. No lights and no one else present, although there was a folding table set up near the holy water font. A few small stacks of announcements, one with a drawing of the church's exterior at the top. A flyer about the church's history and medieval layout. Nothing with that symbol on the paper she'd found at the museum. The schedules showed the only Masses offered here were at different times from those on her scrap of paper, and all were on Sundays. No paper with scriptures, either.

As she checked for wall boxes where something similar might be held, the door behind her opened and a woman covered completely against the rain ducked into the foyer. The woman shook her open umbrella, stamped water off her boots, and pushed her hood back off her head. Only then did Katherine recognize the woman from Beaune who had been at her house so recently. At the same time, Josephine Lacrois noticed her and exclaimed, "Madame Goff, how lovely to see you. I had no idea anyone else was here yet. I came to lay out materials about some lectures in Beaune that I think the locals might want to attend." She approached, detouring to one side to dip two fingers into the stone font and touch them to her forehead as she made the sign of the cross.

"I didn't realize you were Catholic," she said as she unbuttoned her coat.

"Oh, I'm not. I just stopped in to see . . ." Katherine stopped. She wasn't ready to share the paper she'd found with Mme Lacrois, nor explain where she'd found it or why it interested her. "To see if there's a Christmas Mass here in Avallon even if there won't be any in Reigny. I like the pageantry."

"Of course, although our faith is less about pageantry than piety, and a special concern for the poor around the world."

"I do understand. I suppose I'm thinking more of the U.S., where there is sometimes an acting out of the manger scene, you know, with children and singing." Katherine chided herself mentally for her description, which didn't do the holiday proceedings justice, but focused on the topic of her visit. "Here in Burgundy, you have such ancient traditions, and a rich heritage, and a vast trove of art to draw on. I recently saw a handout with some kind of scripture and a lovely piece of medieval iconography on it."

"I suppose it could have been ours, the group I belong to, although that group meets in Beaune, not in Avallon, and most certainly not in Reigny-sur-Canne, which seems to be without any interest in the good works of the Church. So disappointing, but what can you do?"

Josephine frowned and fluffed up her hair before turning back to Katherine. "The priest I told you about visits our group, to keep us informed. Such an inspiring figure." She looked past Katherine with a beatific smile, as if seeing this great man over Katherine's shoulder. "There is such need and we are blessed to be able to help. Here, I'll show you." She opened the cardboard box she had packed in plastic and handed Katherine a flyer.

Bingo. It was almost identical, although the verse may have been different from the one in Katherine's tote bag. The little flyer was tucked under the flap of a donation envelope. "Yes, it looks very like the one I saw. May I keep it?" Katherine said.

"But of course. This is my first time meeting with the women's group here and I thought I would bring these to share. And, while the Reverend Father won't be in Avallon, I shall invite you to drive down with me to Beaune in a few weeks to hear him in person when he speaks to us about his work in Africa. I am sure you will be moved. Maybe you can bring your husband?"

"Oh, I don't think that's his sort of thing," Katherine said.

"You might tell him there are several men who attend the missionary lectures. Although," Josephine said, "I am sympathetic. My own gentleman friend will not venture anywhere near the church." She turned a bright smile on Katherine. "But I will prevail one day, you shall see."

"That's lovely, the boyfriend, I mean. Will he be visiting Reigny?"

Josephine's attention was distracted by her box of leaflets, and when she had pulled a stack out and put them on the table, she only said, "Well, lovely to see you again, and do tell your husband about the lecture."

"Thank you," Katherine said, already practicing her excuses for declining the offer of being cooped up with the devout new neighbor. "I will mention it, but, I realize I'm late picking up Jeannette—you haven't met her yet, I don't think, she's the only teenager in Reigny—and she'll be standing in this rain waiting."

Katherine didn't appreciate the big, American-style supermarket that had come to the outskirts of town. She had gotten used to the regimen of stopping in a handful of market stalls and specialty shops that constituted the traditional European method of shopping. Hand-wrapped roasts and farm-fresh cabbages, lovingly displayed tomatoes handled only by the bustling farmer's wife after you pointed to the ones you wanted, and little baskets of fragile, early strawberries from Switzerland tempted her more than plastic-wrapped meats with congealed liquid trapped inside, and tumbled bins of well-traveled apples. But she did occasion-

ally slink into the massive store when her shopping list in-
cluded staples, always hoping she didn't bump into someone
she knew.

It was ridiculous, of course. If she did chance on Mme
Robilier or the charming young man from the pharmacy, it
was because they, too, wanted cases of Badoit water rather
than the few bottles they could carry back from the little
épicerie closer to home. Still, she hurried as much as possible,
and was glad to get out of the gigantic parking lot—another
untraditional feature of French contemporary life—and
back on the road. She had almost left town before she remembered she was to pick Jeannette up, and she circled
back from the main road into the cramped old streets, preparing her apology for being late.

Jeannette was nowhere in sight, not huddled under an
awning or fooling around with friends. In fact, there were
no students on the street. Katherine glanced at her watch
and squeezed into a space half on the sidewalk, prepared to
wait. The girl wouldn't have taken the bus, would she? If
one of the boys from school was on it, perhaps? She decided
she would wait for thirty minutes. If the bus didn't come, it
would mean it had already been through, and Jeannette was
certainly on it. But if the girl was sitting in a café, paying no
attention, this would give her a whole half hour to remember the meeting place.

Forty minutes later, the bus had come, but gone again.
No Jeannette. Katherine was annoyed. She walked to the
two closest cafés and peeked in, then looked in the clothing
store, the hat shop, and a tiny newspaper and magazine shop
wedged in between them. The light was failing, the dogs
would be hungry, and the house dark. Jeannette must have

gotten a ride or perhaps there was an earlier bus. She couldn't wait any longer. Thankfully, the rain had stopped. A few early stars winked from a break in the clouds as it got darker, and it even looked as though the weather was changing, no warmer but at least drier for a few days.

After she had put away the groceries, fed Gracey and Fideaux, and opened a can of sardines as a treat for the yellow cat, Katherine exchanged her wet boots for woolen socks and the funny Dutch clogs, as always a *vide-grenier* purchase, in this case for almost nothing because who, other than that eccentric American artist, would think of walking around on clunky wooden shoes? Her small feet had a tendency to slide around in their carved cavities, and they made a lot of noise that had none of the rhythm of her tap shoes, but she enjoyed the conceit of being a Dutch girl on occasion.

A veal chop cooking in a bath of white wine, carrots, and potatoes gave off a comforting aroma, and she had time to read and sip some of the same wine while they were gently stewing. The problem, she admitted to herself after ten minutes of restlessly moving between the kitchen and her cozy chaise, was that she was not going to rest until she knew Jeannette was home, doubtless having forgotten all about their plan to come back to Reigny together. "It's no use, Gracey. Why doesn't Jean buy a cheap phone? Never mind," she said as she pulled on her boots and buttoned up a coat that wasn't wet, "I know he can't afford the monthly charges and can't figure out a way to steal them."

Turning the burner down as low as it would go, Katherine banged her way out the door and walked rapidly downhill and around the corner. The lights were on at Jean's house and she could hear the little boys chattering and arguing, as usual. The dogs barked as she got to the gate and before she could call out, the front door opened and Jean peered out. *"Qui est la?"* he shouted into the night air.

"It's me, Jean. Katherine Goff. I came to make sure Jeannette made it home."

Jean, the sleeves of his shirt rolled up and a cigarette hanging from his lips, darted out and met her at the gate, shushing the dogs roughly. He opened it for her and she followed him back into the house. It didn't surprise her to see that the interior looked a lot like the tangle of secondhand objects that littered his courtyard. In this case, it was clothing and food boxes and newspapers and odds and ends of every kind—broken toys, a fishing pole, some big plastic jugs, a lamp with no lamp shade. Her brain tried to sort everything she was registering, but it was too much. She turned her back on it and the boys who had stopped shouting and were looking at her with intense curiosity.

"I came to make sure Jeannette got home safely."

Jean looked warily at her. " 'Nette's with you, isn't she?"

Katherine's heart fluttered. "No. She was supposed to meet me on the same corner in Avallon where we usually meet, but she wasn't there."

Jean took the cigarette out of his mouth and stared at it as if it held the answer to this puzzle. "Then where is she?" he said, squinting at her.

"I hoped she was here. I waited for over half an hour until the second bus came and went. I—I—hoped she had come home on the first one. Could she be at a friend's?"

" 'Nette doesn't have any friends," said the older of the two boys, at which good joke they both started laughing and poking each other.

"*Tais-toi,*" Jean said—shouted really—at the boys. They stopped laughing instantly and retreated to a worn sofa in the corner. There were many ways to say "shut up" in French and she would never know all of them. This version was clear, however, at least in this household.

Jean was, Katherine reminded herself, not the worst father a girl could have. He was no role model, being a small-time property thief and only occasional breadwinner, but he did love Jeannette and, presumably, the boys, in his way. Jean looked worried now, and Katherine was too. It had been almost completely dark when she had given up and come back, and there were no more buses this late. "So, could she have gone to someone else's house?"

"She always comes home in time to cook dinner," Jean said. "And everyone she goes to school with lives too far away to walk. If she didn't have a bike, she couldn't go to a schoolmate's house in the next village." At the mention of dinner, the youngest boy got up and edged toward the kitchen. His brother was too engaged in following this de-velopment—a missing sister—to budge or speak.

Katherine explained where she had looked for Jean-nette. "I wonder if she could have stayed late at the *musée* doing something for Madame? I didn't think to go back there. I believe I can reach Madame by telephone. Shall I go home and try?"

Jean nodded and reached for a jacket hung on a peg by the door. "I will drive to her school friend's house in L'Isle-sur-Serein and ask. Roger," he said, turning to the older boy, "find something to eat but do not turn the stove on. If 'Nette comes home, go up to Mme Goff's house and let her know."

"And I'll come back and leave a message about the museum," Katherine said. A hard knot was forming in her stomach. It wasn't like Jeannette to disappear. Sure, she hid in trees in the good weather, and had been known to slip around town after dark to peer in people's windows, although the girl didn't realize her neighbors knew that. But she was a good girl and always came home to take care of the motherless boys. Katherine made a promise to herself that if Michael's finances improved, she would buy the girl a mobile phone and pay for the account. It was intolerable that no one could reach her.

They parted at the gate, not before Katherine heard the boys begin to squabble. Back at her house, shivering from the colder air, possibly due to the clear skies and lack of rain, Katherine checked on her dinner, then got out her little address book and looked up the listing for the Musée du Costume. No, Madame said, having answered the phone in a quavering voice. "You frightened me, dear Mme Goff. No one ever calls me this late. I was afraid it was the gendarmes again. But the girl came only for a few minutes today, with your friend, and then they left."

"My friend? Who do you mean?"

"That very tall one who knocks into things, the English. Jeannette said she wanted to see the salon where, well, you comprehend."

Katherine did comprehend, all too well. If Pippa had pulled Jeannette away from their meeting place, and caused all this worry and fear, Katherine was going to have a hard time not showing her anger. *"Merci, Madame,* I am sorry to have bothered you, but this is helpful. I live close to Mme Hathaway, and I will go look for Jeannette there right now. *Bonsoir,* goodnight, and thank you again."

The smells from the kitchen should have been enticing, but Katherine had lost her appetite. If Jeannette wasn't with Pippa, there would be an all-out search, possibly involving the gendarmes. If she was with the writer, probably being grilled about the murder scene, Katherine would be furious with both of them for their thoughtlessness.

She remembered the two little boys, probably looking for cereal or crackers, maybe even a bit scared under their childish swagger, and looked at the veal bubbling on the stove. "Oh, to hell with it," she said to no one at all, and pulled out a casserole dish. Five minutes later, she parked at Jean's house and headed through the gate with the dish and a baguette. In their father's absence and undoubtedly without his approval, they had let the dogs in, a mother and her two nine-month-old pups. She knocked, then opened the door to find them piled on the couch. As she suspected, the little one was eating crackers out of a box and the older one, Roger, was drinking a bottle of chocolate milk. The TV was on.

"Good news. I think I know where Jeannette is, or at least who she's with, a neighbor. In the meantime, Roger, you get out two bowls and have some of this delicious stew, all right?" The boys didn't have to be invited twice. Their faces lit up like Christmas morning and in a moment they were sitting at a table, forks at the ready as she dished out her dinner into two big bowls. "Now, if your father comes home before I'm back with Jeannette, you tell him I think I have found her, okay?" Roger nodded, his mouth too full of food to answer, and Katherine left, telling herself she was not going to take two more of Jean's children under her wing. One was plenty, as tonight proved.

Pippa's car was in her driveway, the lights were on in the house, and, sure enough, when Pippa answered her loud knock, there was Jeannette visible, slumped on a chair, eating an apple. Katherine's first impulse was to rant at them both for scaring her and Jean, but she counted to ten as fast as she could before saying, "Everyone's looking for you, Jeannette. You were supposed to meet me in Avallon, remember? Your father's gone to your classmate's house in L'Isle-sur-Serein looking for you."

Jeannette jumped up. "*Merde*," she said, "what time is it? I need to get home before Papa does." She grabbed her jacket and backpack and pushed past Pippa and Katherine into the dark without waiting for a response.

Katherine let her go. It was only a few minutes' distance and would give the girl some time to realize how many people she had frightened. Instead, she turned to Pippa. "What were you thinking? Did Jeannette not mention that I was planning to pick her up at the bus stop hours ago?"

Pippa's eyes had gotten bigger and she put a hand over her mouth. The color rushed up into her face, which wasn't, Katherine took time to notice, terribly flattering to her. "No, I had no idea," she said, stammering. "Will you come in? I am so sorry. She didn't say anything about meeting you."

Katherine stepped over the threshold so Pippa could close the door against the chill that was wafting in. But she was angry and in no mood to cover it up. "You have a phone. I have a phone. Even if Jeannette's family doesn't, you could easily have let me know. As it is, Pippa, you've scared us all—Jeannette's brothers, me, and even her father, which is saying something."

"I am dreadfully sorry, really I am, but I had no idea anyone would be looking for her. I say, it's rotten. No wonder you're mad."

"What happened?" Katherine shook her head at Pippa's invitation to take off her coat and have a cup of tea.

"Well, you see, I was walking past the bus stop and thinking I might drop by the museum to find out if there was any news, and it was raining, and when I saw Jeannette, I stopped to say hello. I asked her if she'd like some hot chocolate. She said yes."

"I looked in the windows of the cafés near that corner and she wasn't there."

"I expect we'd already left by then. I asked her if she'd come with me to the museum and perhaps let me see the room where the murder took place."

"Again? The police haven't said that's where it happened," Katherine said, and immediately regretted it.

"Really? What have they said?"

"Never mind that for now. Did Madame let you in?"

"Her daughter did when she saw it was Jeannette. I think she, well, perhaps both the director's daughter and Jeannette, really, thought I was a bit strange for wanting to see the room, but the daughter said I wasn't the only one, that maybe they should charge extra or something, according to Jeannette. Anyway, Jeannette took me up."

She sat down in the same chair Jeannette had vacated and began to drum her fingers on the table. "Jeannette told me the things the mannequin had been modeling were strewn around. There was so much happening, and I didn't notice details." She sighed. "I don't know what I expected to find, but there was nothing to see. Oh"—her face brightened—"but I did ask Madame's daughter if the mannequins were ever dressed with gold crosses. She said that wouldn't be correct for the periods, even if they did use real gold jewelry, which they never would. So, not all was lost." She looked up hopefully.

In spite of herself, Katherine said, "And the wig? Has it shown up?" Pippa had talked about the damn thing so often that Katherine realized she was accepting it as a clue even though it had no bearing on the case. Maybe Pippa was a better mystery writer than she gave her credit for.

"Jeannette never saw one, although the shoes the mannequin had been wearing were across the room. The police looked at them, but left them behind since it was obvious Madame hadn't been wearing them."

"Obvious? And how did you hear all this?"

"The curator's daughter told Jeannette, who told me. The shoes were tiny and narrow, too narrow for a middle-aged woman who stood on her feet all day, I should think. She's annoyed—the daughter, that is—because the wig cost money. Jeannette said it was brown, and might have looked like a dead rat if the garbagemen saw it." She shuddered.

Katherine's anger had drained away. Jeannette was home safely, and all she wanted to do now was get back to her house, fix another omelet, since the boys had gotten her dinner, and fluff pillows or something in honor of Michael's homecoming.

"Why don't you take your handsome namesake cop out for coffee and grill him?" she said, managing a smile.

Pippa smiled back. "Blimey, as they say back home, I might just do that."

Katherine opened the door behind her and said, "Next time you're inspired to lead a teenager astray from her commitments, call me first, okay?"

"Next time I know she has a commitment, I will," Pippa said, her head tilted to one side slightly, her spiky hairdo and round eyes making her look just a bit like a cheeky cockatoo. "I hope you'll talk to the girl and explain that she upset you."

"Right," Katherine said, and closed the door.

CHAPTER 16

Katherine rarely bothered to put on her watch, but she had this morning right after her bath and now she checked it every ten minutes. The train wasn't due until four but she was dressed and had cooked her own recipe, a combination of a traditional French Bourguignon and the simpler stew she normally threw together—the difference being a shockingly expensive amount of mushrooms and half of a fifteen-euro bottle of red wine that was only possible because she put it on the magic credit card. It was bubbling quietly in the oven. The dogs, sensing something was up, or possibly only smelling the beef, were prowling, bumping up against her, staring at her through the tangle of their bangs. The yellow cat, in contrast, was sound asleep in her chair, close to the heater, and had been since breakfast.

There had been frost on the grass when Katherine first got up, but it was gone now except in the shadiest part of the garden, where it clung to the withered hollyhock stalks that Katherine had neglected to chop down before the rain began. She wondered if she should go out and start the car, to make sure it would be ready for the twenty-minute drive to the train station, but dismissed that as anxiety rather than prudence. She stood staring out the window at the mess that was a winter garden, wondering if all gardeners had the bouts of depression that she did in December and January. By the middle of February, she would have begun to plan for the season ahead and there might be days when she had the energy to do the garden cleanup, rake the decomposing pear tree leaves that blanketed the ground between the house and the gate, cut the roses back, and daydream about the lilacs in the corner. The lilacs would surely do better this year. After all, she had been talking to them earnestly for many months, promising them more sun and attention.

When the phone rang, she jumped. When she jumped, the dogs began to bark. As she hurried to get to the little table that held the phone, she banged into the cat's perch and it raised its head long enough to give her a slit-eyed look of irritation.

"Hello? Madame Lacrois? Yes, this is me." The woman's voice filled her ear with what seemed at first torrents of words, but slowly organized themselves into sentences that Katherine understood, more or less. "Ah, I see. You want to know if I'd like to ride with you to Beaune tomorrow? To hear Father . . . I'm afraid I—"

The voice rode over her attempt to explain for another few minutes. She grasped that Josephine would be meeting her gentleman Catholic friend for lunch, since he lived in Beaune and never came up to this little outpost of rural civilization, and Katherine was invited. When Madame stopped, Katherine began again, in French and slowly, to be sure she was saying what she intended. "You are very kind, but I'm afraid I can't. My husband is coming home shortly and tomorrow will be the first day we've had together in weeks. So much to take care of, you know."

Mme Lacrois began again and Katherine couldn't resist glancing at her watch. Really? Had it only been five minutes since she last checked?

"Thank you, thank you so much. As I said, religious events are not really my—" How did one say "cup of tea" in French and would the French understand that? "—my particular interest, but I do appreciate your thinking of me."

More talk, the summary of which seemed to be that this was different, really quite thrilling. Katherine finally made it clear she wasn't interested, and old man Lacrois's granddaughter gave up, at least for today. Katherine also gave up waiting and decided she would drive the twenty minutes to the train station and sit in the little café across the street with her book and a café au lait and wait for Michael. It was only an hour and a half until the train arrived, no time at all.

The sun was shining, or, if not precisely shining, was aiming its weak December rays in the direction of Burgundy's pastures and tidy forest fringes. The drive was a pretty one, even when the fields were barren. The gently swelling hills and specks of towns visible, each with its church spire rising modestly, were daily inspirations for her oil paintings. Katherine took a moment to thank fate and Michael for depositing her here amid the placid, white Charolais cattle and the abundant local cheeses and the narrow roads and cobblestone streets of this ancient place. Amazing, really, to think that Joan of Arc might have seen some of the same views as she marched through Burgundy.

Daydreaming, she almost missed the sharp turn that

took her into the homely town where the train stopped. A series of twists along the last mile of the route and counter-intuitive turnings finally brought her to the station parking lot. This was the station for the fast train from Paris, not the station that served Avallon. As she sipped her coffee and looked out the window at the tracks, she wondered if the Americans from the Bellegarde tour had all made their connections home. They seemed so determined to leave and Katherine hoped they wouldn't take away only the impression of the salon and the corpse, but admitted if she had been one of them, the memory hardest to ignore would be that of finding a dead body in such bizarre circumstances. They would likely tell the story a score of times in the next few weeks.

Katherine had not said anything to Michael. When they had celebrated his news and she had extracted as much about what it could mean from her husband, then she would fill him in. By that time, the gendarmes might have arrested the killer and Michael would not be tempted to admonish her to stay out of it, as he was wont to do, well, had at least done last summer.

Several people in the café got up suddenly and Katherine noticed a flurry of car traffic across the street. The train was coming. Hastily paying, Katherine joined the small group headed across the road, her heart beating a little faster. The sleek train pulled slowly into the station and she waited in a clear spot where Michael would be sure to see her.

Katherine giggled, and Michael raised his head from the pillow to look at her questioningly. "Oh dear, if I go into

Avallon tomorrow I must be careful not to walk past the chocolatier's shop."

"I know this means something, but I wonder if I want to know what." Michael grinned at his wife, rolled over and sat at the edge of the bed. "Much as I hate to do it, the dogs need a walk before it gets any later."

"Do you think that's why they're scratching at the bedroom door? I think it's that they missed you as much, or almost as much, as I did." Katherine reached over and ran her hand down his back, reveling in the shape of his shoulders and promising herself she would paint him, undoubtedly clothed since he would be shocked to be asked to model nude.

The beef and mushrooms had been perfectly delicious, tender, with the wine infused into every bite. She had served the plain boiled potatoes Michael liked with the stew, and the rest of the red wine had paired nicely with the pear tart at the end of the meal. It had been a warm homecoming, with the big black dog and the small white one taking turns laying their heads on Michael's lap and gazing up adoringly at him. Even the yellow cat had deigned to come down from its perch and join the family celebration from the top of a bookcase behind his chair, its tail swishing rhythmically.

Michael had talked about the good news in bits and pieces, about Eric's seeming sincerity about having Michael and Betty Lou open for them, backed up by the delivery of a contract covering the tour, the shared expenses and revenue, the ability to sell CDs and sing "Raging Love." Having heard Betty Lou and Michael's arrangement of the song,

Eric thought it would be cool—his words, Michael said—for the band to then play its version. Fans, he told Michael, insisted on that song anyway. It was one of their anthems.

"How did you feel, hearing that?"

"A lot better with the new agreement in hand. I'll be getting royalties from the new version and J.B. tells me the more the Leopards play their version, the more listeners will play the new one, so it's a win all around."

"And playing before the big crowds at a Leopards concert. Are you nervous?"

"Damn right. I'll have a knotted gut, at least at first. But Betty Lou and I are working on that. She'll say hello and talk about us first and will open with one of her old songs to warm up the crowd. I'll play backup but not sing. Then, here's hoping, I'll kind of drift in to the next song and we'll move through the set."

"And the big number?"

"We'll end with that, we think, although J.B. isn't sure. He might have us do that next to last and finish with a faster, upbeat song. Betty Lou would like that. She doesn't want 'Raging Love' to be the last thing audiences hear from us before the Leopards do their version."

Katherine was happy listening to Michael. In the space of six months, he had grown in confidence and ambition, from sitting on the patio tinkering with new song ideas and no way of getting them in front of people in the business to this, energized and planning the details of an exciting opportunity, way beyond his and, to be honest, her dreams. "My husband, the rock star." She got up and pulled a robe around her, not feeling the cold draft that had depressed her for the past several weeks.

"Yeah, well, at least you don't have to be embarrassed when Emile magnifies my status. Does he still have that big dog?"

"Oh yes, and don't even try to walk Gracey and Fideaux past there."

"At night, in this cold, the poor dog's outside?"

"It's a guard dog, remember? In case thieves and murderers decide to sneak up in the night and slit Emile's throat and take his accordion."

"I wish someone would take his guitar and that cheap amplifier. You might have a word with him. Tell me the animal at least has a doghouse."

Katherine laughed. "You're such a softie. Yes, there is a doghouse, and I scolded him so much when the rains came that he bought a dog bed for it. And he admits, looking quite embarrassed, that he lets Napoleon—yes, that is the creature's name—in when it gets too cold."

As Michael slipped into his jeans and boots, grabbed his Stetson, and clattered down the steep stairs calling for the dogs, Katherine wondered when the right time was to tell him about the murder of the butcher's wife. Maybe not tonight in case he disapproved of her interest in the investigation. She didn't want to spoil the mood.

CHAPTER 17

Katherine was happy. Her husband was home. Someone else could roll out of bed early to take the dogs on their first walk of the day. She could hear humming coming from the kitchen, and smelled coffee. Michael was having a one-sided conversation with the animals when she finished dressing and joined him.

"Your rock-and-roll-star husband needs to lug more firewood in while it's not raining and fix the tarp over the storage shed roof that got loose while I was gone. Okay with you," Michael said, his mouth full of brioche toast, "if I hang around today and do stuff like that?"

Should she give him a list of chores, Katherine thought as she sank into the chaise with a cup of Michael's strong coffee, only partially tamed with copious quantities of hot milk? Would it dampen his enthusiasm to know the fence bordering the alleyway was leaning dangerously, dragged down by the climbing rose she had not gotten around to pruning? Or that the gate was squealing terribly? "That's fine. I have plenty to do today myself."

As she sat jolted by the caffeine but before she could

organize her day properly, there was a knock at the kitchen door. Michael opened it and Pippa stepped back from the threshold. "Oh, I say, I didn't realize you were home. Maybe I should come back later."

"Howdy. Come on in," Michael said, brushing the crumbs from his hands. "How's the book doing?"

"Coming along rather well, I think, although some days I'm ready to toss the whole thing into the rubbish bin." Pippa ducked her head as she crossed to the main room where Katherine was now kneeling in front of a bookcase jammed with volumes of every size. "I read in a magazine that it's normal to feel that way right about this place in the story, which helps. Katherine, I was going to ask if you wouldn't mind driving to Avallon with me today. I might need some translating help." She gave Katherine a look that Katherine interpreted as meaning there was a special purpose in the request.

"I was hoping not to go anywhere today," Katherine said, pulling herself to a standing position and reminding herself a little yoga now and then wouldn't be a bad idea for aging joints.

"Don't stay here on my account." Michael reached around her to take an old jacket off a peg on the wall, leaning in to kiss her on the cheek as he did. "Once I get going, I'm going to be all mud and grumbling. You know me. I'll keep finding things that need fixing. You go if you like."

"Have you told Michael about the murder?" Pippa said. "Does he know what we think?"

Michael stopped in the act of putting on his Stetson and turned to look at Katherine.

"I was going to," Katherine said as heat rose to her face,

"but it doesn't really touch us and I didn't want to worry you while you had more important things on your mind."

"But we found the body," Pippa said, oblivious to the rapidly changing climate in the room.

"You found a body?" The hat returned to the peg and its owner swiveled his head from one woman to the other, his mouth tightening. "You'd better explain because I don't know what you're talking about."

Pippa opened her mouth, but Katherine jumped in first. "It was only a coincidence. The woman was already dead and the whole tour group saw her in the salon. I was with the group. So was Pippa, but everyone actually discovered her, if you see what I mean."

"Which I don't," Michael said.

"It wasn't in Reigny, if that's what you're worried about," Pippa said. "It was at the museum in Avallon, and we think the police suspect the butcher, but we aren't so sure."

"The butcher?"

"The poor man is gobsmacked. It's clear he couldn't have strangled her. And then there's the mystery of the mannequin in the river." Pippa ran a hand through her spiky hair. "It is rather confusing, I know."

"You could say that. Katherine, you realize this is making no sense to me. Were you even going to tell me what's going on?"

The warm mood that had prevailed since he got home was gone and Katherine could have strangled Pippa for spoiling it. She had planned to tell Michael, but in a way that minimized her connection to the crime, and made it clear she had no interest in solving it. Taking a deep breath, she said, "It only sounds like I'm involved. I thought I'd tell you all about it later, when we weren't so busy, maybe over dinner."

Pippa seemed to realize belatedly that she had caused something between husband and wife, and started to back out of the room. "I'll come back later, shall I?"

"No," Katherine said. "Sit. I'll make you a cup of tea. Michael, please believe me, this is a police investigation, we are casual bystanders who got caught up in the drama for an hour or two, and it's only because the town is buzzing that we're still talking about it."

"You want to tell me who died at least, and why someone suspects the butcher?"

"It's the couple who own the business, the Sabines. She was strangled, maybe at the Musée du Costume, or maybe brought there after she was killed."

"Dressed up in a costume," Pippa said. "That's why the mannequin was dumped, you see."

"I'll tell this," Katherine said, shooting a look at the young woman.

"Oh, right."

"Wait, this is the shop on the main street that sells my veal sausages? That couple?" Michael sat down. "I can't believe it. And the police think he killed her?"

"We don't actually know that," Katherine said. "The police aren't saying much and the town's full of rumors. You know, serial killers on the loose, or a crime of passion—you name it."

"A crime of passion? I hadn't heard that," Pippa said. "Does that mean he thought she had a lover? I wouldn't think there was enough privacy around here to carry on an affair."

Michael lifted both hands. "Hold up, you two. Katherine, give me the basics, in some kind of order. And please tell me you are not poking around thinking you can solve whatever it is."

Katherine handed a sheepish Pippa a mug of steaming tea—herbal as a punishment—took a deep breath, and recounted the sequence of events, eliminating every ounce of drama she could. She left out her recent visit to the museum, the scrap of paper she had taken, and the gossip she had happened to hear at the dentist's and the chocolate shop. Nothing had happened when she dropped by the gendarmerie, so she didn't think there was any reason to mention that.

"And what was that about a store dummy?" Michael said when she was finished, turning to Pippa.

The budding mystery writer paused before answering. "It's only that when whoever did it substituted Madame's body for a costumed mannequin, they decided to take away the mannequin and dump it in the river at L'Isle-sur-Serein."

"Why would anyone do that?"

"That's it, of course. No one knows."

"No one? How do you know that?"

"Well, you're right, of course. Perhaps the police do know, but they're not telling us."

"I wonder," Michael said, "if this means you've asked. I'm just guessing here."

Again, Katherine beat Pippa. "Of course not, although the gendarmes apparently questioned Pippa since she happened to be there when they pulled the dummy out of the river."

"Another coincidence?" Michael said, getting up and

reaching for his hat. "I've made an executive decision. I know I can't stop the two of you from whatever amateur snooping around you decide to do. Three rules only for you, Katherine. Don't do anything that brings the police or Reigny's sheriff to the door. Don't do anything that puts you—or Pippa—in danger. And remember to be home by dark. Otherwise I'll worry about you."

The door closed behind him. Not slammed, Katherine noted, which was a good sign. He either didn't take them seriously, or he trusted her. She decided not to spend any time figuring out which was more likely.

Pippa had cajoled every bit of the crime-of-passion theory proposed by the chocolate shop owner out of Katherine before they reached the outskirts of Avallon. Katherine, glad to confess to someone who would understand, told her about the scrap of paper that turned out to be related to a church group in Beaune. "It was probably dropped by one of the church ladies during their tour of the museum, so it means nothing."

"Ah, but it means the police didn't do a thorough job of searching the salon," Pippa said, the eagerness in her voice unmistakable. "It could mean that the missing wig is still there."

"I don't know why you attach so much meaning to it," Katherine said as the young woman edged her bright red car in between two others along the main street, not far from the museum. "What will it mean if it shows up in the river, or in the street, or in the salon?"

There was a pause, then a sigh. "I don't know. I don't feel I have a firm grip on this."

Katherine bit her tongue. Really, the two of them were equally foolish. Michael's implication that they were chasing something they knew nothing about and had no capability to solve wasn't far from the truth. Why did she let herself get so caught up in it? Was it perhaps to prove something to herself after last summer's debacle? That, maybe, she wasn't a complete idiot?

She was saved again from uncomfortable self-examination by her more optimistic neighbor, who had jumped out of the car and was shifting impatiently from one foot to the other. "First, can we get the local paper and see what news there might be?"

They ducked back into the comparatively warm car so Katherine could scan for an update on the murder. "Ah, here it is," Katherine muttered as she translated the story. "As best I can figure out, the investigation is still open, the police have satisfied themselves that the husband's alibi during the time in question has been substantiated. At least that's what I assume the word means since it's the only conclusion I can draw from the rest of the sentence. 'Alibi,' at least, is the same."

"So they don't know who did it, but it wasn't the husband." Pippa tapped her front teeth with a fingernail. "Do they say where he said he was?"

"If they do, I'm not seeing it. I still have a lot to learn about the language. But in the States, I'm not sure they'd say that in a newspaper comment anyway." She turned the page. "Oh, wait. Look, here's a picture of M. Sabine and a different story. It's an interview."

Katherine was silent for a few minutes. "Okay. Says something about if he'd known of danger to his dear wife, he wouldn't have been at his 'jeu de cartes.' Hmmm, I'll check my dictionary when I get home but I think it means his poker game."

"Well, that's that, then," Pippa said. "Unless it was solitaire, there was at least one other person present. So, jolly for us. One suspect eliminated."

"He says something about the memorial service and that he is praying the *monstre*—the monster—has left the area." She folded the paper. "I have an idea. Michael could hardly object. We should go to the service, to pay our respects."

"And look to see if the monster is there? Yes, I've read that killers sometimes come back to the scene of the crime, although I'm not clear on why." Pippa's voice trailed off, and she pulled out her notebook and scribbled something.

She turned to look at Katherine, grimacing slightly. "I say, have you ever had the feeling someone was following you? It's only that I've felt that way recently even though there's nothing I can prove. It's odd."

"I'm sure it's your imagination, Pippa. You've gotten caught up with all this murder investigation business. Maybe you should quit, and get back to the book. You don't want to get paranoid."

Pippa nodded. "I'm sure you're right. After all, I never saw anyone, or a car, that I could honestly say stayed behind me for long. All right, then, onward, to the museum."

They stopped at a *boulangerie* for a paper bag of round, crusty rolls, which Pippa had discovered were Madame's favorites, and made their way toward the museum. "Your discovery means there may still be something that the police have overlooked."

"I seriously doubt it, Pippa, and I'm afraid Madame and Josée will refuse to let us in again. We're as much of a nuisance as the police."

"Oh, no, Madame always nods and smiles. I only wish I understood French."

"Suggestion," Katherine said as they walked up the slate path to the museum's front door, "take French lessons in the new year. If you want to live among the French, it's only fair."

The door opened before Pippa could answer and Katherine had to admit the welcome was warmer than she would have expected. Madame peeked into the bag Pippa thrust at her and cooed, pulling the two visitors in and locking the door behind them. *"Bonjour, bonjour, mesdames. Le temps est si froid, n'est-ce pas?"* Katherine agreed that it was cold and Pippa pantomimed being chilly.

Josée came out from behind the curtained doorway to the apartment. Her pleasure at seeing them was explained when she said she had to do some errands for her mother— the post office, the pharmacy, the shoe repair shop—and she didn't like leaving the older woman alone so long. Her mother beamed, made a two-handed gesture that dismissed her daughter's concerns, but added that she would love company in any case. "The museum needs to close in the winter because I will have all of the salons to redesign for the next show, and Josée and I will have to mend costumes and fit the models, so many of them. But I do miss the tourists who like so much what we show them. It is quiet in winter."

Madame's comment gave Katherine the opportunity she was looking for and without stopping to translate for

Pippa, she posed a question. "What about the costume that was so roughly put on poor Mme Sabine? Will you be able to repair it?"

"Sadly, no," Madame said, shaking her head. "It was torn beyond repair, especially since it had so many tiny sequins on the bodice. Ruined, and such a unique dress too."

"Unique?"

"Did you notice how demure it was, much more than other dresses of the day? The bodice was high, no décolletage, the skirt was not close fitting, and instead of gloves, it had long sleeves of plain black satin. No, this dress belonged to a well-known Burgundian lady who was famous for her modesty."

"I hadn't noticed," Katherine said and translated the gist of Madame's comments to Pippa.

"Yes, religious she was, known for bringing baskets to the poor and supplying the church where she lived with a stained-glass window. There weren't many society ladies in her time who dressed as she did. It was quite a find and my dear Josée is desolate. The gendarmes took the dress away as evidence or I would show what was left of it to you."

"I suppose all the dresses were made for wasp-waisted women so nothing on display would have been a more logical fit."

"Josée says the terrible man who did this chose it because he needed to lay poor Mme Sabine down and this figure had been on the chaise. Although why he needed to bring her into my beautiful museum, my treasure-house . . ." Madame trailed off and her rheumy eyes filled with tears.

Katherine reached for the old lady's hand. That was the question, wasn't it? she thought. The victim had no more connection to the museum than anyone else in Avallon who might have come for a tour. And then, why take the mannequin and throw it in the Serein? The whole business was so melodramatic and seemed designed to make a statement. What if the crime of passion had been committed not by the husband but by a jealous lover? The man in Beaune that someone had seen with Mme Sabine. Maybe he was in the same church group that Josephine Lacrois and the victim had been in, which could be how they met. She'd have to check, ask Josephine some discreet questions.

While she had been wandering mentally, the museum curator had disappeared into her apartment. Now, she came back with a photograph of a mannequin dressed elegantly. *"Ici,* here is the dress. Beautiful, isn't it? We take photos of everything before each exhibit opens, and I create a catalog for the archives so we know what we displayed each time. After so many years, I need to aid my memory."

Katherine passed the picture to Pippa, who made appreciative noises and said, "Dark brown wig and piled into some kind of twist. Can you ask her if the wig was like that or if she put up the hair?"

"No, I am no good at that," Madame said when Katherine had translated as best she could. "There was a lovely lady who had a wig shop here in Avallon years ago. Alas, the business did not do well and when she closed she offered me a good price on any stock I liked. I think Josée and I picked out a dozen or more. Such a bargain and you know we never have much money. Of course, none of it was real hair, but that is good for us, less upkeep. We have so little storage that we glue the pieces on the mannequins permanently and change the style if we must. This was one of them, a classic twist."

Pippa got up and, in a lively game of charades, asked and received permission to go once more to the salon. Madame lifted her palms and shrugged. Clearly, she didn't understand Pippa's obsession for the room where the body had been discovered, but by now she had gotten used to the young woman.

Katherine trailed Pippa up the stairs, which were dark since Madame was understandably frugal with electricity when the building wasn't open to tourists. At the doorway of the infamous salon at the top of the stairs, Pippa pulled a small flashlight from her coat pocket and began probing into the darkest corners. "I knew I'd need a torch," she said over her shoulder. "That wig must be somewhere. You're right that I don't know what finding it would prove, but I can't help thinking it might carry some clue, especially because the killer must have pulled it hard to get it off the mannequin's head, right?"

"If you find it, then, don't touch it," Katherine said. "If you think the murderer handled it, his DNA might be on it. You wouldn't want yours on it too."

"I should say not, especially since Philippe thinks I might be the killer."

"Wait," Katherine said. "What are you talking about?"

Pippa got up from the floor, from where she'd been shining the light under a deep armoire, and dusted her pants. "I haven't had a chance to tell you. Philippe came 'round to my house and asked me a lot of questions that I think mean he, or at least the police in charge, is suspicious of me. You know, having been here and then in L'Isle-sur-Serein at the right times?"

"Well, that's ridiculous. I hope you told him so."

"I did, or at least I think I did. I was so rattled, you know. Embarrassed, really. Katherine," she said, coming over to stand with her in the doorway, "I'm not sure I did the right thing. Seeing as how he was so suspicious already, I didn't dare tell him about the cross, or show it to him. I mean, if he saw I had it, and if it was hers, I think he might have arrested me."

Katherine privately wondered if Pippa was right. There were some aspects of Pippa's activities that were hard to explain unless you knew her. "Look, you have no motive unless you thought she cheated you over the price of some pâté."

"Pâté? Are you daft? I can't afford pâté. The most I ever bought from them was a few pork and apple sausages at a time."

Katherine clapped her hands together and said, "That's it. We have to go to the police, give them the cross, and explain that it's curiosity on your part. I'll make sure the man in charge knows you could not possibly be a credible suspect. If necessary, I'll track down the lieutenant who managed the investigation last summer. He turned out to be quite reasonable in the end."

"That's good of you, but I don't have the cross with me. I tucked it inside my manuscript notepad where it would be safe."

"Then we'll tell them about it, and your handsome Philippe can drive out with you and pick it up. Michael was right, you know. On the off chance that the person who did it is in Avallon, we don't want him to know you and I are too interested in this."

"Wait. You told me I was being silly to think that."

Remembering Pippa's worry that she was being followed, Katherine nodded. "Maybe Michael's made me think twice, although I know no one has followed us when we've been together, so I do think it was your imagination."

"I've decided it was the lover in Beaune, and he's far from here by now," Pippa said. "Let me finish searching this room, and then maybe we can go to the police, but only if you're with me. Please?"

"Of course. We'll even have lunch first at a bistro I like. I need to buy fresh eggs and perhaps a piece of fish at the lovely indoor market which is close to where we can eat. Michael and I finished the beef stew last night. Silly me, I had thought there would be leftovers. In two weeks, I forgot how much he eats." She smiled, glad again that her husband was home even if he was already disapproving of her interest in the affair of Mme Sabine.

CHAPTER 18

There is nothing quite like onion soup on a cold December day, Katherine thought. Slivered onions simmered for a long time in broth and white wine, scented with thyme, topped with thick slabs of baguette and French Comté cheese, then toasted under a broiler and served in bowls decorated with the melted cheese. This bistro's version was perfect, testimony to the experience and patience of the chef, a bald, middle-aged man who popped out of the kitchen now and then to call out *"Bonjour"* to another regular customer. His wife, or at least Katherine assumed it was his wife, bustled around the small restaurant, setting up tables as soon as they emptied and bringing fresh glasses of wine to the happy diners.

"I've never been here," Pippa said, her face flushed from the heat in the room, or maybe from the warmth of the soup. "I think I could order it myself if I came here on my own. I've been too shy to try it. My French, you know?"

"Onion soup is onion soup. You can't mess that order up. But it really is time to take lessons. It's not possible to appreciate France if you can't talk with people, even if it's only in simple sentences. You can't even flirt with your gendarme without some conversation. I'm no good as a teacher, but there must be someone." Pippa agreed although she reminded Katherine she lived on very little money. Perhaps, she said, her father would give her some extra money at the holidays.

Later, over slices of warm pear tart and espresso, the two women rehearsed in low voices their visit to the gendarmerie. "I want to find out if there was anything we should have seen right when we came on the body, something obvious that it was our duty to make note of and inform the investigators."

Katherine was dubious that Pippa's approach would get them past the gendarme at the reception window. "I think you're going to have to say you have evidence in the murder case. Ask for your policeman by name, so they realize you're already involved."

"I can't do it unless you'll translate for me," Pippa said, beginning to look nervous.

"I'll do my best although my French for criminal activity is a little sparse. Don't worry, we'll manage. Are you ready to go into the lion's den, as they say?" Katherine lifted a hand to get the server's attention. The women split the bill and gathered up their coats. *"Courage,"* Katherine said in French, patting Pippa's shoulder as they left the warmth of the bistro.

There was more than courage needed at the gendarmerie. A different but no more helpful officer sat behind the window, peering up at them as Katherine explained more than once why they were there. It was only when Pippa fished Philippe's

card from her wallet that the man on duty seemed to understand they had a possible reason for showing up in his
kingdom. *"Ah, oui, Philippe. Bien sûr. Un moment, mesdames."*
He picked up his phone, talked rapidly into it with great
feeling, and replaced the receiver with a small bang. *"Un
moment,"* he said again as he waved them to a couple of
wooden chairs across the room from him.

It was much more than a minute, but eventually a door
opened and the handsome policeman peered around its
edge. "Ah, hello. Yes, you are here, Madame Hathaway, perhaps to assist us again with this tragic case?" he said in English, a small smile flitting across his face before he replaced
it with a stern frown.

"This is my friend, Katherine Goff," Pippa said, waving
an arm loosely and almost knocking Katherine's hat off.
"She found the body too, you know."

"Really? How strange. Two of you."

"Actually, a whole van full," Katherine said. "On a tour
of the museum. It was a terrible shock."

"Of course, of course. And you have something to
share?" he said, turning back to Pippa.

"Perhaps we could speak in your office?" Katherine said
when she saw Pippa's hands were shaking and she was biting her lip.

"Office? I am afraid I do not have an office, Madame. But
someplace less public, *bien sûr*. Please," and he opened the
door to whatever lay beyond the reception area. As they
passed through it, Katherine noticed the officer on duty scru-
tinizing them.

It proved hard to begin. They were in a large room with
a dozen or more desks, a noisy copy machine making what

might have been a hundred copies of something, men and one woman talking and laughing from their desks. Katherine and Pippa perched on two more wooden chairs, as uncomfortable as the ones in the lobby, and tried to tell their story in low enough tones not to be overheard by anyone who wanted to listen. Judging by the curious looks other uniformed officers shot their way, there was at least some interest. After all, how many murders were there in a small city like this one, and how many non-French people were involved in Avallon's crime scene?

Pippa asked about the missing wig, explaining only that the museum's director had described one and that it didn't appear to be in the salon where the murder took place.

"A *perruque*? The false hair on the *makeen*? Do you know where it is?"

Pippa seemed lost in her thoughts, gazing at his face. Either she couldn't understand the French words for "wig" and "mannequin" or it was his extraordinary eyes, Katherine thought. "No, she doesn't, but you see Pippa thinks it might be important, that for some reason the man who did this terrible thing to Mme Sabine might still have it." Philippe looked genuinely confused.

"You haven't found it, then?" Pippa said, shaking herself like a dog getting rid of a flea itch. "You see, if it wasn't simply discarded, he might have kept it, or it might even be in his car or something. It could be a clue."

The gendarme didn't seem as excited as Pippa was by this insight. Across the room, a pretty young policewoman was glancing at the trio, her mouth twitching to subdue a smile. Katherine saw her bump an elbow into a man near her, then whisper something in his ear, at which he turned and stared directly at Pippa. This wasn't going well.

"Pippa, you had something you wanted to share with the gendarmes?"

Pippa's misery was evident. She rubbed the fingers of one hand with the other, slumped in her chair, looked at the far wall, but said nothing. Philippe looked puzzled, and turned his head from one woman to the other.

"If there's something—"

"Not really," Pippa said, and jumped up, knocking her chair into the corner of the closest desk with a loud bang. "Honestly, I can't think what good I thought coming here could do. Come on, Katherine. We'd best get back. Thank you." She held out her hand and pumped the one Philippe was forced to offer. He and Katherine stood up and followed Pippa, who was moving fast. Not fast enough to keep from bumping into the policewoman who had been watching them and who had strolled over to intercept the trio.

"Sorry," Pippa stammered as she backed away and shifted to go around the block.

"Ah, *l'écrivaine, oui*? The crime fiction, yes? You have more to teach us today?" Her smirk was accompanied by a wink at Philippe.

"What? Oh, hello. I remember we met in Serein." Pippa was so obviously eager to leave that Katherine felt pity for her. Whether it was a crush on Philippe that was upsetting her, or this unfriendly gendarme in her face, Pippa was about to lose it.

"Come on," Katherine said, taking her arm. "*Merci, Monsieur*, thank you for your time. I didn't realize we have to be someplace soon. You were good to see us." With that, she pulled Pippa through the doorway, only to be dragged by Pippa all the way to the lobby, with Philippe following.

The same gendarme was on duty, cleaning his finger-nails with a pocketknife. As they pulled on their coats and hats, an old man opened the outer door and staggered in. The gendarme on duty shouted something at him that seemed more affectionate than threatening, and the old man hiccupped and collapsed into a chair. Drunk, Katherine decided, and the bright color of his nose suggested this might be a frequent condition. Philippe made as if to say something to Pippa, but she was tugging the outer door open, and he shrugged instead. As she followed Pippa out the door, she heard Philippe say something to the old man. She turned, and he had gone to stand in front of the drunk's chair. Philippe looked once in Katherine's direction, his brow creased, then turned back to the new visitor.

"Stupid, stupid," Pippa was muttering as Katherine caught up to her and walked beside her. "He'd think I was daft if he knew me better." Her eyes were shining with tears, and her head was down. "I'm going to throw that bloody cross away, into the Serein maybe, and be done with this. It's too stupid."

She paused for breath and Katherine said, "I don't know. You did choke up back there, but I doubt he thinks you're stupid. He was listening carefully. I admit it's going to be harder now to tell him about the cross. He seems nice, which is more than I can say about the woman. What was up with her?"

"She was at the river that day. I tried to tell her about the mannequin and how I thought it was connected to the murder." Pippa stopped near the car, now hemmed in even tighter than it had been when they parked. "I told her I write murder mysteries. I wanted her to understand I wasn't an ordinary bystander with crazy ideas, you see? But my French wasn't helping so she called him over. That's when we met. Or, I met him. I know I was some silly English girl to him, to both of them."

"We've had enough of this town for one day. Let's go home and we can think about what we know and how to get that cross to your gendarme without a fuss, okay? I don't know about you, but I'm freezing standing out here." Katherine smiled and rubbed her gloved hands together. What she wanted was to go home to a cozy house with a bright fire, a smiling husband, and the motivation to cook a lovely meal for two.

Pippa nodded and pulled the car keys out of her bag. Katherine grabbed the passenger door handle, prepared to open the door when her friend unlocked it. Pippa swung her door open. Suddenly, swiftly, she jumped back and began to scream. She didn't or couldn't stop. Katherine couldn't see through the side window so she ran around to where Pippa was standing in the middle of the street, still making loud, incoherent sounds. And no wonder. Lying outside the car, grinning up at Katherine with half-closed eyes, its tongue hanging out, was the bloody head of a pig. A real pig, a large pig, a recently deceased pig.

Katherine heard a new scream and realized it was her own.

CHAPTER 19

Pippa was only aware of chaos. First, people running out of the shops along the street, yelling, pointing, waving at cars to stop so they didn't hit the pig's head. Or, maybe it was her they were trying to protect. She wasn't sure how she had come to be sitting in the middle of the street, and she couldn't seem to control her own weeping. The sound of police car sirens only made things worse. It looked like two police cars were edging their way into the confusion. Several uniformed officers spilled out of the cars, waving and shouting. What if it wasn't only that ugly head? What if all this fuss was because there was a dead body somewhere?

Several people tried to help her, but they only made her feel claustrophobic with their hovering. "My friend, where is she? Is she all right?" Pippa said through her hiccupping sobs, hoping her voice was loud enough to be heard. She stood up on weak legs and lurched toward the sidewalk. A man steered her to a spot at the curb that she collapsed onto until she realized she was looking directly at the pig, which was leering back at her. She stumbled to her feet again, fought to quell her stomach, and pulled away. "No, no, I need to find my friend," she said, "please let me go." Shaking off the would-be rescuer's grip, she made her way toward Katherine, who was leaning against a building wall thirty feet away, surrounded by onlookers.

The policewoman who had been so unfriendly at the station a short time ago appeared next to her. Ordering the bystanders away in a tone of voice not to be disobeyed, she put her hand on Pippa's shoulder and patted her gently. Pippa looked over and saw Katherine coming toward her. She grabbed her friend in a hard hug. "Oh, Katherine, I'm so sorry," she said in a wobbly voice. "I've never been so frightened in my life. What was it? Is that . . . that thing . . . still here?"

"It was a stupid joke," Katherine said in a scratchy voice. "In very bad taste, of course. Are you all right now?" Turning to the policewoman, who was listening but who might not have understood all of what they had said, Katherine said something in French, then turned back. "I told her you need some strong tea and asked if we could sit in the café over there while they check this out."

Tea suddenly sounded essential to Pippa. New tears clouding her vision, she said, "I was so afraid something had happened to you. I couldn't think straight. Even now, I can't bear to look at my car." But she did feel a bit more like herself. The sights and sounds around her were coming into focus, as was the reality of what had happened.

At that moment, Philippe joined them, his face pale, speaking first in rapid French to his partner, who nodded and hurried off. His eyes were flashing and Pippa felt dizzy again. She noticed other policemen examining the car. Someone in a uniform was crouched by her door with a video camera. The watchers had been shooed off, although some were still standing at a distance, talking animatedly among themselves and staring at her.

Philippe touched her arm to get her attention. "Will you come back to the station with me? I think we can find some tea for you both. You will need sugar too, for the shock, I think." He looked genuinely concerned as he held out his hand, but when she reached for it, she was too blinded by tears to make contact, and crumpled back again to the cold pavement. It was too much. Her stomach was still unsettled and her legs hurt and the kinder Philippe was to her, the stupider she felt. She heard Katherine accept hot tea for both of them, and when her friend and Philippe together hoisted her to her feet, she held on to Katherine's arm and ducked her head, hoping Philippe wouldn't see her looking so ugly. They slowly walked the block to the gendarmerie, her legs threatening to go weak again at every step.

"Convenient that this happened right next to the police station," Katherine said in a low mutter that was probably meant to convey humor. For Pippa, the coincidence was no laughing matter. She was relieved that after the first minute, she hadn't needed to do anything. The car, the mess, the crowd, all of it was too much. She wanted her father, in truth.

The lobby was swarming with uniformed police, all in action on their cell phones, or shouting to one another, or putting on jackets and hats. Pippa and Katherine followed Philippe into the big room where they had met earlier. He pulled up two chairs next to his desk and the women sank into them.

"Do you have your car keys?" Philippe asked Pippa

gently. "We will want to check out the car for fingerprints and any sign of who did this, and then bring it to our garage."

Pippa shook her head as much to get rid of the buzzing in her ears as to answer him. Feeling for them in her coat pockets, she said, "I must have dropped them."

"She's in shock," Katherine said to Philippe. "She needs that sweet tea before anything else." Yes, Pippa thought, please, please.

"Of course. *Bien sûr.*" He waved at an older officer who was standing in the doorway and in a few minutes the man returned with two mugs.

The three of them sat without speaking for a few minutes. The tea was helping. Gradually, Pippa felt warmth returning to her limbs and her face. Her stomach stopped flipping as long as she blocked the image of the pig's bloody head from her mind.

The light outside the window had faded and Pippa noticed a single strand of holiday lights visible in the storefront across the street poking out through the gloom. Philippe left them to confer with other officers in the hallway, their voices low and less urgent now that the shock of the moment was over.

"Oh, I say, should you call Michael?" Pippa said into the silence, jerking upright from her slump in the uncomfortable chair with the sudden realization that while she might be alone in France, her friend wasn't.

Katherine had been staring into her mug. She looked tired and Pippa noticed lines on her face that she'd never seen before. "I've been postponing the moment. He'll be worried now that it's dark. Since he doesn't usually answer the phone, I have to hope he'll guess it's me and pick up. He'll be upset when he hears about this."

"He should be. I'm so sorry I dragged you into this. I had no idea anyone would get angry at me."

"You think it's related to our asking questions about the murder?" Katherine said, keeping her voice low. "I thought it was a prank, or at least I want to think so. We haven't been doing anything dangerous, as far as I can see. We certainly don't know who killed Mme Sabine."

Pippa wondered if Katherine was rehearsing what she would say to Michael. He was a lovely man and one didn't want to say bad things about a celebrity in the neighborhood, but he could be a bit of a dragon at times.

"They found your car keys next to the car," Philippe said, taking long strides from the doorway back to his desk. "That's a good thing, yes?" He smiled at Pippa.

"Gosh, yes. I guess I lost them when . . . well, you know. I can't remember much about the first few bloody minutes. I'm so glad you found them. May I have them back, and can we go now? I am feeling much more like myself. Katherine is too, aren't you?"

"I would ask you to stay a little longer, if you will. My boss wishes to ask you a few questions. Then, someone will drive you—both of you—home to Reigny."

"I can't take my car? Is it, uh, dirty?"

"We have to inspect it for clues. When we are done, we will let you know and you can pick up the car. Or, someone from here can escort you back, if that will help. But in the meantime, we must do everything to learn who did this to you. Do you have any idea why someone chose your car to defile?"

Philippe was kind. He would understand and not judge her. She wanted to tell him everything. But if she did, she'd have to explain the gold cross and the thought of doing that closed her throat as if she, not Mme Sabine, was being choked. "No, not really. I only know one teenager here and she's not the type to be cruel."

"You think it was *ados*?"

"Adolescents, you mean? Not necessarily," Katherine said quickly. "I'm sure she didn't mean that. But vandals of some sort. Have there been other incidents like this recently?"

Pippa understood. The last thing Katherine wanted was to have the police interview Jeannette. The girl had gone through enough drama last summer, and everyone knew her father's business practices couldn't bear much official scrutiny. "No, I didn't mean schoolkids, not really. My mind's gone blank, that's all. I can't think of a soul who would do this. Maybe it was random."

Philippe made a sound as if to say her theory was worth considering, drummed his fingers on the desk for a few seconds, then said, "Let me take you up to meet Captain Borde."

The captain, an older man who looked as if he enjoyed his lunches a great deal, invited them into a smaller office, where he closed the door after waving them to upholstered chairs that were a little more comfortable than the plain wooden ones in the lobby and the officers' big room. Rubbing his hands together, he greeted them politely but with no warmth.

"We met before," he said, looking at Katherine. "At the museum, you recall? This new incident was remarkable, *mesdames,* and quite an upset for the people on the street who saw it. I wonder what can have caused it? Do you know?" He spoke in French.

Pippa stared at him, willing her brain to decipher what his mouth was saying, to no avail. Katherine stepped in, said something in French, then in English, "It was even more of a trauma for us, I assure you."

"Ah, no French, Madame?" he replied, switching to a heavily accented English. Pippa silently swore she would either learn some French, dammit, or go back to King's Cross and never set foot in this country again. But not today. Today, she had to keep her wits about her until she knew if she was in danger.

"It was your car?" The gendarme swiveled his stare to her and she felt suddenly like a bug under a magnifying glass.

"Yes, mine."

"It appears that your car door was opened illegally. There are scratches where something was jammed into the window sleeve."

"Is it a mess, the inside of my car, I mean?" She looked up at him, shoulders hunched against what he might tell her.

"Well, we won't worry about that right now, will we? What I'd like to know now is if you knew M. and Mme Sabine? Did you shop there?"

"Not often. But do you mean had I ever been in there or seen them? Yes, on the rare occasions I couldn't live without a French version of bangers and mash." Pippa tried to smile. Her attempt at a mild joke fell flat. Perhaps it was a translation problem.

"And did you ever see either of them outside of the shop?"

Now she was puzzled. "No, not that I can recall."

"You're single, if I understand correctly," he said, leaning back in his chair, fiddling with a pen. "Have a boyfriend here?"

"No." What was this? she wondered. Had the policewoman been gossiping about her? Did everyone know she thought Philippe was cute? Why would this man take it so seriously?

"Maybe have one back in England?"

"I really don't see—," she began before he sat forward, the chair legs thumping on the floor.

"I am wondering if you had some interest in M. Sabine. He is, after all, an attractive man."

Pippa noticed Katherine was looking alarmed, and now her friend spoke. "Now, wait a minute. You sound as if you suspect Pippa of being involved in the death of Mme Sabine, which is not only preposterous but impossible."

Involved? How could he think that? Pippa thought, and her breath became labored. "See here," she said, feeling her throat tighten. "You're frightening me. My car was vandalized. I can't see how you could possibly suggest that because someone broke into my car that I, or it, have anything to do with the murder of that woman." She should have felt righteous anger but Pippa was terrified. Terrified without reason, she tried to remind herself, but to no avail.

"There was something else in your car. Perhaps you didn't notice it?"

"Something else? How would I have noticed something else after what fell in front of me?"

He said nothing, but looked at her with interest.

"No, nothing else. What was it?" She looked at Katherine, who was frowning. What she needed right this instant was a fresh cup of hot tea. Without it, her brain and her strength were failing fast. And, she noticed, her hands were shaking badly. She shoved them in her coat pockets.

"This," he said and picked up a cellophane envelope from his desk, in which was a single sheet of paper. "It was on the front seat."

"What is it?" Pippa said, reaching for it. But the captain pulled the envelope out of her reach.

"It is a note, Madame, presumably, like the boar's head, addressed to you and put in your distinctive automobile. Shall I read it to you?"

Pippa nodded.

"When I tell you what it says, maybe you can help me understand." He cleared his throat, looked hard at her, and read, 'I know what you're doing. I am watching you.' Now, what could that mean, Madame?"

CHAPTER 20

Pippa opened her mouth but couldn't say a word. This was bad. It could only mean that someone had noticed her asking questions about the wig, visiting the museum, maybe even finding the cross. Had the murderer been in L'Isle-sur-Serein that day? Lurking around the museum? Talking to Madame, the owner?

The captain was waiting for an answer, his gaze sharp on her face. Katherine spoke first. "Was it in French, Captain? You read it in English, but I wondered."

"French, Madame. Short and to the point, I should say. But to what point is what I am asking your friend."

"Yes, I see," Katherine said. "It is a puzzle." Pippa figured Katherine was stalling and she exchanged looks with her co-investigator, wishing she could speak with her privately. She was being threatened by someone who didn't want her to snoop into this death, someone who showed his power with evil flair.

"Yes, all right," she blurted before she could change her mind. "You see, I was asking questions. I just wanted to know more about why poor Mme Sabine was killed and I thought if I could research a real crime, it would help with my book."

"Book?"

"Well, yes, you see, I write detective fiction, or rather murder mysteries, and I—"

He held up a hand in a gesture that he had probably perfected standing at traffic intersections. It worked. "You have been investigating on your own something that is gendarme business? Perhaps following my officers to observe their activities? And why would you do that, I wonder. Would that be for a story or to see if we were getting closer to a solution, a solution that might involve you directly?"

He looked pleased with himself, as if he had pulled a rabbit out of a hat, Pippa thought. His conclusion was so idiotic that it calmed her down a bit. She flashed on an image of Peter Sellers, playing the inept Inspector Clouseau in her favorite childhood films. Once this puffed-up captain understood, he would abandon this theory and apologize to her, and she would be gracious. She drew a deep breath. "Not at all. I think you don't understand how we writers work. We gather information so we can use it, disguised of course, when we make up stories." She even smiled.

He dashed her picture of an easy resolution immediately. "Disguise, invent, embroider, yes, I understand completely. And that is what I fear you may be doing at this moment."

"Now wait," Katherine said, squirming in her chair, "this is silly. Pippa was in the van with me before the body was found that day. She only saw the corpse when the rest of us did, and she never went into the room."

"That may be, but the crime happened before you found the body, some time before, we have deduced."

Pippa was startled into a protest. "I didn't know the Sabines beyond hello, I would rather die myself than kill someone, and you need to be focusing on whoever did this to my car. Whoever it is might or might not be trying to implicate me, but I think it's likely it is the killer who left the note. You must see that." She wasn't altogether sure he did, but he seemed to have run out of steam for the moment.

Katherine cleared her throat. "Okay, I need to call my husband now. We live in Reigny-sur-Canne. He'll be worried. He could come pick us up if you need to keep the car. Pippa's right, you know, although I don't like the idea. Someone's been watching her and wants to scare her off. She should have police protection at home, don't you think?"

The captain frowned and shook his head. "I am prepared to let you return home for now, but I cannot spare anyone to spend time in Reigny watching for troublemakers. If—and I emphasize if—there is even a soupçon of truth in what you say, the person who did this will have made his point, especially since you will be doing no more research, as you call it. If we need you, we will be in touch.

"Madame," he said, turning to Katherine, "you will be driven home also, although we may need to speak to you again as well. I have been told your husband is famous but, *je vous assure,* it will not protect you if you are part of a cabal."

"A cabal? Really?" Katherine said, and Pippa shook her head so violently that her vision blurred for an instant. "I think your impression of this has inflated its importance.

Either that or our mutual awkwardness with each other's language has garbled our explanations."

The captain only grunted in a noncommittal fashion. But he did point to the cell phone Katherine had in her hand and tell her she could use it. And he left the room, leaving the door open.

Pippa chewed a fingernail while Katherine talked to Michael. Pippa could tell he was mad, but when she hung up, Katherine gave her a weak smile and said he was on his way.

"What we both need is a hot bath and a good sleep. We can talk tomorrow. I'll be happy to drive you in to pick up your car when they release it to you. This is all so silly and I bet the captain sees that in the morning too."

"I hope so. But what should I do about the cross?" Pippa had dropped her voice to a whisper.

"Tomorrow. We decide tomorrow."

Philippe was nowhere in sight and a different gendarme walked them to the door of the gendarmerie and waited with them until Katherine saw Michael pull up. The policeman escorted them to the car and hardly glanced at them as he opened the door. Pippa noticed the watchers had all gone, and the street was empty of pig's head and red car. She felt disoriented, as if it had been a bad dream, at least until they got under way and Michael's angry voice penetrated her exhaustion.

Their argument was a repeat of his irritation from the morning, but amped up with the drama of the evening. Katherine was meek and apologetic, too much so, Pippa thought, given what had happened. It was hardly their fault someone had thought to put an animal's severed head in her car, was it?

She tuned out their talk as much as possible and thought again about the note. The fact that there was a message had disturbed her so much that she hadn't thought seriously about it. What had it said? Someone was watching her, someone who thought he knew what she was trying to do. But was that likely? She hadn't done very much, if you thought about it. Went back to the museum a few times, watched along with at least thirty other people when the mannequin was fished out of the river. What had made someone so worried?

Michael spoke her name. "I'm sorry? I'm so wrung out I was in a bit of a daze back here." She leaned forward from the backseat to hear him better.

"Do you want me to check out your house before you go in? If the cops aren't going to keep an eye out, it might be smart to make sure the same bastards that messed up your car didn't also decide to trash your house."

"Oh, crikey, I hadn't thought of that. I'll do it with you, but yes, I'd appreciate it. Then I'll let you two get home. I have good locks and I'll make sure I'm tucked in safely."

"Do you want to have a bite to eat with us first?" Katherine said, turning in her seat.

"No, but ta. I have some soup I can heat up. Then, like you said, a hot bath and to bed. My cats will guard the house. Really," as Katherine laughed, "a few of them are real tigers when they think someone's coming to the door. It's all an act, really, but tonight, I'm grateful."

The driveway and the house were completely dark. At Katherine's direction, Michael drove slowly down the driveway so as not to risk hitting a cat. Katherine elected to sit in the car.

"Thank heavens I don't keep my house and car keys on the same ring," Pippa said as she turned the first lock, then used a second key on a deadbolt-style lock. She reached inside the door and flipped on a weak outside light and a stronger one in the hallway. Michael edged past her and peered into the living room.

"Looks okay to me. You stay here and I'll check out the other rooms."

Pippa thought for the first time in hours about something ordinary. She hadn't made her bed, and she was very much afraid there were underthings drying over the bathroom shower rod. Well, he was a married man, so it wouldn't shock him. He might decide she was a messy housekeeper, but right now that didn't matter.

He sprinted up the stairs, calling to her that the kitchen and dining room, which was actually her writing office, looked fine.

She heard his cowboy boots clacking on the bare floors and then he was down again. "Nope. Nothing's torn apart, the windows are all locked tight, and the only closet I saw had shelves filled with clothes. Anything else to look at?"

"No. Thank you, Michael." As he turned toward the front door, almost tripping over the fat, gray cat that was standing close behind him, staring up suspiciously, she added, "I am truly sorry. Believe me, Katherine was an innocent bystander. Whatever this was, I'm sure it was aimed only at me."

He looked at her and then, to her surprise, reached out and pecked her on the cheek. "I think you two have had a bad shock and didn't deserve it. I'm glad to know this is the end of the amateur detecting. I'm sure whoever warned you off did the job. Not to say I don't hope they catch him and string him up." A small smile fractured the frown he had been wearing since he picked them up in Avallon, and he left, closing the front door behind him.

Pippa counted noses as she opened up a can of cat food in the kitchen. All six animals inside, prowling hungrily, expressing their indignation that she hadn't been back before night descended. She heated her own supper out of a can and it wasn't until she was soaking in the tub, every light in the house on, that she circled back to Michael's comment. Had they—or at least she—really decided not to inquire further? Katherine might feel obliged to end her scouting, but Pippa still had questions. The puzzle pieces were building up in her head. She could be more careful, but should she really give up now?

CHAPTER 21

Wonder of wonders, Katherine thought as she put the kettle on to boil water for the *café presse*. Looking out the window, she saw glittering sunshine, winter-sharp and glassy, striking the slate on the patio. There hadn't been a sunny day in so long that she had forgotten how breathtaking the pale blue sky looked with the outline of bare trees fringing it on the farther hills. After a difficult night's rest, when bad dreams woke her every hour, she suddenly felt a burst of energy to be painting. The cat butted her leg to be let out and when she did, she saw her breath visible as frost. Too cold for painting outside, drat.

She was glad of the warmth offered by the Chinese silk wrapper and large black wool shawl, both of which were gleaned at last year's *vide-grenier* in Grimault, a hamlet so small there was no café, nothing but a jumble of old houses, a decrepit church, and a fenced-off cemetery. "I must come back and paint this view," she had said to Michael as they stood at the metal cemetery gate, looking down the slight incline at the tiled roofs that traced a couple of twisty streets.

Now, she remembered the place and promised herself a visit after the worst of winter had passed.

Coffee in hand, she settled onto the chaise, ignoring the dogs, who were Michael's responsibility when he was home. She could hear her husband banging around in the bedroom above and knew he'd be down in a couple of minutes. She needed some time to think. The heater kicked on with a loud gurgling sound, promising more comfort in a few minutes.

Yesterday had been horrible. Even if it had been a nasty prank, that ugly severed head, the bloody stump of its neck, and the tongue that hung out of its mouth would have been a major fright. But the note confirmed what she thought. They, or at least Pippa, were being warned off shining a light on the murder of Mme Sabine. Why, though? Why bother with a couple of expat amateurs who weren't doing anything other than revisiting the site of the crime and asking a few questions? And, she added to herself, not getting anywhere. Whoever sent the message had to be someone who lived in the area. Otherwise, how would he have been able to watch Pippa? Assuming it was a he.

Michael interrupted her thoughts with a squeeze of her shoulder as he passed her on his way into the kitchen. She knew he was pouring himself a mug of the brew to carry with him on the first dog walk of the day.

"It's cold this morning, honey, best wear the sheepskin jacket. And remember, Emile's poor dog is likely to be outside, ready to warm himself up by barking madly at Gracey and Fideaux."

"I think that dog needs to learn how to get along in this

neighborhood," he said as he doubled back to pluck the jacket off a peg.

"Yes, well, take it up with Emile first. Maybe he'll listen to you now that you're a bona fide rock-and-roll star. Not that he didn't already think you and Mick hang out together on a regular basis."

Michael called to the dogs, waiting anxiously at the door once they saw their master picking up their leashes. A waft of cold air reached into the living room to chill her neck briefly before dissipating in the new warmth of the room. Michael had gotten the heater running properly on his first day back, an occasion for joy since its subtle workings baffled Katherine.

With no need to do anything right away, Katherine turned back to the bothersome questions about why Pippa's car had been vandalized. She tried to replay everything Pippa said she had done since the day of the museum visit. Had she inadvertently crossed the killer's path? Had she speculated out loud in a way that frightened whoever did this? She hadn't been with Katherine when the police inspector saw the garbage truck and got so excited. Yes, she had grilled Jeannette a bit, but the girl was clearly not involved. Had the teenager mentioned Pippa's curiosity to someone in school? Someone who knew someone?

It was all so speculative and unsatisfactory. The note said that someone knew what Pippa was doing. Clearly, she was to stop doing it. The museum curator and her daughter were almost as much victims as Mme Sabine, but perhaps there was a connection through the museum. Katherine poured the last of the coffee and debated making a new pot. No, she'd wait until Michael got back so it would be hot.

The only other place Pippa had been was L'Isle-sur-Serein when the mannequin was fished out of the river and where Pippa had picked up the mysterious gold cross. It must be that someone saw her do it and then saw her talking to the police, which was when Pippa met the cute gendarme who spoke English.

The sound of barking, one deep with warning, one high-pitched and nervous, came through the closed window. She got up, leaving the wool shawl on the chaise, and put the kettle on again. Later today, she would walk over to Pippa's house and share her thinking. Maybe Pippa could remember who else she saw at the river. Katherine realized that she was skirting Michael's intense desire that she abandon this project, but Pippa needed protection. Then, right before the kitchen door opened, as she heard the dogs' claws scratching the slate step, it occurred to her. What if the warning was directed at her too? What if it was aimed at both of them?

Pippa peeked out from behind curtains in a living room window before she opened the door. She was dressed in a shapeless skirt, under which she wore black tights decorated visibly with cat hair, and over which she wrapped a cardigan that had lived long past its intended life. Spectacles were perched on her head and her spiky hair looked as though it hadn't been combed, or whatever you did when you had had an asymmetrical, short haircut gelled to stick out like porcupine quills. But, Katherine noted, Pippa's cheeks were rosy and the haircut gave her a gamine look that livened her face. Did looks matter, though? Maybe Pippa would much prefer to be known as a bestselling author living a romantic life in Burgundy. Romantic, yes. Dangerous, probably not.

"Good for you," she said as Pippa waved her in. "If I didn't have Michael and two dogs, I'd be thinking twice about opening the door today too. How are you this morning?"

"I didn't think I would sleep at all, but I slept like a child. I was so fagged out from everything that I think my brain and my body gave up. You?"

"I woke up a few times, but I'll be fine." Katherine glanced at Pippa's outfit.

"Oh, I know, it's rubbish. But this jumper was my mum's and I keep it around as a reminder. Plus it's Shetland wool, the best."

Katherine processed "jumper" to mean what Americans called sweaters. She wondered what the Brits called dresses that Americans might call jumpers, mostly worn by little girls, but scolded herself to stay focused on the main reason for her visit.

"Tea?"

"No, thanks. I've had my coffee already. Am I interrupting something?"

"I'm working on my manuscript, the one about the killing at the castle, but I keep flashing to the new murder so it's not going brilliantly." The electric kettle steamed and Pippa poured herself a fresh mug. The aroma of strong black tea wafted toward Katherine. "Let's sit in my study. It's warmer there." She led the way and flapped one hand at a black cat curled up on the only seat other than her desk chair. It rose slowly and strolled out, giving the women a look that plainly said it wouldn't forget this affront. Katherine sank into the vacated armchair, realizing at the last instant that the springs were old and that she was a lot closer to the floor than she had anticipated. Good thing, she thought, that she hadn't been holding a scalding mug of tea. Pippa didn't seem to notice.

"Have you decided to abandon your interest in Madame's death?" she asked.

Pippa opened her mouth, closed it, then opened it again to speak. "Not exactly," she said, dragging the word out, "although I fully intend to make it look like I have. I see no reason to speak to the police again. I hid the cross but took a smartphone picture of it first. I won't do anything obvious like go looking for the wig and I promise to leave poor Madame and the museum alone."

"All of that is good, but what will you do, then?"

"Use my brainpower and my computer," Pippa said. "'Love,' I told myself this morning, 'think of it as a new mystery novel.' You know, write out a list of possible suspects, a timeline of what you know, the clues you have, or rather I have, although I rather hope you'll compare notes? And a map of what was found where."

"And you think you can deduce the answer that way, like Hercule Poirot?"

"Why not? All it needs is logic, and I will think more clearly if I'm not looking over my shoulder for a butcher, well, in this case, I mean a butcher of pigs."

Katherine froze. What had Pippa said? "My god, M. Sabine *is* a butcher of pigs. Pippa, think of it, who could get hold of a butchered pig more easily than the butcher? Until this moment, I hadn't put the two pieces together." She shivered.

"But we know he didn't do it. Is there another butcher shop? Would that person be jealous enough of M. Sabine's success that he'd kill half of the competing shop's management?"

"Don't be silly," Katherine said. "I'm probably reaching to mention it. It's a coincidence. The pig's head might not imply anything like that and, anyway, the regular butcher sells entirely different things, roasts and chops and the like. Really, Pippa, let's not stray into fantasies."

Pippa's face as she looked over at Katherine signaled her hurt feelings. At that moment, the older woman was keenly aware of the differences in their ages. Pippa was young enough to be her daughter, but not as malleable as Jeannette. Jeannette had no mother. Pippa's mother, however, was gone and what little Katherine had heard about the woman's father suggested he wasn't much of an influence.

"How about this? The real killer gets hold of a pig's head. It can't be that hard, really, if you think about it. He plants it so we will think it's the butcher."

Katherine had to admit that was a clever idea. "I wonder if the gendarmes are surveying farmers or meat suppliers right now? The scariest thing is not the head, which was there for shock value, but the note. What do we know about it and who knew enough about what we were doing to decide we needed to be stopped?"

"Written in French, so a French person?" Pippa said.

"Yes, most likely. And someone who could get into the car without attracting a lot of attention. Who might that fit?"

"A local?"

"A car thief, who'd know how to break into a car?"

"No," Pippa said. "Anyone who's been locked out of their own car knows how to stick a wire hanger inside the window to reach the latch."

"I don't," Katherine said.

Pippa gave her a pitying look.

"What if the person who did this isn't the killer?" Katherine said suddenly. "Maybe the killer paid someone to do it, not saying why, of course."

"If that person knows French, though, wouldn't he read the note and figure out it wasn't a prank? By now, I expect, he'd be at the police station telling them everything."

"True. I was trying to broaden the possible candidates, but it's harder than I thought."

Pippa opened her laptop and began to type. "A man, because it wouldn't be easy to drag her around." She looked up. "That wasn't a nice way to put it. Sorry."

"Someone who wouldn't make people suspicious if they saw him," Katherine said. "He either came in the front door, and Madame would certainly remember anyone suspicious, or he climbed over a wall or somehow knew about the little door arrangement. And he had to get into your car."

"With a pig's head under his arm," Pippa said, and suddenly the two women started laughing. Once they started, they couldn't stop. One would pause and then get a fresh case of giggles. Almost screeching, running out of breath, Katherine managed to say, "Oh stop, stop. This isn't funny."

And with that, the laughter stopped as quickly as it had started. Pippa wiped tears out of her eyes and Katherine rummaged for a tissue in her tote bag. Silence descended in the little room.

"No, it's not," Pippa said. "But I feel better."

Katherine looked at her watch. "I have to get back, but if I think of anything, I'll tell you when we meet tomorrow to go to the memorial service. I'll drive."

"You'll have to unless someone brings back my car. Can we stop at the police station after the service and maybe they'll give it back to me?"

They agreed and as Katherine left, she did something she didn't always do with Pippa. She pulled the younger woman in for the double kisses. "This will get better soon, I know it will."

CHAPTER 22

Michael was asleep, slumped in the battered upholstered chair he had insisted on buying the first week they were in Burgundy. His legs were crossed, a paperback book lay open, facedown, on his knee, and his booted feet rested on the end of her chaise.

Fideaux lay blissed out next to his master, chin on paws, more relaxed than he'd been since Michael left.

Trying to move quietly, Katherine began chopping onions and garlic for the evening meal. Tonight it would be the *boudin blanc* sausages she had defrosted earlier braised with the Romanesco she hadn't been able to resist at the Saturday market even though it cost way too much, potatoes, a handful of dried herbs, and a little white wine. She was tempted to throw in something even greener, like cabbage, but Michael would complain loudly. Beans were as far as he'd go in the direction of green vegetables. He had explained to her the first time he took her to dinner in Aspen, where he and Eric were performing in cafés for tips, that there weren't a lot of green things other than grass in Montana, where he'd grown up, and he was suspicious of them. "I don't eat green ice cream neither," he had said in his stagiest cowboy voice whenever she had tried to persuade him in the decades since.

The kitchen clock said quarter of five, and she resolutely ignored the impulse to pour a glass of wine for herself now that she had opened the bottle. Five o'clock was the holy hour and not a moment before. She had won the argument with herself last week that a small glass of wine during the day during Michael's absence was an entirely different matter. Her nerves, after all, had been shot after they found the body. And it was partly Michael's fault for staying away so long. But that was the exception to her ironclad rule, or at least one. Rule number two, if someone offered her a glass of champagne at lunch, it would be rude to decline.

She left the vegetables to simmer gently in the wine and went to check on her sleeping man, who was coming back to life, rubbing his eyes and yawning.

"Dang, I was tired. Haven't had to do this kind of thing for a few weeks. It's a lot harder than singing, I can tell you."

"What're you reading? Did it put you to sleep?"

"Naw, a thriller I picked up at the airport, all about cybercrime, good stuff."

"I don't read thrillers, or at least I haven't so far. I'll have to read Pippa's, I know. I hope it isn't awful. I don't lie well." She reached past him for her costume book.

"You may not be much of a liar but you sure know how to dance around a thing. I'm still half-pissed at you for not telling me what happened at the museum. You've let it go, right?" He was looking right at her.

"Of course." The simmering pot called for attention, the sausage needed to go in. If you put them in too early, they burst, but if you waited too long, their wonderful fatty flavor wouldn't meld into the onions. And, it was five o'clock, and not a moment too soon. She spun away and retreated. How would she explain why Pippa and she had to go to the memorial service tomorrow?

With a glass of wine in hand, she wandered slowly back into the living room to find Michael shrugging into his warm jacket. "The dogs missed me. I know you don't let them off leash, but they've got me trained well enough that I know exactly where they want to take me for a run." Gracey looked up adoringly as Michael settled his Stetson. "C'mon, mutts," he said sternly and they rushed to the door. "See?" he said and grinned at Katherine. "Back in fifteen minutes. Whatever you're cooking smells fantastic, by the way."

With a bit of time to think it through, and the smallest topping off of the glass, Katherine was in good spirits when Michael and the dogs burst through the door, bringing with them cold air and the smell of dead leaves. His favorite sausages pleased him, and after checking his emails, he suggested playing the rough cuts from the new album that he had sent himself as MP3 files.

There were a half dozen. Michael explained the last layers hadn't been added to the others and that J.B. had promised to forward them in a day or two. When the last note of the last song ended, there was silence.

"What do you think?" he asked, and she could hear nerves in his voice.

She got up and came over to his chair. She eased onto his lap, something she hadn't done in years because it was for young people, and put her arms around his neck. "What do I think? I think it's magic, pure magic. Oh, Michael, I am so proud of you."

"I guess you'd have to say that."

"I'm saying it and I mean every word. Betty Lou's voice is a perfect complement to yours."

"Or mine is a complement to hers. She's the big name." But he was smiling.

"Together, you sound great. And the band—who are those people? They're fantastic."

"Memphis is loaded with talent. Actually, a couple of the guys are with other bands but they do side stuff like this. Since Betty Lou hasn't done rock before, we needed to make damn sure the band had, you know?"

Once he got started, Michael wanted to tell her everything about the experience. Listening to his descriptions of the way they built up the tracks, the sophisticated equipment that evened out the sound, the fun of making music with a dozen people, she realized how hard he must have struggled to maintain his professional motivation sitting on the patio or in the little living room working on his own week after week for years. Her eyes teared up, and she went to the kitchen so he wouldn't see.

"Dessert?" she said while refilling her glass.

"Only if you have that fancy French gingerbread."

"*Pain d'épices?* Of course. With Christmas coming, all the *boulangeries* and patisseries have it. It's a Burgundy tradition. Coming up."

She waited until he'd had a bite, then said, "By the way, I'll be going to the memorial service, well, really not a service since there's no priest, but a gathering anyway, for Mme

Sabine. It's tomorrow at four in Avallon." She had kept her tone casual and decided to mention Pippa only if he asked.

"Is Pippa going too? Is this something I should worry about?"

Maybe she had been too quick to wish him home so soon. "She may. I expect a lot of their customers and other store owners will be there. My dentist was in the same church group, so I'm sure she'll be there. She was well liked, you know."

"No, I didn't, but it doesn't surprise me. I have a general sense that she was pleasant and professional. Should I go?"

Katherine knew he hated events like this. "I don't think it's necessary. I'll be there for both of us. I have a little bit of Christmas shopping to do and then straight home, I promise."

"Dang, I almost forgot," he said, getting up and going to the small work table crammed in a corner of the living room that served as his desk and repository for mounds of paper that Katherine had long ago learned not to touch. He rummaged around, dug into a backpack that lay under the desk, and said, "Close your eyes and hold out your hands. Consider this an early Christmas present."

She did as she was told, pretty sure she knew what was coming.

"Now," he said. She opened her eyes. Yes, an Elvis bobblehead doll, as kitschy as it could be, with an exaggerated pouty doll's mouth and a black painted pompadour rising to an improbable height. Elvis sneered at her as he shook his head. "Like it?"

"How could I not?" she said. Under the doll was a business envelope. "And what's this?"

Michael's eyes twinkled as he said, "Open it, sweetheart, before I grab it back."

A check made out to her husband, several thousand dollars, from a company she'd never heard of. "What? Who?"

"Small advance, the most I'll get as a newcomer, from the company that will distribute the songs to the streaming services. Royalties to follow, fingers crossed. I'll sign it and you can deposit it tomorrow. That way, the credit card bill I have a hunch I'll see at the end of the month will be covered, at least."

Inwardly, Katherine sighed with relief. But this also meant she could get Michael the warm sweater she had seen last time she was in town. And maybe some decent wine, and the ceramic angel in the *brocante* window unless someone had already snatched it up. All she said was "Christmas is coming and this is perfect timing." She kissed him and he squeezed her arm before going over to pull one of the guitars from the lineup along the wall.

"Gotta get in some practice. By the way, Emile's dropping by later. He wants to show me his new guitar and I couldn't say no."

"Softie. We'll invite him to stay for dinner as long as he's here. This cold weather keeps me in and I'm feeling out of touch. Tomorrow morning, I'll drop by Mme Pomfort's house and Yves's bookshop. I might walk over to see Adele and Sophie, if Sophie's down from Paris. After lunch, it's over to Avallon for the memorial and some shopping. And, no, you may not come with me. Santa has to have some secrets."

CHAPTER 23

Mme Pomfort's living room was dimly lit and felt like a mole's hole to Katherine. The old widow was surrounded by framed photos on every surface, interspersed with small figurines of seventeenth-century noblemen and women in frilly costumes. Her furniture was upholstered and heavy, the drapes thick like those at the museum but not as rich, the lamp shades darkened by age from what was once probably cream to a dull tan. Today, the shutters on her living room windows were open, which helped, but Katherine couldn't live without more light. She speculated, as Madame fussed over a tray of Marie biscuits and coffee, if the gloom might explain the stern demeanor of Reigny's social lioness.

Mme Pomfort spent the first fifteen minutes of Katherine's visit criticizing the newcomer to Reigny. "If you ask me, that Josephine Lacrois doesn't care one bit for her poor old grandfather. You watch, she'll sell his house to some foreigner an hour after he's laid to rest."

Like Michael and me? Katherine thought. But that had to be better than seeing the building continue its slow crumbling into the rocky earth. Instead, she said, "How is he?"

"Not good, not good. His lungs, you know. I remember when he was quite the man, running his tabac, knowing everything that went on in the town, quite the life of the party then."

This cast not only M. Lacrois, whom she had only seen a few times, in a shabby sports coat and wooly scarf, slowly negotiating the badly paved road near his house, but Madame herself in a different light. The life of the party? Was this a party at which the stern Mme Pomfort was also a guest? Katherine tried to picture her as a young woman but got nowhere. "Did you know his wife?"

"Poor thing, she died of the pneumonia after the war. We had nothing then, you see, everyone so poor, the Germans having robbed us of our livestock, our crops, even our cars and trucks. When they left, we had to start all over again. Those were bad years, the children didn't have milk, and so much sickness." She shook herself. "But let us not dwell on what we cannot change, Mme Goff."

"We may lose a resident when M. Lacrois dies, but we will be gaining one soon since Marie and Raoul are about to become parents."

"Yes, that will be something to celebrate. She is a good girl and he, well, he may be a farmer one day. But they respect the ways of their elders."

Katherine smiled. So there was a way to get into Madame's good graces. Be French, have relatives from Reigny, fit in without making waves, and bring new life into this old town.

They chatted a while longer and Katherine asked if Madame was going to the memorial for the slain butcher's wife. "No, she was not from here and I didn't know her other than to say hello on my market days. She made the finest pâtés in the region, although they were too expensive, and I expect her reputation as a *charcutier* is one reason people will attend. That and to gossip about her killer." She paused. "Nevertheless, her cooking talent should be recognized." It came out, as most of the things Mme Pomfort said, as a statement of protocol, a dictum laid down by some ancient Reigny-sur-Canne social magistrate, whom it was Madame's duty as a distant descendent of the Bonapartes to uphold.

The mention of talent did give Katherine the opening to brag a bit about Michael's news, most of which seemed to go over the old woman's head. Streaming songs? American concerts? Country rock music? She nodded her head in the appearance of interest but made only a few noncommittal sounds before signaling that the visit was over by standing abruptly.

Back on the street, Katherine wondered at her own meekness around the woman. It had started when she and Michael arrived in Reigny, all smiles and American casual manners, and had been instantly and completely snubbed by Madame and, as Katherine learned, therefore almost everyone else. Last summer, her offer to manage the entertainment portion of the town fête had helped, although it was the trauma of an unexplained death that had finally made them allies. The good news was, once you were on Madame's good side, she explained to Michael, you were pretty much assured to be there forever unless you tried to claim the church garden.

The bookstore was dark and the "Fermé" sign Katherine had painted for Yves was hanging from the nail. Katherine realized that Pippa might be waiting for her, so she pulled out her cell phone and dialed the writer's number. There was no answer. Pippa might be in the bath, or out for a walk, so she left a message saying she'd pick her friend up at one and trudged up the hill to Château de Bellegarde. The housekeeper who answered the door was no friendlier than on any other visit, but said Madame Adele was in the sitting room.

"Katherine, my dear," Adele Bellegarde said, rising from her chintz sofa and coming over to kiss her guest. "How lovely, and perfect timing. Will you have a glass of sherry with me to take off the chill of the day?" Pulling Katherine over to sit with her, she asked for all the news. "I don't get out much, you know, and no one comes to see me."

Katherine noticed immediately the new lines on Adele's face, and the thinness of her hand as the older woman patted hers. "Is Sophie here?"

"Only for a short visit. She will go back to Paris on the morning train and take Yves with her. Thankfully, I have my books and my house projects to work on, but a widow's life is a lonely one. Ah, there you are, *chérie*."

Sophie, trailed slowly by Yves, had come into the room, rubbing her hands together briskly. "Katherine, it is so good to see you. I hear Michael has returned. Has he finished his music making?" She kissed Katherine and sat next to her.

"Just the recording. The concert tour hasn't started and I confess I'm not looking forward to it. He'll be gone so long."

"Ah, but you will go with him, will you not?" Sophie looked surprised, probably imagining, Katherine thought, something far more glamorous than red-eye bus trips and fast-food meals. She thought Michael wanted her to come, but guessed he'd feel differently if it didn't go well. And there was the matter of Eric, who would be the big star at the concerts. She and Eric had minor history, only one foolish night before she and Michael got married, but given what Eric did to Michael by pushing him out of the band and stealing the hit song Michael wrote, it was sticky. How would she behave if—when, really—she saw Eric?

For now, she only said, "Too early to know. And then, there are the animals. They must be fed and walked and that means we can't close up the house. I really need to think it through."

Yves poured his fiancée and himself generous glasses of sherry, and slumped into a deep chair, yawning and scratching his head. "But you must go, dear Katherine, so you will have stories to tell us when you return." He lifted his glass in a careless toast, then drained it.

Sophie glanced at him. "Maybe we should come to a concert? Oh yes," she added as Katherine made a questioning noise. "After all, our company has a major investment in the recording studio and it might be a way to combine a meeting with the pleasure of seeing Michael onstage in America. What do you think, Yves?"

He brushed a strand of dark hair from his forehead and frowned. "Will Michael be in Hollywood? I would very much like to see that. But it is a long trip and I do not like the idea of flying so much, you know?" He looked at Sophie.

She smiled and Katherine saw the iron underneath the turned-up lips. "Yves has been telling me we need to visit Playa Blanca, a nice idea if I can get away from the office for a week."

Yves jumped up and went to a window, staring out at

the woods beyond the driveway. "It is a good thing to keep your father's business going, but surely there are others who could do that as well as you."

A small silence settled in the room. Sophie looked thoughtfully at a large painting over the fireplace mantel and sipped from her glass. Adele's eyes jumped back and forth between the couple, and she clasped her hands in her lap. "Well, we shall think about it," Sophie finally said. "But what has happened about poor Mme Sabine? I do not spend much time here and Maman has no visitors to tell her the latest news."

Katherine said as little as possible and quickly steered away from a discussion of Mme Sabine's death. Adele had experienced too much of death this last year. Instead, she talked about the coming baby in Reigny, Mme Pomfort's delicate friendship with her former garden rival, and Michael's work in the Bellegarde-funded studio, without mentioning his producer or Betty Lou by name.

From his spot at the window, Yves spoke. "I'm sure there are lovely places in America, but once you have lived in France, it is hard to consider leaving."

Katherine hid her smile. No use describing sunsets in Malibu or walks on the rugged trails in Big Sur.

Adele said, "New York is such an exciting place."

"You've been to Manhattan?" Katherine said.

"Once, with my parents, after the war. So much abundance, hard to take it all in, given our condition here. But the Americans we met were friendly and generous. Indeed, it was rather uncomfortable to be treated as though we were poor, as so many people did, not realizing how prominent our family is."

"How did the Bellegardes fare in the war?" To Katherine, it was a simple question, but somehow it misfired. Adele drew herself up to her full height, became busy with the soft throw she had put over her legs, and asked how Jeannette was getting along in school. In a few moments, she rose and explained she had some correspondence to deal with and thanked her neighbor for dropping in. Sophie rose too, and said she had phone calls to make to Paris. Only Yves remained, offering her a refill of the sherry. The sherry, Katherine thought, was excellent, but the message was clear. For the second time that morning, Katherine was dismissed.

Finding herself deposited outside the massive wooden doors of the château, she wondered about the history of the Bellegardes. There had been some gossip about Adele's late husband, a naturalized French citizen of German origin, last summer but she thought it had been unfair, triggered by the always present memories of the Nazi occupation of the region.

She checked her phone but there was no message from Pippa. It was time to get home and change. She would wear the slightly witchy, black bouffant skirt that someone had decided to part with at a summer flea market with black tights and the ruffled black coat. That is, if it wasn't covered in dog hair from the time she left it on the chaise and Gracey turned it into a nest of sorts.

The sound of a guitar being strummed and Michael singing softly welcomed her as she came in the kitchen door, pulling off her boots. It was a sound she had been so used to hearing every day for three years. Today, it sounded fresh and his voice more polished. The house smelled like coffee and wood smoke. It was warm and cozy, such a treat after so many days alone. She kissed the top of his head as she slipped past his chair to warm her fingers and toes by the fire.

"Heaven," she said, speaking to the whole house and everything in it. The dogs briefly opened their eyes to stare up at her, but were too content lying along the hearth to do more. "What are you up to?"

"I'm trying to figure out how to do this song for the Christmas show at the church if it's going to be a duet with Emile. There must be some key he can sing in."

"Good luck with that. You played and sang last year so you know it's likely to be a handful of the oldest, deafest residents, everyone freezing in that unheated building, impatient to get to the *mairie* and the potluck dinner."

"I don't perform without rehearsing even if it is for people who have no clue about the lyrics or the importance of chord changes. They will want to sing a couple French songs and Emile will lead that."

"You're a darling to take it seriously."

"You fixing up that Madonna painting?"

"Unfortunately, yes. Tomorrow I'll touch up that hideous thing, as promised. I might take a stab at the old stations of the cross if I have time. They're frescos, painted directly on the walls, and so faded that I can hardly pick out the images. But one of the old ladies told me she gets distracted because the paintings annoy her so much, so maybe that will be my present to her, even if she's the only one who cares."

Michael turned in his chair. "You're a good woman, you know that?" He turned back and Katherine, warm in body and heart, went to the kitchen to find something to snack on. He called from his chair, "You're driving today, right? Because I thought I might go buy some firewood from that funny old farmer who lives near the truffle town in the next day or two."

"The truffle town" was Noyers-sur-Serein, a tiny town that came alive on a specific day in late fall when the truffles were gathered and sold from the courtyard of an old school in a frenzied atmosphere. Katherine could never afford to buy, but she had gone this year to see what the fuss was about, and found it extraordinary. Michael had driven and while she was squeezed in the crowd, he had walked around, and found a man working a field who cared as little as he did for the earthy-smelling fungus. The man had instead done a good job of convincing Michael of the superior quality of his firewood, and the two had struck not only a bargain but the kind of man-to-man friendship Michael seemed to thrive on, one with very little talking, lots of posturing, and many hand signals.

"Can it wait 'til tomorrow? Pippa needs a ride so she can pick up her car, and I intend to stay in Reigny all day tomorrow."

"Sure. By the way, the phone rang a couple of times. I didn't answer it. Too confusing."

"Probably Pippa wondering where I am. I'll change and get going. But maybe this will be the winter you learn to say hello and goodbye."

"Problem is everything that comes between hello and goodbye," Michael said to her back as she headed up the stairs.

CHAPTER 24

The woman in her dream was hitting her with a gnarled stick, so hard that it made a thumping sound. Pippa struggled to stop her and came awake feeling sluggish and disoriented. The banging didn't stop and, clued in by the presence of all six cats in her bedroom eyeing her with alarm, she realized it was the door. Throwing on her old robe, she stumbled down the stairs, calling out that she was coming. It wasn't like Katherine to be insistent. Maybe something was up.

But when the door swung open, it was Philippe, in uniform, who looked back at her without expression but with a flicker of warmth in those beautiful eyes. Behind him on the path stood his partner, lips in a tight line. She pulled her robe closer around her and did a fast inventory. Bed hair, unbrushed teeth, old pajamas, bare feet.

"May we come in?"

She stood aside as the two of them walked in, picking their way around the suspicious cats, who were not about to let anyone forget it was time to eat.

"Yes?" she said, standing in the middle of the room,

wishing she could run upstairs and get dressed after erasing her image from their brains. "Did you bring my car?"

Philippe cleared his throat. "No, it is the car and what was in it that we need to discuss with you." His partner's silence carried waves of suspicion.

"Look, I just woke up. Can I get you tea and then get dressed? And I have to feed the cats or they won't leave us alone." That latter was obviously true. Two of the felines had taken positions near the woman's feet and were rubbing up against her navy blue pants. She was trying to kick them away discreetly.

Philippe exchanged glances with his partner and shrugged. "Quickly, please. We must interview you."

Pippa ran up the stairs, threw cold water on her face, and pulled on leggings and a big sweater, one that her father said brought out the greenish gold in her eyes. A swipe with the hairbrush did no good, but another swipe with the lip gloss helped a bit. Shoes—where were the ballet slippers?

Back downstairs, she put the electric kettle on, dished out cat food as quickly as she could without slopping it on the counter, and grabbed three mugs. Irish Breakfast for strength, tea bags in mugs, pour water, and back to the living room, where Philippe and the woman, whose name she didn't know, were sitting on the edges of her mismatched chairs. Until that moment, sinking into the remaining chair, Pippa hadn't had time to ask herself what they needed to interview her about, or why they still needed her car. Now, she began to worry. Sipping the hot liquid, she waited.

Philippe cleared his throat. "We need to go over the time between your finding the body at the museum and when your car was vandalized, in detail." His partner stirred, and pulled out her notebook.

"Why?" Pippa said. "I don't understand."

He didn't answer but said in his accented English, "You went to the museum with your friend on that day. But had you been there in the days before that, perhaps even that Tuesday?"

"No, why would I? Aren't they closed Mondays and Tuesdays except for special events? Anyway, I'd already seen that exhibit with Katherine, at least a month before. Really smashing, you know. I don't know how she does it, exhibit after exhibit. I only went along on the day Mme Sabine was found because I needed a ride. My car was in the shop in Avallon."

"What shop?" Philippe said and the woman gendarme raised her pencil. "How long was it there?"

Pippa told him the name and said it was only in for twenty-four hours, something to do with the clutch. "I never understand these things. But they'll tell you if you check."

Philippe had not touched his tea. He now said, "You were not part of the Catholic women's group that toured the museum?"

"No," she said. "I'm Church of England through and through. When I can be, of course. Not possible here."

"And what of the days after the museum? Where were you?"

Pippa shut her eyes, trying to recall. Ticking off the days on her fingers, she walked through the past ten days as well as she could. Philippe and his partner had seen her in L'Isle-sur-Serein and in Avallon. There wasn't much else to tell.

"And your friend, she is your only alibi for those days?"

"Alibi?" A sudden chill gripped her. What was this about? "The policeman in Avallon seemed to think I needed an alibi too. But there's no reason I would possibly have for killing that woman. What can you be thinking?" Her eyes fell on a gaggle of furry animals milling around the door. "I have to let them out," she said, pointing.

The woman cop shuddered slightly and nodded. Pippa made sure all six were out before shutting the door slowly, all the while wondering what she should do. In England, she'd say she wanted a solicitor if they were going to suspect her. Was this about that note in her car? Would it be best to explain what she and Katherine thought it meant, even if it made them look more foolish than ever to the coppers?

"Look," she said, "let's walk this through again. I've said before that I hardly knew the woman. Maybe my curiosity got the better of me because I'm always looking for ideas and scenes for my murder mysteries, the stories I make up. You understand that, right? That's the only reason I came to L'Isle-sur-Serein when you were there. It's why I went back to the museum after the body was found. Looking for inspiration."

"Inspiration?" the woman said, twisting her mouth into an expression of severe disbelief. She understood at least some English.

"It sounds silly, but think. I live in a town full of people who don't speak English. How am I supposed to make up stories if I can't get ideas?"

"You live in France," she thought she heard the woman say under her breath.

Philippe stirred. "Your car was in your possession all

the time except when you parked it on the street the day it was vandalized?"

Pippa stopped to think. "It was in the garage that day before. I have to park it if I have an errand nearby. I drove to Auxerre for a propane canister last week. Why?"

"You took nothing from the museum on any visit?" Philippe said, ignoring her question.

"No, I'm sure not." She didn't mention Katherine having taken the slip of paper. That wasn't what he asked her, fortunately.

"Then why, Madame, did the gendarmes find the missing wig from the mannequin in your trunk?"

The gendarmes left thirty minutes later with no answers. Pippa's pulse was still elevated although she had stopped shaking by then. She had assured them several times that she had no idea, that the vandals must have planted it, which meant they were the criminals involved in Mme Sabine's death.

The wig had been under the carpet in the boot, jammed up against the jack, and had only been found when the car was being searched minutely for traces of the vandals themselves. The museum curator had identified it as the one the mannequin had been wearing in the exhibit. There were no fingerprints on the inside or outside of the boot, or indeed anywhere on the car.

Pippa had pointed out it was cold that day and everyone was wearing gloves and scarves. Philippe explained that the wig did hold a few threads of fabric that might—or might not—belong to whomever stuck it in the wheel well. He asked for the gloves she had worn and Pippa was relieved to tell him her gloves were leather, not fabric. He had asked her to give him any fabric gloves or scarves she had, however, and she had reluctantly handed over at least a half dozen items, any one of which might implicate her falsely.

"What if you find a thread from when I had to pull the jack out six months ago so the farmer in Reigny could change my flat tire?" She was near tears.

"We'll deal with that when we come to it." But he looked at her and must have seen her panic because his voice softened and he came closer to where she was standing near the doorway to the kitchen. "Look," he said in a kinder voice, "this may not mean anything. You may be right that someone is targeting you and hoping to distract us. But, never fear, we will discern the truth of the case before we are done." He even smiled a bit and tilted his head as if to say she should trust him. But she couldn't have her car yet.

"You must have more believable suspects than me? Isn't there someone more likely? I read that the butcher had an alibi, but are you sure about it?"

Neither of the gendarmes wanted to discuss the case with her, but Philippe took pity on her and said, "If it were that simple, I assure you he would have been arrested by now. As I said, we will find the culprit and we are investigating every small piece of information we have."

Pippa slumped into a chair as the door closed on them. When Philippe's partner had opened the door to leave, two of the cats had streaked in and one now began to sharpen its claws on the arms of the chair.

What she wanted more than anything was to be in her father's house in London, with the TV blaring in the background, and the smell of a shepherd's pie baking in the old

AGA. She thought about calling him, but the thought of explaining everything over the phone stopped her. Her Chunnel trip was in four days and surely the police would have caught the real killers by then. For now, talking to Katherine would help. Michael might even be a good substitute for her father since he was determined Katherine—and, she hoped, by extension, herself—should be as far away as possible from this investigation.

Katherine's phone rang and rang. They must be out walking, or up at the *mairie* on some business. She could never remember all the forms she was supposed to fill out until the day they were due, or worse, the day after that. Reigny's mayor was impatient, she could tell, when she dropped by to ask for his help deciphering the official letters she received. Maybe she'd best dress in something more suited to a funeral than the rags she was wearing (any hope she had of attracting Philippe's positive attention was surely crushed after he saw her looking like an old hermit) and walk up to Katherine's to meet her.

As she pulled the hood of her anorak up, lamenting the loss of her wooly scarves, she gave herself a stern rebuke for the thoughtless way she had blundered into this whole mess. Maybe if she read more murder mysteries, she wouldn't be tempted to get into the real world to pick up ideas. Maybe she should move back to London. Katherine had once asked her if she wouldn't find more to think about among the daily crimes committed in a big city, and she promised herself to think seriously about that as soon as this crisis was over.

While she walked, she ticked off the possible suspects. The butcher had a firm alibi, the newspaper reported early on. He had been playing cards all Tuesday evening. There had been no other crimes suggesting a maniac on the loose. The theory of a lover was taking on more credibility, although definitely not because the nosy, invalid wife of the chocolate maker fantasized about sex from her second-floor window. Someone had seen the victim on the street in Beaune, holding hands with a man. The cross might suggest some connection to the church group, except they were women and dragging the victim around the salon would surely have caught Madame's attention, even though she was several floors below. So, perhaps a man who knew the women, maybe met Mme Sabine through the church? Whoever it was must have carried the dead woman into the salon or killed her right there on the chaise, and Pippa realized that had to have happened on Tuesday evening because Philippe had asked her where she was on Tuesday. Pippa shivered. Crikey, the dead woman must have been lying in the cold room until Thursday. It didn't bear thinking about.

Katherine had wondered about the pig's head, most easily procured by a butcher. Who were the other butchers in the neighboring towns? That might be the best place to start. She paused, her hand on Katherine's gate. What was she saying? Already she was thinking about continuing her investigation.

CHAPTER 25

The church was lovely inside, obviously cared for and used for Catholic services, unlike Reigny's sad building. The mostly twelfth-century, crusted and chipped stone exterior gave no hint of the polished stone and soaring arches that seemed to collect light and sound. The rose window sparkled in the afternoon sunlight and neat rows of straight-backed chairs were arranged to leave a long center aisle that led to a set of windows behind the altar and, above it, a half dome with faded artwork that was sepia-colored in the shadow.

Katherine and Pippa had stopped to decipher a worn stone tablet outside the church. Pippa had suggested doing it and explained she would take pictures of Katherine whenever anyone who looked the least suspicious approached the open doorway. "They'll be in the background and I can load them onto my computer so we can look at them later." She seemed to think this was a brilliant move and Katherine didn't have a better idea.

There was a small but steady stream of people entering the church, many of them stopping on the steps to chat.

Katherine was about to suggest they go in when Pippa said, "Don't turn around now, but here comes the butcher. I wonder who that is with him?"

Katherine turned her head as discreetly as she could to see the man. "Someone told me M. Sabine had a brother, but he doesn't live around here."

"Wait," Pippa said, whispering. "You don't think the brother is the one she was having an affair with? He's quite good-looking, although he's obviously knackered. Point at the stone bit so I can shoot. Rats." She pulled the camera away from her eye and made a face. "Both of them looked at me right at the moment I took the picture."

"I was afraid of this. We've upset M. Sabine on an already unhappy day. Enough, Pippa, let's go in." Katherine turned for a fuller look at the stranger and sucked in her breath. It was, she thought, the man she had run into near the museum on that rainy day. He had tucked his head down behind his open umbrella and walked away quickly, but she was almost sure it was he. There was probably a simple explanation. He might have come to Avallon after the murder to tend to his grieving sibling. At that moment, as he stepped into the church, his eyes darted around and she thought he looked hard at her. Then, he was out of view.

The recorded bells began to chime. Pippa tucked her camera away and the two hurried in to take seats on the aisle near the back. There were about thirty people clustered mostly in front rows. No coffin. Perhaps, thought Katherine, they hadn't released the body yet. Or maybe M. Sabine had made arrangements for a cremation.

The bells stopped ringing and a woman Katherine had never seen before stood up from the front row and walked forward to the lectern. Without the help of a microphone, she read something in rapid French, then nodded at the audience and walked back to her seat. Josephine Lacrois was next, her high-heeled, fur-topped boots clicking as she came up to read. Gold earrings sparkled, her lipstick was a cheery red, which stood out in this gray space, and she looked younger and more chic than she had at Katherine's rustic lunch. She crossed herself before she began and again when she had finished, a rather showy gesture, Katherine thought. As she walked back to her seat, her smile was rich with sympathy aimed at the butcher and the man sitting in the front row of chairs.

Pippa leaned toward her and whispered, "Do you think I could take a few pictures now?"

Katherine shook her head vigorously. Honestly, Pippa sometimes had no sense at all. She assumed the widower would speak, but to her surprise a man in a bulky suit stood up, spoke in a gravelly voice with a rustic accent Katherine couldn't decipher, gestured toward M. Sabine, and said something that let everyone know it was over.

"No priest, no hymns?" Pippa said in a low voice as the people who had been sitting silently stood up, shaking their coats into shape, pulling on gloves and beginning to head back up the center aisle. The natural light had faded, the rose window held its secrets again, but the ugly fluorescent tubes that stuck out from the pillars to break the harmony of the medieval design had not been turned on. "I say, I'd rather no one tried to do me a memorial if this was the result. Too depressing."

"I didn't catch much of the readings, but perhaps if we had the language, we would have found some spiritual value, or at least poetry, in what Josephine Lacrois and the other woman shared."

"Maybe," Pippa said, but she didn't sound convinced.

Katherine saw Josephine cross the center aisle to grasp the widower's hands and bestow on both men another dramatically mournful smile. Then she did something that startled Katherine. She placed her hand under the sleeve of the taller of the two and looked up at him with an expression that was so intimate it stopped Katherine in her exit. Did Josephine know M. Sabine's brother? Was he the boyfriend from Beaune she had talked about? If so, why had she never mentioned the coincidence?

She jumped as something clattered onto the stone floor, the noise loud in the space. A few heads turned to see what caused it, and then turned away again. The sound came from a mass of golden curls only partly tucked into the collar of a rather shabby parka. "Jeannette?" she said, crossing the aisle to look down at the teenager, who was picking up a handful of coins.

"*Bonjour,* Katherine," she said, standing up and pushing hair back from her face, which was pink, either from having been bent over or from a sudden moment of awkwardness at being caught at an adult event.

"What are you doing here?"

"I knew her. Maybe only a bit, but I am sorry that she is dead." Jeannette looked as though she was ready to defend her position.

"That's thoughtful of you, *chérie,*" Katherine said, wondering if behind that innocent explanation and the suspiciously cherubic expression there might be some other motive, perhaps a wish to entertain her after-school friends

222

with an account of the event. "Do you want to ride back to Reigny with me? I have only a couple of short errands to do first."

"Yes, thank you," the girl said. "I will visit my friend Amelie at her parents' store while you shop." In front of Katherine, a couple of people had stopped to talk to the widower and his friend. Glancing their way as she and Katherine edged past, a puzzled look swept over Jeannette's face. She did a quick double take.

"Oh, Mme Goff," a voice trilled behind Katherine. She turned to see Josephine headed her way. "How kind of you to come. I'm sure the family will be pleased. There was a good attendance, don't you think? I'm sure it would have been even more, as I told M. Sabine, had it been on a weekend day or perhaps at lunch when the shopkeepers were free."

"Yes, I'm sure you're right. Josephine, who is the man with M. Sabine? I don't think I know him."

"I didn't know myself until recently, but he is the brother."

"Of Madame?"

"No, M. Sabine's brother, half brother, actually. Such a coincidence, isn't it? I know him in Beaune, where he lives, but he has a different last name and she never introduced me to him so I never connected them. You can imagine how shocked I was when I saw him here, but he has explained it all to me. And he is so worried about his brother's health, of course."

"Yes, both of them look distressed," Katherine said, but she was distracted. She needed time to process what Josephine had told her. It seemed there were connections among the four—the victim, Josephine, the charcuterie owner, and this new man, the half brother. What did it mean, if anything? Eager to leave the cold church and collect Pippa, Katherine added a few words about the late, lamented Mme Sabine and eased away. That explained why she had seen the man around Avallon recently. He must have come to help his brother. Another bit of information for Pippa's "little gray cells" worksheet.

She looked around and saw Pippa and Jeannette in a dark side chapel at the rear of the church, their heads together. Katherine walked over to them. "I'm headed back to the main street. Are you two coming?"

Jeannette gave Pippa a conspiratorial look that Katherine couldn't decipher, then reached over and kissed Katherine, bobbed her head in Pippa's direction, and promised to be waiting at the car in a half hour before pulling up her collar and taking off.

"What was that about?" Katherine asked as they passed through the massive wooden door with its iron scrollwork.

Pippa said, "I'm not sure," and tripped over the uneven stones, making a choking sound. Katherine looked at her, then at where she was staring. The captain who had accused Pippa of being romantically interested in M. Sabine and Philippe's partner were leaning on a police car parked across the street, watching the people leaving the church. They had seen Pippa, and the woman gendarme had her hand in front of her mouth as she leaned into the older policeman to tell him something. He looked hard at Pippa, who had turned away from the street and was fumbling with her camera, head down.

"Let's get out of here," Pippa said in a panicky voice, "they're looking at me. Quickly, please."

"Absolutely not. Walk slowly, chat with me, do not look so guilty, for heaven's sake. Let's check out this stone plaque again. We'll wait until most people have left and then stroll to the car. Right now, you look like you're waiting to be handcuffed."

The tablet was as mysterious as before, Gothic-looking script so smooth it was not readable in some places and, where she could make out a few letters, still meaningless to Katherine. The pamphlet she had paid a half euro for said nothing about it, although other descriptions suggested that being part of the original wall meant it dated from 1170, which was so long ago that Katherine couldn't quite conceive of it.

They carried out their charade for such a long time that the butcher and his brother left, accompanied by the man who had spoken and Josephine Lacrois. Josephine snatched back her hand from the brother's arm when she saw the police standing across the street and busied herself looking in her handbag. As they moved off, she leaned in to whisper something to the Sabine brother. He swiveled his head toward Katherine and Pippa huddled near the church wall. Almost handsome, Katherine thought, and definitely the man with the umbrella. His face was mottled red, though, and his eyes were puffy from the emotion of the memorial service. The butcher was sagging, pale and visibly exhausted. The three mourners stood on the steps as Katherine steered Pippa to the sidewalk, while pretending to be engrossed in the former priests' house that abutted the church. The gendarmerie captain pushed himself off the car's side panel and crossed the street, not toward Pippa, but toward the widower and his party. As she and Katherine reached the comparative safety of the corner, Katherine said, "See, they're not interested in us. I can't wait until this is over and they've arrested someone."

"As long as it's not me," Pippa said.

They had parked nearer to the police station than the church, although the two were close to each other. Avallon was a small town for all that it had everything Katherine needed most days. After the police station, she could easily stop at the bookstore and go down a block and around the corner to reach the *maître chocolatier*'s shop, whose window now featured brightly dyed miniature fruits and vegetables sculpted out of marzipan. She would get a small box of them as a treat for Jeannette and her brothers.

For a moment, the two stood on the sidewalk near the gendarmerie, calming themselves. Pippa had told Katherine everything about Philippe's visit and the gendarmes finding the wig on the short trip to Avallon, and Katherine was as worried as Pippa. Someone was not only trying to derail them with warnings, but was trying to frame Pippa.

It wasn't credible that Pippa had any role in the crime, of course. A few times, Katherine had snuck a peek at her companion as they sped toward the town. Yes, she looked a bit scattered, and her explanations, especially in translation, were apt to raise a few eyebrows. Yes, she probably annoyed the gendarmes with her complete lack of French and her lack of a solid French history that they could verify with the mayor or the sheriff. Her face had an unfortunate tendency to telegraph what might read as guilt, although Katherine knew it was only a version of her normal self-deprecating, apologetic personality. The police were doubtless getting pressure from the mayor and their own higher-ups to close this case, which had been dribbling on for almost two weeks. Pinning it on a foreigner, someone not even from Avallon, would be a relief.

"Listen, Pippa, you have to be more assertive, and look people in the eye and say again and again that you didn't see Mme Sabine during the times in question, that you don't know her husband, and that you will have to call the embassy if the police don't stop harassing you."

Pippa looked at her with the same liquid expression the cows in Reigny did.

"No, that won't do. Head up, posture straight, pretend you are already a celebrity author coming to accept a prize, or something. Right now, you look like a victim."

"I am a victim—," Pippa began, but Katherine interrupted her.

"No, you're a resident who was minding her own business until you were put in a compromising position—as we all were—by coming across the tragic sight of a dead woman. Someone's trying to trick the police, and you need to let them know you expect them to get to the bottom of it soon." Katherine hoped her voice carried enough backbone to support the younger woman.

She needn't have bothered. Philippe wasn't in. The chief investigating officer was, they already knew, at the church. There was, the gendarme on duty at the window explained, no one available to see them. No, he had no idea where Madame's car was but since the incident had happened over the weekend and the experts who would do the detailed search for the evidence didn't work Sundays, and today was only Monday . . . He looked up at them through the window and shrugged. There was nothing to do but leave Pippa's name and promise to come back the next day. It was getting dark and Katherine wanted very much to be home.

This time, Jeannette was where she was supposed to be. Katherine shared her disappointment that the sweater she had hoped to get for Michael was already sold. "Probably best. The last time I saw him in a sweater, he was valiantly trying to get down a beginner ski slope in Aspen. I think sweaters bring back memories of his first and only time on the slopes."

Pippa sat staring out the window and chewing her thumbnail.

Jeannette was silent too, probably stumbling over too many unfamiliar vocabulary words in Katherine's story. It was almost dark when Katherine dropped both passengers off and entered her warm house, where music she recognized as a song from the new album was playing.

"How was it?" Michael said from behind his computer screen.

"Short, cold, and I could barely understand the speakers," Katherine said, shedding her coat and hat and swiveling back to the kitchen for her five o'clock wine. "You didn't miss anything except that I think I've come across the butcher's brother before and didn't realize it."

"Ummm," Michael said, a long-standing clue that his mind was otherwise occupied. He was staring at the screen and listening to the music coming from his computer, head cocked, his old stopwatch in his hand. "Damn, there it is." He pressed the button on the watch. Rising, he came over to make a mark on the sheet music propped up on the stand that had resumed its place of honor in the middle of the cramped living room the same day he got home from Memphis.

"Problem?"

"I hear an extra note coming from a backup guitar. It's filling what should be a silent beat."

"I didn't hear it."

"Yeah, well, you wouldn't. I have to email J.B. It's not hard for the engineer doing the mix to wipe it out."

"If it's that noticeable to you professionals, maybe they already have."

"Ummm," he said, back at his computer.

She wasn't upset, but it did annoy her the tiniest bit to be dismissed so quickly. After all, she did have ears. She did listen to music. She was her husband's staunchest supporter. Was this the new version of Michael, focused on something apart from their life together, paying her less attention? She got up and went to the kitchen, where a newly opened bottle of five-euro pinot beckoned, as did the need to introduce the carrots and potatoes to the plump chicken breasts so they could all cook gently in chicken stock, a bit of the wine, and a handful of tarragon she had dried from her jungle of an herb garden.

CHAPTER 26

From her perch on the ladder Michael had carried down to the church for her, Katherine squinted, then dabbed more blue paint onto Mary's robe. The painting of Madonna and Child she was trying to repair had been bolted in its frame to the wall, which was one reason it was in such bad shape. Moisture, heat and cold, dirt and crumbles of stone had rendered the original, amateur artist's work even less appealing than it must have been when it was new in the late nineteenth century. In the cold morning light, the Madonna looked thin and stressed, the baby uninterested, staring blankly away from his mother. No joy, no mystery, no magic. She would give the project another fifteen minutes, then move on to the stations of the cross, a series of faded pieces that were probably older, but no more masterpieces than the one she was working on.

"Jesus's face," someone said, and Katherine turned slightly, careful not to overbalance on the narrow step of the ladder. "Jesus looks like an old man."

It was Mme Pomfort, and with her, Mme Robilier, who

nodded vigorously. M. Robilier, wrapped up in a long coat, muffler, and knitted cap, looked up at her, a slight frown on his face. Everyone knew he had dementia and that his wife kept a close watch for fear he would wander off into the forests of the Morvan if left too long on his own. He smiled up at Katherine suddenly, and his smile reminded her of Jeannette's, a sudden ray of sunshine. She smiled back.

"I'm not sure what I can do about that unless I paint right over the original artist's work. I'm only touching up the color and bringing a few details into sharper focus."

"You may paint over that monstrosity. We want a baby Jesus without wrinkles and a long face."

"Yes, we do," Mme Robilier said, "*bien sûr.*"

It wasn't that Katherine didn't agree with them, but how was she supposed to get to all those stations and get done by lunchtime? One didn't just slap on a coat of paint and, voilà, a portrait of the savior of mankind appeared. "I'll see what I can do." Maybe the other pieces would have to wait until after Christmas. The stations of the cross were more of an Easter thing anyway, weren't they? "Have you seen Marie today? I haven't wanted to be a pest, but I thought she was due a couple of days ago."

"It's her first. She will be late," Mme Pomfort said, with authority.

"The baby Jesus?" M. Robilier said, entering the conversation from a different point on the compass.

"*Non, chéri,*" his wife said, shushing him with a firm pat on the hand. "I'll explain later." He nodded, looked into her eyes with that bland, innocent smile. Katherine thought there were many ways to be a loving couple.

Mme Pomfort announced that she had to freshen the paper wreaths for the *mairie*'s community room in preparation for the dinner, and the floor there needed a good scrubbing. "The *pétanque* group met there recently and they left muddy footprints everywhere. I really don't know why the mayor lets them use the room. A disgrace, really."

"They weren't playing the game in there, were they?" Katherine could imagine Emile trying to talk the mayor into letting the men use the room as an indoor court, but couldn't imagine the mayor agreeing. Of course, Emile might not have asked first. He took his role as president of the club seriously. The three or four farmers who played regularly were happy to let him take the lead on everything including maintaining the smooth sand surface of the court, preferring to simply show up on foot or in their battered cars on late afternoons when the weather was fine.

Mme Pomfort expressed the firm opinion that walking inside in muddy boots was as bad as rolling balls across the floor and that she intended to speak to the mayor's wife about banning the *pétanque* members from the building altogether. At that, Mme Robilier looked dubious, but held her tongue.

Katherine had turned back to the painting and was mixing colors for the baby's skin, wondering if the churchgoers in Reigny would appreciate a swarthy Jesus, or if she had better play it safe and give them a pink-cheeked cherub. When her cell phone rang, she jerked slightly. "Michael, you startled me. Is everything all right?"

"I wanted to give you a heads-up. A couple of cops came by looking for you. One spoke some English. I told them you were at the church. Hope that was okay. Want me to come down?"

Before she could answer, the police in question had come into the church vestibule, a paltry spot only separated from the small church proper by a half wall. Philippe and the captain who had interviewed them and who apparently suspected Pippa of being in love with the butcher. "They're here. All's well, sweetie, thanks. I intend to stay on my ladder."

Mme Pomfort sat down on a wooden bench with an audible thump. Katherine wondered if the police would be able to dislodge her without a direct order when it was obvious that something interesting might happen. M. Robilier looked uneasily from his wife to the uniformed Philippe and back at her again. He began to rock back and forth in agitation. Mme Robilier was clearly torn, wanting very much to hear what was happening, but feeling her husband's restlessness. True to her promise, Katherine remained on the ladder, paintbrush in hand, and said only, *"Bonjour, messieurs."*

The senior officer clasped his hands behind his back and cleared his throat, looking pointedly at the old woman dressed in black, seemingly attached to her seat. She sat staring back at him implacably, her lips pursed, her posture straight. Katherine turned back to the painting to hide a smile, applying a beige base coat to the oval of the baby's face, rounding it slightly so it looked less like that of an aggressive lawyer's she remembered from L.A. "Already better," she said under her breath.

The standoff below her continued and the policeman

blinked first. "Madame Goff, I thought you might know where your friend is, the Englishwoman? She's not in her house."

Katherine wanted to believe they were returning the car and not in Reigny to harass her again. "I don't. She hikes the area and, stuck without a car, I imagine that's what she's doing. It's a decent day for a walk."

"Have you seen her today?" It was Philippe speaking this time, and there was a worried note in his question.

"No," came the answer. Mme Pomfort had spoken before Katherine could, pleased to have an opportunity to inject herself into the importance of a gendarme inquiry.

"No," Katherine said, "but I don't see her every day, you know? It's only because she needs rides into Avallon while you have her car—" She stopped. If Mme Pomfort didn't know Pippa was a suspect in the murder, Katherine didn't want to let it slip.

The older woman's body twitched and she rotated her head between Katherine and the gendarmes, triumphant. This would be news worth having, whatever it was. Katherine hoped the police knew a busybody when they saw one, and that they would be more careful than she had been. Poor Pippa wouldn't last long in the shunning Mme Pomfort could orchestrate if it was known she was a suspect in a murder case.

"Have you brought back her car?" Katherine said, hoping her nosy neighbor would assume it had merely broken down somewhere.

"May we speak with you privately?" the older policeman said in French, looking up at Katherine and then down at Madame. Since Mme Robilier and her husband had slipped away as soon as the policemen planted themselves in the church's aisle, the implicit message could only be aimed at Reigny's leading citizen, and she didn't look as though she was going to go without a direct order.

Katherine wasn't going to budge either. "I'm in the middle of painting this and the pigment will get harder to manipulate if I stop now. And, anyway," she switched to French, "Jesus needs a face and I'm running out of time."

"Madame," the captain said, turning to the old woman. "We need the building. I must ask you—"

"I am late for the *mairie* as it is. You shouldn't have kept me here," Mme Pomfort said, "if you did not need me. Sometimes I wonder why we even have gendarmes if they cannot carry out their duties without inconveniencing people. Mme Goff, you may continue with the Madonna and Child." She swept out of the church, head high, her role as the unofficial art committee chair—and her dignity—intact.

Philippe went to close the heavy, battered door, and then came back. Katherine put the base coat on Jesus's hands and feet. The Madonna's makeover would have to wait for next year. She decided to come down off the ladder. Her feet hurt from standing on the narrow step, and her hands were cold.

She sat on the bench Madame had vacated and the captain came to stand in front of her. "We have brought her car back, although there are still questions. We hoped you might be able to clear a few things up."

"What can you still want to know that I can help with? I've told you I think it's impossible, stupid, really, to think of her as a possible murderer. She is, I admit, a bit clumsy explaining herself. She wishes she had more French. But she is a sincere person who only wants to be careful in her research, and I think she needs protecting right now rather than being badgered as a suspect. Someone is trying to frighten her and even to frame her. That seems obvious to me." Having said her piece, Katherine took a deep breath and waited.

The older policeman nodded at Philippe. The younger man looked so handsome in his blue bomber-style jacket and narrow trousers, standing at attention, that Katherine was reminded of an old World War II image of RAF pilots. No wonder Pippa stammered when she mentioned him, and blushed.

"We are coming to the same conclusion," he said in English. He must have been designated beforehand to interpret, which meant her own French wasn't anywhere near as good as she thought. "We cannot share details of our investigation, Madame, but *je vous assure,* our investigation is turning in different directions. However, we must speak to Mademoiselle Pip—your friend. It is essential that we ask her a few things that will help us go forward." He shot a look at his boss, who did not seem to have noticed the slip into Pippa's first name.

"Then I'm especially sorry I don't know where she is at the moment. I'm sure it will relieve her mind greatly. It certainly eases my concern. Will you leave the car at her house?"

"I myself will be waiting with the car for her return," Philippe said, straightening his shoulders and lifting his chin.

The captain grunted again and spoke rapidly to his junior officer. Philippe translated. "The captain wishes to know if you saw anything unusual when you were at the museum the day he came upon you?"

Suddenly, Katherine was on shaky ground. That was the day she found the scrap of paper, the clue she hadn't shared with the police. Both she and Pippa had made things more difficult for themselves by holding back their finds but, like Pippa, she couldn't see how to admit it without bringing down the wrath of the gendarmes. And, she argued with herself, who knew if it was evidence of anything? "Not that I can recall. There were bits of things all around, weren't there? Hard to know if anything had special meaning. By the time I entered the salon, the police had been through it more than once, Madame Roussel told me."

"You didn't see, for example, regular women's clothing?" Philippe said.

"No." Katherine was taken aback at her own stupidity. "Oh, of course. What could have happened to what she was wearing? I hadn't thought of that at all."

"It wasn't visible when you were there?"

"There wasn't anything more than some long gloves, I recall, shoes and odd bits, and everything was vintage. I'm curious. Can you tell me what you decided about the wig?" Katherine spoke in French, not ready to admit linguistic defeat, or how to communicate the planting of evidence versus what she knew better, the planting of roses.

Whatever he thought she meant, the senior policeman only said, "That is police business, Madame." He turned and spoke rapidly to Philippe, and the two thanked her and hurried out.

Odd, Katherine thought, slowly climbing back up the ladder. Good news that they didn't think Pippa was credible as a killer, but nothing to hint at what they had learned from the wig or the horrible defacing of Pippa's car. She was torn between a desire to know more and the shame of having deliberately held back information. Not lying, exactly, she told herself. If they had enough to point them in some other direction, they could hardly need her little religious tract, if that's what it was. She wished she could talk to Pippa but, having no idea where the writer had gone, and recalling Philippe's declaration that he was, in effect, staking out Pippa's house, she couldn't think of anything to do that would be more useful than giving the baby Jesus pink ears, a turned-up nose, and a smile she hoped wasn't insipid. A definitely European infant, undoubtedly what Mme Pomfort had in mind.

Later, over a cobbled-together lunch of leftovers, Katherine shared the good news with Michael.

"Wait. Someone thought she killed the butcher's wife? I thought she was the potential next victim."

"It's complicated."

"Yeah, I guess so," Michael said as he wiped his mouth and stood up. "The less I know, the better, I think. I'm headed over to Noyers to pick up the wood. Need anything?"

"Something nice from Millésimes? With the Sabines' shop closed, I don't know where else to go other than the *supermarché* in Auchan."

"I guess we can splurge a little with Christmas coming. The big chain doesn't have my sausages, anyway."

"Do you have to bring the wood back in the car? I was hoping your new friend would deliver it."

"He'll deliver the rest, but you may have noticed we're

about one fire away from freezing on the next cold night, which is six hours from now." He put on his Stetson and called to Fideaux, whose idea of Christmas and birthday wrapped up in one was to ride along in the front seat with the window open and his ears flapping in the breeze.

The house was quiet after Michael left and Katherine felt restless. She had done all the painting she was up to this morning in the church, although she would go back to look at it later to see if she'd made a mess of it. She picked up the costume book, but it couldn't hold her attention.

She knew what it was. The little piece of paper. Was it important, a clue the police should have? And the gold cross Pippa found? And, the big question, who were the police looking at? Maybe they had found fibers they could tie to someone else on the wig that someone had stuffed in Pippa's car. She picked up a sketchbook and on the back of a clumsy sketch of Jeannette's face, she began to write.

> *Mme Sabine's missing clothes*
> *The cross*
> *The mannequin in the river with no wig*
> *The wig in P's car*
> *The religious note*
> *The locks on the doors*
> *The trash pickup?*

The last item puzzled her. She could understand why the captain thought the path the trash men took was important, but, unless the killer lived in the house next door, not why he was so upset. Maybe they had found footprints or DNA on the gate, although from the little she had seen, she didn't think the local gendarmerie was anything close to the flashy CSI shows on American TV.

Actually, as she squinted at her list, everything puzzled her. She was glad that she had no pretentions as a crime writer because she would never get past chapter one. That reminded her of Pippa and Pippa's determination to make her own lists and solve the mystery à la Hercules Poirot's "little gray cells." She wondered if Pippa had gotten home by now. If she had, perhaps she and Philippe were having a romantic moment, so maybe Katherine shouldn't intrude. But if not, there was a lot to talk about. Michael wouldn't be home for an hour and she and Gracey could use a walk.

From the top of Pippa's driveway, she glimpsed the car, and Philippe leaning against it, smoking a cigarette and talking on his cell phone. Her watch marked midafternoon, so Pippa was still hiking. She'd better be on the way home. Clouds were massing again, and it was getting colder.

CHAPTER 27

Katherine and Gracey turned and headed back up the hill. On impulse, she ducked into the café, where the only occupants were the owner and a farmer in a shabby jacket, who was making an espresso last and telling a story that he illustrated with chopping motions. The café owner looked bored but laughed obediently now and then, all the time swiping a wet rag back and forth over the already clean counter.

Katherine picked up her *café crème* from the counter and sat by the window. There were no fresh-baked pastries, *désolé,* but the owner brought her a small plate of chocolate biscuits, compliments of the season, she thought he said. Her short time painting in the church had reminded her it was time to make career plans for the new year. She would visit the gallery in Vézelay that had given her a show last summer to see if they might be willing to look at new paintings. After all, they had sold a couple, so she was not a complete bust. She would read papers from other Burgundy towns of some size and make a list of galleries to call on.

Once Michael knew definitely about the tour, she would organize the household so she could come to a couple of venues midway through Michael's absence.

Briefly, she wondered about Eric, the charismatic leader of the Crazy Leopards, the lead guitarist of one of the most enduring bands, hardly an adult when they met and possessed of a huge ego and a mean streak. Michael's enemy for so long, now, supposedly, a friend again. How would she feel seeing him? If she had gray hair, so did he, and he might be married or at least settled down with someone. Maybe she'd search for him online as a way to prepare. It was only that she'd slept with him once, after Michael had proposed but before they were married. That, she told herself, was a bad case of pre-wedding jitters, fueled by too many tequilas, never repeated, never even wanted again. But still, a problem?

More realistic to worry about who'd take care of the dogs, she chided herself. Jeannette most likely. The girl was the only young person in town, poor thing. No wonder she was hanging around the bus stop with her age mates in the pouring rain, showing off by recounting her version of the murder in the museum. Katherine could picture the scene as she walked toward the group of teenagers, Jeannette's exaggerated response when she realized M. Sabine heard her tale, and the girls dislodging the man who had been sitting quietly in the bus shelter. Something tugged at her about the picture. Yes, that was it. The stranger in the bus shelter was the butcher's brother. So, they may both have heard the teenagers talking about Mme Sabine's death.

But what of it? Jeannette hadn't been harassed. There was no obvious connection between the girl and Pippa. Somewhere in all that she had seen and heard, Katherine was sure there was some clue as to why Pippa was so cruelly targeted, if only she could see it clearly.

Katherine warmed her hands on the coffee cup and looked out the window without seeing the bare trees and the tufts of brown grass alongside the pavement. There must be something. There was the captain's exclamation when he saw the trash truck in the alley. The fact that the trash made it to the street through a side door into the yard of the vacant house must have been the trigger for his outburst, but it hardly explained anything. The police must have asked Jeannette if there was anything incriminating in the trash can like the missing clothing or the wig. She had said she put the remnants of the ladies' party in the can Tuesday afternoon and hadn't been able to clean the murder room since then. The body was discovered Thursday.

That meant that anything thrown into the trash later on Tuesday would have been there until it was picked up a few days later. The police would have searched Thursday after the body was found. Katherine had a feeling she was close to understanding something important, but it was frustrating.

The café owner flicked on the lights. Her watch said it was not yet five o'clock but Katherine realized the winter solstice, the shortest day of the year, was only a few days ago. She put on her coat and roused the dog, who had fallen asleep under the table. Time to get home so Michael wouldn't fret. As she opened the door, a figure materialized.

"Jeannette, *bonjour*. Are you just getting home?"

The girl shook her hair free of a stocking cap. "*Oui*. Papa sent me here to see if they have a baguette." She poked her head in and repeated the request to the man behind the bar, but he shook his head. "It is my fault. I forgot to get one in Avallon after school." She looked unhappy.

"Those brothers of yours are growing so fast. They need all the food they can get." Katherine smiled. She admitted only to herself that she worried about them, living the unorganized life their father seemed to provide. "Tell you what. I have an extra loaf I got yesterday. Walk up with me and I'll give it to you, along with a little Brillat-Savarin to make it special."

Jeannette fell in beside her and Gracey, and Katherine was reminded of the summer days, so recently, when Jeannette would appear out of nowhere to link arms and accompany her on walks. Time passes so fast when they become teenagers, she thought.

"Jeannette, I think the police have someone in mind as a suspect and I bet the case will be solved soon. I'm trying to make sense of the bits and pieces I know about, like why the mannequin wound up in the Serein, and why the wig disappeared."

"I too have the puzzles," the girl said from behind the turned-up collar of her coat.

"Like what? I thought Pippa Hathaway and I were the only ones who kept poking at the mystery."

"Poking?"

They had reached Katherine's gate. Gracey, let off her leash once they were inside the garden, shambled up to the kitchen door. Lights shone from inside and the delicious smell of wood smoke perfumed the air.

But Jeannette stopped and pulled the cloth away from her mouth. "Katherine, can you tell me who was the man in the church sitting with the butcher?"

"His half brother, is what I heard. Mme Lacrois told me he lives in Beaune. Why do you ask?"

"He lives in Beaune? But that can't be. He works in Avallon."

Katherine opened the door and gestured for Jeannette to come in.

"That you, Kay?" Michael called. "You get a break from cooking tonight. I got something wonderful in Noyers."

"That's a first," Katherine said, laughing and unwrapping her scarf as she eased around the dog. She turned, expecting Jeannette to be right behind her, but the girl had stopped at the doorway. Michael was saying something, but Katherine turned back to Jeannette. "What were you asking?"

"*Rien*, nothing. I can talk with you tomorrow."

Michael's voice was louder now. "Kay, wait 'til you see what J.B. emailed me."

"In a minute," Katherine called out, and to Jeannette, who was backing toward the kitchen door, "Wait, the bread."

"*Merci*, Katherine," Jeannette said, taking the loaf and the slab of paper-wrapped cheese with a hasty kiss, closing the door behind her.

"Who was that?" Michael said, coming to stand in the kitchen doorway.

"Jeannette. I gave her the extra bread I had. They ran out at home and of course the café didn't have any."

"Watch out or you'll be feeding the whole family one of these days." He kissed her cheek to take the sting out of his words.

Katherine was about to say she had no intention of getting involved further with Jean's family when it hit her.

"Hold it," she said, and spun back to the kitchen door, darting out into the cold night air. "Jeannette, I need to ask you something." She hurried down the slate steps to find Jeannette at the open gate, looking up at her.

"Say again what you said. About M. Sabine's brother." A gust of wind struck the back of her neck and she shivered.

"He doesn't live in Beaune. He can't." Jeannette shrugged. "He's a garbageman. No one would drive from there to Avallon to work at the *poubelle*. It makes no sense."

"How do you know this? Please, it's important." Katherine's teeth had begun to chatter, either from the cold or from something like fear.

"I saw him at the museum. He took the trash away."

"I don't understand."

Jeannette shifted her weight from one foot to the other, tucked the bread under her arm, and pulled her collar higher against the wind that was gusting more now. "He come—came—through the side gate and takes the cans."

"Is there more than one trash can? I didn't realize that."

"No, only one from the museum and one from next door."

"Next door? Are you sure?"

The girl shrugged and hunched her shoulders against the cold.

"Did you tell the gendarmes about the man? This is important, *chérie*."

"I told them someone picks up the trash, yes, but I did not know it was this one."

"Okay, let me ask this. Has he been back this week?"

With a shift of weight from one leg to the other, Jeannette signaled her impatience. "I do not know. I do not see them most days, you know."

"What was he wearing?" Katherine saw that Jeannette was torn, wanting to get away from the interrogation, but curious too. "Please, tell me that and then you'd better get home."

Jeannette squeezed her eyes closed and said, "Nothing special. The vest, you know, the bright one they all wear? Maybe a cap, but it was quick. I am not usually there when they come and I did not hear the truck beyond the wall. It is too high to see. But he came again, not on the regular day. I saw him the day you found Mme Sabine."

"Still with the vest?"

"*Mais oui*, yes, otherwise I would not have known who he was."

"And where was he that day?"

"At the corner of the alley and the street, that is the only reason I saw him. You sent me to the patisserie up the street for madeleines, remember?"

"Was he lugging a trash can?"

"*Non.*" Jeannette looked at Katherine as though doubting her sanity. Katherine gritted her teeth and tried to stay calm. "They can't carry the cans far, only to put them on the truck that waits in the alley." She made a move to go through the gate.

"And did you see the truck?"

"No, it must have been on the next alley and he was behind in his work, you know?"

"Thank you, Jeannette, this was important and a big help. Go home and don't mention this to anyone, all right?

I'll explain later. Now, go." She made a shooing gesture that was somewhat jerky because she was now shivering, and ran back up the steps as the gate clanged behind the teenager.

"Michael," she said, trotting into the living room. "Listen, I know who killed Mme Sabine."

CHAPTER 28

"Quick, we need to find Pippa."

"Whoa," he said. "Slow down. Why are you even trying to figure it out? It's police business, remember?"

"No time to argue," she said, panting. "I swear, I know, and I don't think the police have the information."

"If you think you know something, call the police."

"It's not that simple. My French won't do it, and they don't like me there, anyway."

He opened his mouth, probably to ask why that might be, but Katherine was shrugging into her coat and digging gloves from its pockets. "I'm going to Pippa's even if you don't want to help. She needs to know this too since the killer was threatening her." She spun to the shelf where the car keys lay.

"Hold on. If you're going to do this, I'm coming with you. I don't know where the danger's coming from, but I don't like you anywhere near it. Pippa either. Turn off the stove first. Don't want the house to burn down while we're chasing after her."

He seemed to be moving like molasses on a cold day,

she thought as they went to the car. It couldn't have been more than three minutes before they got to Pippa's, but to Katherine it seemed forever. Philippe was gone. The house was still dark and when she knocked on the door, cats materialized from the darkness to crowd her on the step, meowing.

Katherine pulled out her cell phone and punched in Pippa's cell phone number. She knew the young woman hadn't bothered to get a land line. It rang five times, then Pippa's voice came on, cheerfully telling her to leave a message.

The car's headlights were on and the engine running. "Nothing?" Michael said, sliding out from behind the wheel and coming to the door. He banged harder on it, then put his ear to the wood. "Her car's not here. Maybe she's left for the holidays?"

"Don't be silly, she wouldn't do that without telling me. And she certainly wouldn't leave the cats out at night."

"Okay, then where else could she be?"

"I don't know," Katherine said in a voice that quickly became a wail. "I'm frightened, Michael, I really am. She's kind of clueless at times, and she's really naïve, but she's been focused on this murder for days and I'm afraid the man who did it thinks she's on to him. He might, I don't know, he might kill her."

"That's pretty extreme, Kay. Who is this guy anyway?"

"He—"

At that moment, another car turned into the driveway, partly concealed by the trees. Katherine felt a scream building inside her. That man, had he come to threaten her too? She shut her eyes and turned into Michael's protective arm. A pulse of light behind her closed eyes, what was that? A heart attack beginning? But wait. She opened one eye, peeking around Michael, who let her go suddenly.

"The cops. Good. You can tell them your story."

The blue light on the top of the gendarmes' car rotated as both doors opened. Philippe and his partner got out, right hands bent as though to be ready to draw their guns. Katherine realized that Michael was a stranger to them, a man in a big hat, and he was holding someone. She stepped around her husband and said, "I'm so glad you're here, Philippe. I'm Mme Goff, remember me? Please, you have to listen, and find my friend."

They let their arms fall to their sides and came closer. The woman gendarme flicked on a flashlight so powerful that it blinded Katherine when it shone on her face. Putting her hand over her eyes, she said, "This is my husband. We came down because I'm sure I know who killed Madame. Now I can't find Pippa and I'm frightened that he has done something awful to her." Her voice was high and pinched, and she had to work not to start crying.

"You haven't heard from her?" Philippe said.

"No, and she's not here."

"I waited until near the end of my shift," he said, "but she never returned. It didn't feel right. Marianne and I decided to come back tonight." He motioned for Michael and Katherine to move off the step, then banged hard on it with an open hand, shouting that it was the gendarmes. When he got no answer, he looked at his partner and pointed to the back of the house. She nodded. She pulled out a cell phone, spoke into it so quietly that Katherine couldn't pick up a word, then moved off into the darkness. "*Merde,*" came a low voice from the side of the building and a cat yowled and bounded back to the driveway.

Philippe motioned Katherine and Michael away from the front door and pantomimed for them to get in their car. Michael nodded and grabbed Katherine's arm. She twisted away from his grip. "But don't you want to know who the murderer is? I learned something tonight—"

Philippe spoke in a low voice, his head cocked. "We know who killed Madame. We know everything. Now, please move away." There was a soft whistle from behind the house. "Now. You must get back," he said, and Michael pulled her over to the car.

"In. They know what they're doing, Kay." He closed her door and was inside himself in an instant.

"Did you hear? They know who the killer is." Katherine's brain wasn't taking it all in. "But I have new information."

"Ssshh," Michael said as Philippe yelled again, and then drew his gun. Before Katherine could take in what was happening, he fired a shot at the lock, then kicked the door open. Cats streaked past the headlights and into the woods. Katherine would have liked to do the same.

"What's happening?" she said, as much to the universe as to Michael.

CHAPTER 29

Pippa concentrated on her breathing, trying to remember her yoga instructor's soothing voice. Slow, steady, not too deep because her mouth was covered and the only air she could get was through her nose. She was desperate to tear the wooly fabric from between her teeth, but he had grabbed the old jumper from the back of the chair and knotted one arm of it around her face as a gag when she began to shout. She tried not to think about the cat hairs and worse that were undoubtedly being sucked into her throat with every breath. Before being silenced, she had tried to find out what he wanted, but he spoke at high speed, entirely in French, and seemed close to hysteria. Important not to panic. The man pacing back and forth in front of her was panicked enough for both of them and he was doing all the talking. And crying now.

Pippa couldn't understand most of it. Occasionally, he would twist toward where she sat, one foot tied to the bed leg with her old tights, her hands pinned behind her with a rope he must have brought. He brandished the fireplace poker from downstairs now and then, although it was such a general motion that she thought he'd only hit her if he did it by accident. With his free hand, he rubbed his hair, wiped his eyes, and occasionally slapped his forehead. She bloody well understood that he was frightened, that he blamed her for something, and that he might at any moment, if he focused on her long enough, bash her with the fireplace tool.

Her eyes followed him around the perimeter of the room. Being an involuntary listener seemed to be the best option right now, but oh, how she wished someone would come and rescue her right this second.

He dragged over the only chair in the room to where she perched and sat abruptly. He said something at warp speed that sounded like a question. She looked at him and shrugged to show she didn't understand. She wondered if this was the same fail that plagued the Neanderthals when they came upon the species that would eventually wipe them out. Bloody, bloody hell, how was she supposed to reason with a lunatic when she had a gag in her mouth and no French even if he took it out?

As they stared at each other, Pippa accepted that she was looking into the face of a murderer. His skin was slick with sweat and mottled, his eyes were red, there was a little mucus coming out of one nostril. Something to think about for the book, a small part of her brain noted. If I live that long, she pointed out to herself.

"Understand, yes?" he said at last in heavily accented English.

All she could do was shake her head. No, she didn't understand anything. She had no effing idea what was happening, nothing since she had opened the door without checking first, so sure it was Katherine or Philippe, and this man had come barging in, scattering cats, slamming the door and pulling her up the stairs. She had flailed her arms in his direction and kicked at him, but he was strong.

"You come. No hurt," he had yelled.

"You're hurting me right now," she had shouted back.

At first, she had been sure he was going to kill her in spite of his words, but he seemed distracted by his thoughts.

"What is it you want? Aren't you the butcher's brother?" she had stammered. "You need to leave here at once."

He raised his arm and made a fist, and Pippa screamed. At that, he had grabbed her stupid jumper, which belonged in the dirty clothes hamper, if she was to be honest. When he was satisfied she couldn't move or speak, he slumped on the other edge of the bed for a few minutes, mumbling to himself. Her tights were stretchy and she had begun to wiggle her leg free. But he noticed and ran down the stairs, stomping heavily up again with the stupid poker and bottle of water that looked like what she kept in the refrigerator. As he swigged it and rubbed the plastic bottle against his forehead, he talked, calmly at first, almost as if he were explaining something to a friend. Then, his phone rang. All he said was, *"Non, non, non,"* a word she actually knew. After the call ended, he began pacing back and forth, seeming alternately to plead with her and to wave the poker at her.

Now, he said, "I go soon. You be okay, yes?"

Really? she wanted to answer. I am tied to a bed, can't talk, can hardly breathe, and you think I'm going to be all right? You think bloody Superman is going to fly through the window and rescue me after you toodle away? Not bloody likely.

"I go," he said again, nodding and pressing his hand against his forehead. "*Les flics,* they will come to you, yes?"

What a cock up, Pippa thought. He's counting on the police to come looking for me when they're more likely to come and arrest me. Although, she realized, even that would be a rescue of sorts. The trick was not to upset him, though, so she nodded and tried to smile under the gag.

He leaned so far in to her that his nose almost touched her cheek. Breathe, breathe, she reminded herself. If I'm calm, maybe he'll see I'm no threat. "I no do it," he said, his words slow but strong. "You understand, I no do it."

Bollocks, she thought, but she nodded. What else could she do? Of course he did the murder. Why else would he be here, threatening her and acting like a crazy man? Too bad she couldn't ask him why.

Quiet descended on the old house for a moment, broken only by the sharp meow of a cat coming from somewhere outside. Poor things, Pippa thought. What will happen to them if I don't get out of this alive? The thought, which she'd been avoiding, made her gasp for air, yoga techniques forgotten. The man jumped up and would have spoken if there had not been a loud noise like a firecracker, sounding like it was right in the room with them. Before she could recover from the shock of the sound, Superman appeared in the doorway, gun held steady in front of him, eyes on her captor, who crumpled to the floor, yelling and weeping, his hands covering his head.

Philippe had arrived.

CHAPTER 30

"He's good with a gun," Michael said, "and I think the cavalry have arrived."

Katherine followed his glance in the rearview mirror and, sure enough, there were flashing blue lights and headlights and, soon, a handful of men in bulky black outfits moving quickly and silently down the driveway, guns pointing at the house. Katherine gasped when one of them pulled her car door open. "*Vite, vite,*" a woman's voice said, and almost dragged her from the car. She looked at Michael for help, but he was already out of the car. One of the gendarmes marched them up the driveway and onto the street, where the captain who had interviewed her and Pippa was standing next to an unmarked car.

"What's happening?" Katherine said, going up to him. "Is Pippa all right?"

He held up a finger but said nothing, listening instead to his cell phone.

There were shouts and slamming noises coming from Pippa's house, and the closer sound of static and garbled speech. The captain barked something into his phone and

walked away from Katherine. Their minder indicated a police car that was vacant, its rear doors open. *"Ici, s'il vous
plaît."*

"Come on, Kay," Michael said in a gentler tone than she
was used to. "You've done all you can. We have to stay out
of the way. If Pippa's in danger, they'll find her."

"Danger? Oh, Michael, you don't think she's in there, do
you? If she were, wouldn't she answer the door, or yell or
something? Unless . . . oh, Michael, you don't think she's
dead, do you?" And, to her shame, she began to cry.

She heard loud, hiccupping sounds coming from her
own mouth, and she put her head between her knees to
drown out the sound. This was the worst, the very worst
thing that had ever happened. She couldn't seem to stop
crying. There was shouting outside the police car, running
feet, and into every corner those rotating blue lights that un-
nerved her. She put her hands over her ears, ignoring Michael's murmured comfort. Her nose was running and her
hair had fallen in her face. Pippa, the silly, sweet woman,
gawky and shy, and so determined to do the right thing. Why
hadn't she insisted Pippa leave this dangerous business
alone?

"You must let me see her." A plaintive voice, cracked but
familiar. "I say, Katherine, it's all right, truly."

Katherine pulled herself into a sitting position and,
looking through her tears and the strands of loose hair that
half-covered her face, she saw, of all people, Pippa. Philippe
and his partner were holding her up, one on each side, and
Philippe was looking into her face, his eyebrows drawn into
a single line of worry. Pippa's mouth looked raw and she
stumbled as she approached the open door of the police car.

Katherine tried to wipe her face with the sleeve of her coat, and she managed to say, "Is that you? You're alive?" before crying again, this time with relief.

"She will be all right," Philippe said, his own voice gruff with what Katherine felt was emotion. And Marianne, on Pippa's other side, said, "She is one—how do you say—the very brave?" Then, they bore her off to an ambulance that stood at the end of the line of police cars.

"What happened to her?" Katherine was suddenly so tired she could hardly hold up her head. She wanted to know everything, but couldn't form words. Michael, who had gotten out and come around to her side and was squatting next to her open car door, patting her awkwardly, said, "Someone was holding her, but he didn't hurt her. See? There he is."

Katherine stood up, leaning on the car door for support. Michael pointed in the direction of a small knot of policemen holding a man. Yes, it was the butcher's brother. "I was right," she said, but her words were slurred and it was doubtful even Michael heard them.

"Sweetheart, you've had a rotten night. Pippa's all right and the police say there's no danger. Someone told me they have the killer in custody in Avallon. But they're taking Pippa to the clinic in Auchan to watch her overnight. She had quite a shock. You need some looking after yourself. Let's go home."

"But, no, I need to talk to the captain," she said, pulling her arm away from his hand.

"Tomorrow, Kay. They have this under control. You need quiet, and maybe a glass of wine."

Because their car was parked in by at least four others, a gendarme offered to lock it in place for the night and ferry them home. Katherine was only dimly aware of the activity around her, but how could it be that police didn't realize who the killer was? And, something was bothering her. "The cats," she said out loud to no one and anyone who would listen. "Pippa's cats."

The gendarme sat her gently in the backseat of his car. *"Les chats? Oui, Madame.* Your friend said the same thing. Someone will feed them, although they cannot go in the house until our investigation is complete."

"Oh," she murmured, "I'm not sure . . ."

"Honey," Michael said, "I'll bet you a silver dollar they'll sleep under our car tonight. Safe, dry, and the engine is still warm. We have you to take care of and you'll need more than a warm engine tonight. I think you're in shock."

Later, after she had taken a hot shower, he tucked her under two duvets, with a cup of sugared tea and a small glass of bourbon. She felt sleepy, but whenever she dozed off some unnamed fright woke her up with a start. "She's really all right?" she said more than once.

"She is. Remember, the cop who drove us home said she was tied to a bedpost, a cloth gag in her mouth, and her hands were bound? But she wasn't hurt."

"She must have been terrified."

"He says she told the police that she was more frustrated than frightened. The man who tied her up apparently talked nonstop, but in French, for hours. She thinks he wanted her to know all he needed was a little time to get away."

At that point, she had faded away, but a few minutes later, she jerked awake again. "But the murderer is out there somewhere. We have to tell Jean so he can protect Jeannette. She knew something too."

"No, sweetheart. Remember, I told you the bad guy is in custody. The guy in Pippa's house is his brother."

"Yes, I knew that. That's what I figured out tonight from what Jeannette remembered."

"You knew that the butcher killed his wife?"

"What? No, it was his brother."

"I don't think so, although you know my French isn't any better than Pippa's. But we'll find out more tomorrow. You know, you're not such a bad detective, figuring out that something was wrong at Pippa's house. But please don't take that as my blessing to get yourself in a situation like this again, you hear?"

"Ummm," she said, drifting off again. Had he put something in her tea?

The next time she woke up, the house was dark. Michael was in bed with her, his arm around her, and there was something pressing against her knee. Raising her head a bit, she saw the yellow cat curled up there. When Katherine moved, the cat opened its eyes, stared meaningfully at her as cats do, to say she should not move. "All right," Katherine said. It was an honor, really, the yellow cat coming onto the bed for the first time to guard her. She smiled in the dark. "Thank you."

CHAPTER 31

When she opened her eyes, the smell of coffee was strong. Michael, already dressed, was standing in the doorway with two steaming cups. "Ready to face the world?"

"I guess so," she said, smiling sheepishly as she held out her hand. "Did I make a fool of myself?"

"Compared to when you insisted on tap dancing on Richard and Mickey's coffee table at the party in L.A.? Not so much." He grinned, but she noticed the dark circles under his eyes.

"I'm sorry if I scared you."

"Don't be. If the butcher hadn't been eaten up by guilt and confessed everything when the police brought him in, they wouldn't have known about the brother, and he'd be on the loose. Then, you would have been Miss Marple, saving the day." He grinned and sat on the bed to kiss her.

"I'm nowhere near as old as Miss Marple, thank you. But I'm confused. Didn't his brother do it? Please, what actually happened?"

"They didn't tell me, sweetheart, only that both men are locked up tight. I called the clinic and managed to make myself clear enough that they put me through to Pippa. She says to tell you she's really sorry she scared you, and that Philippe will bring her home later today."

"She has nothing to be sorry about. She could have been killed, for heaven's sake. You know, Michael, I really like her. She hasn't got the sense of a toddler at times, but she's good-hearted and, who knows, maybe this mystery writing will take off? She's determined when something excites her."

"As are you. Which reminds me, you had a caller earlier. The local witch came to find out how you were and to tell you that the young couple, well, the wife anyway, is in labor."

Katherine threw off the covers. "Marie's having the baby? I need to get dressed and go down to their house."

"Why? She's going to have that baby even if you're not there. Besides, I think the old dragon said she's in the hospital. You need to start slowly, Kay. Look at your face. You look like you've been through a war."

Katherine wondered if, given his description, she wanted to see herself, so she sat on the edge of her bed, drank her *café crème*, and made a plan for the day. Cold water compresses for her eyes first. Then, she'd call the gendarmerie and ask to speak with Philippe. Since she didn't know his last name, that might be hard. Perhaps his partner then, Marianne. There couldn't be too many Mariannes at the police station in Avallon.

She had to struggle for a moment to remember what day it was. Wednesday. Jeannette would be in school, so talking with her would have to wait. The two boys would be also, which meant Jean might be out making a living in a way she wouldn't look at closely unless Michael's new wheelbarrow went missing.

She'd leave a message for Pippa to call her when she got home, probably after checking on her cats. She felt guilty for not pulling herself together last night. She could have done something for the poor, frightened creatures. That reminded her. "Sweetheart," she called. "Have you gotten our car back yet?"

"I thought I'd walk down there now and check. You stay here. You need to rest, Kay, and I don't want to see you getting all lathered up for a while."

"Check under the car and under the hood before you start it up." She had to raise her voice to be sure he heard her downstairs.

"Yes, ma'am."

She heard the sharp knock at the front door, but not more than some murmuring until Michael's voice said, "Wait there and I'll ask her." He bounded up the stairs, his cowboy boots hitting the steps in a rapid beat. "It's against my better judgment, but there's a reporter outside who wants to talk to you about what happened."

"How could that be? I was just a weeping wreck off to the sidelines. Who could have sent him here?"

"Her, and she told me. In English, by the way. I'll give the French this. They're a lot better at learning my language than I am at learning theirs. It was your biggest fan, the queen of the village, Mme Pompadour, who sent the newspaper person your way."

"Mme Pomfort? How on earth . . . ?"

"She who knows everything. Want me to send the reporter away?"

"Yes, I think you'd better. The police need to be the ones talking about the crime. Pippa and I weren't exactly official." She looked up and smiled. "Okay, we were being nosy. But I'm not going to let the reporter see that. Please tell her I can't help her."

In the end, she didn't have to call the police station. Pippa knocked on the door not long after she had made the best of her face, using more makeup than usual to take attention away from her red-rimmed eyes, and come downstairs. Michael had checked to see that she was okay being on her own for a few minutes, then left to pick up the car and had bumped into Pippa and Philippe on their way up to the Goffs'.

Pippa's mouth was bruised and she kept rubbing her chafed wrists, but she swore she was all right. "I was scared at first, but I could see he was in worse shape than me. I think the stupid bloke hadn't thought anything out before he agreed to his brother's demands."

"Demands? Can you say anything?" Katherine had turned to Philippe after giving them coffee.

He blushed and said, "I should not share police information, but since you have been so involved . . ." His voice trailed off and he looked earnest, and somewhat conflicted, Katherine thought. "But Pippa already knows some of it from Marcel."

"We never could have guessed," Pippa said. "Philippe says Mme Sabine had been giving away the money they had saved for retirement—"

"—the little house in Provence. I remember hearing how passionately he looked forward to it," Katherine said.

"Yes, I guess that was it. Anyway, there was this priest

in Beaune who convinced her to keep giving more and more for his work in—"

"—Africa. Oh, why didn't I pay more attention?" Katherine said, jumping up and handing Philippe the piece of paper she had put in a drawer in Michael's desk for safe-keeping.

"What's this?" he said, then read it carefully. "Where did you find it? Is it related to this case?"

"In the salon where it happened, but long after the gendarmes had finished their searches. Yes, I think so, although I wasn't sure how. I'll explain later, but first, please tell me what you can."

Pippa gave her a look. "Maybe you should finish," she said.

"No, no, please. It's only now that you're describing what happened that it's dawning on me that all the pieces were there. Please, tell me." Katherine sat back down and leaned forward.

"Well, Marcel—that's the brother's name—was pacing back and forth, after he had gagged me so I couldn't ask him to let the cats in even if he didn't want to feed them—"

This time, she was interrupted by a gargling sound from Philippe.

"I say, I don't have to continue if neither of you wants to hear from the person who spoke directly to the accomplice." Pippa's cheeks were bright, and her eyes were glistening with tears.

"I do, I do," Katherine said, reaching out and pressing the young woman's hand. "Accomplice, not the person who actually did it?"

Haltingly, awkwardly, occasionally interrupting each

other or both going silent at the same time, Philippe and Pippa filled in the details they knew. M. Sabine had found out that his wife was "a saint" for her charity from someone else during the church ladies' party at the museum. After the others left, he had cornered his wife in the salon and demanded to know what she had done. She had told him how much more important God—or maybe it was Africa—was than his fantasy about living in Provence. To his shock, she had admitted their retirement savings account was mostly gone.

Marcel told the police what he had probably confessed to Pippa in his panic, that his half brother had strangled Mme Sabine in a blind rage when she admitted what she had done, and, afterward, enlisted Marcel's help covering it up.

"He told me he didn't do it," Pippa said. "He said it in English. He was falling apart. He seemed like a weak man, to tell you the truth, and I wonder if he got bossed around by his older brother."

"Me, I think M. Sabine thought no one would ever suspect his brother, since he lived in Beaune and had a different last name, so it was all right to have Marcel working to cover his brother's tracks. No one here knew Marcel, or even knew he existed," Philippe said.

"Except Josephine Lacrois," Katherine said. "She dated him in Beaune, but she didn't realize the man paying such flattering attention to her was related to the woman she knew only from her trips down to the church there."

"She may have known," Philippe said. "We will talk with her, to be sure."

"If she had known," Pippa said, "she might not have

wanted a boyfriend whose brother was a butcher. She seemed a right snob to me."

"So many small things and that is how we usually catch our villains," Philippe said. Katherine noticed he was sitting closer to Pippa than the chaise longue they were sharing required. "What we didn't understand until Marianne interviewed Jeannette and Mme Roussel a second time the other day was that whoever committed the crime made use of the empty house next to the museum. My boss realized how possible it was when he saw the man from the *poubelle* using the neighbor's gate and realized he was emptying a trash can from that spot even though no one was resident there."

"Aha, so that's what excited the captain that day, when we both stood at the window," Katherine said. "Why didn't I figure that out?"

"Yes," Philippe said, "that is the container the victim's clothes were stashed in and where Marcel took the mannequin until he could get it away. He now says he thought it had his brother's fingerprints on it, which is why he dumped it in the river a few kilometers above where it washed up."

"Do you know why they dressed poor Madame like that and left her there?"

"I am guessing that the butcher realized he had to get out of the museum quickly and there was no place to hide Madame's body. We will find out more as the interviews progress."

"But how did he get out? Dear Mme Roussel is a tiger with those locks of hers," Katherine said.

"Pippa knows," Philippe said and looked at her with pride. "She told us last night at the hospital when the boss went in to see if she understood any of Marcel's ravings."

Pippa squirmed. "I meant to tell you, Katherine, but we kept getting interrupted by other things. The time her daughter took me upstairs, she told me her mother's arrangement was so clumsy, having to do and undo all the locks, and wasn't really necessary. Her mother's hearing isn't great, so if she went into the apartment to use the loo, or to warm her hands at the heater, Josée would sometimes only close one deadbolt, the easiest one."

"He went out the door, as simple as that?"

"Sometimes the simplest answer is the right one, *n'est-ce pas*?" Philippe said. "We learned that in training."

Pippa looked at him with what Katherine could only call adoration, forgetting that she had a cup of coffee in her hands. As it tipped and coffee spilled onto her lap, Philippe made a sound, and righted it for her. Pippa stammered, tried to stand, and almost tripped over the small white dog that had been listening from under the table, or appeared to be listening, his head swiveling from one speaker to another. Philippe handed her a towel, or what he thought was a towel but was really a scrap of fabric Katherine had wanted to use for a pillow, then grinned at Katherine and rolled his eyes.

"See, it is nothing," he said, bending toward the young woman and patting her hand. "Anyone could do that. Your mind, it is on the bigger things, yes?" Pippa turned scarlet.

"And the wig in Pippa's car?" Katherine said, determined to hear the entire mystery explained even at the sacrifice of this unusual courtship.

Pippa sat up straight. "I thought he said something about it. *'Toupee'* is wig, right? He seemed to be apologizing, by his gesture. But . . ." Pippa lifted her hands in confusion.

Philippe kept his eyes on her hand and on the cup and when he seemed satisfied nothing was about to move, he spoke. "The boss interviewed him last night and I was present to take notes. Marcel said he found it in his car after dumping the mannequin and didn't know what to do with it. Later, he decided to put it in your car to implicate you. But that was a stupid mistake. He brushed it with his coat sleeve and left so many fibers that he would have been better off depositing it in the trash anywhere in Avallon."

"But I still don't understand how you came to suspect him enough to make those coat fibers useful."

"Oh, we suspected the husband from the start. A crime of passion, *mais oui*? It is traditional."

So French, Katherine thought.

"His alibi was only a friend with whom he played cards, yes? He named this man, but never said he was related to him. In any case, that meant we had to suspect that person as well. We watched them, and soon we realized they were not casual friends. They did not share the same surname, but it was not difficult to discover Marcel's blood connection to the murderer when we checked his background, and so we collected the evidence, bit by bit. We will continue until the case is proven beyond any doubt, *je vous assure*."

"Then why did you investigate me?" Pippa said, saying precisely what Katherine wanted to ask.

Philippe looked sheepish. "My boss thought you might be having the affair with the butcher. I did not, but there you were, wherever something was happening. Marianne was suspicious at first, but she decided you were only a silly foreigner. I agreed—not that you were silly—," he added after catching her look, "but that you had nothing to do with it.

After all, you told us from the start you composed *la littéra-ture de gare,* the crime fiction."

"Well, I guess that's something," Pippa said a little uncertainly.

"*Oui, oui,* I read mysteries all the time. Maigret, Fred Vargas, Japrisot. I am impressed to meet a British author." He beamed at her. She beamed at him. They were both blushing now.

"I'll make more coffee," Katherine said, looking from one to the other, "and then you can tell me the rest."

The rest was simple except that the gendarmes watching him lost Marcel. A car crash on the A6 diverted the team following him long enough for Marcel to come back to Pippa's house, which he had scouted before. The plan was to keep her from sharing anything she knew with the police, then anonymously frighten Jeannette into silence before the butcher and his brother vanished to Belgium, where they had relatives. M. Sabine was captured as he loaded his suitcase into his car and crumbled within minutes at the station.

Marcel had been hanging around the bus stop in Aval-lon, planning to slip a threatening note into Jeannette's backpack, when he saw four gendarmes banging on the door to the apartment and fled, landing without too much thought at Pippa's house to complete his job of silencing her long enough to flee the country.

"After a bit, I didn't think he would kill me. He was al-most as frightened as I was," Pippa said. "But it was scary anyway."

"They were amateurs," Philippe said, with the naïve dis-dain of a rookie cop, which made Katherine smile inwardly. "When Marcel went back dressed as a garbage collector to retrieve the things in the vacant house can, he realized the girl probably saw him. She will be an important witness," Philippe said.

"Will she be in any danger?" Katherine said.

"No, the two men are the only criminals who were involved and they cannot escape the law, not with the butcher's confession and what Marcel told Pip—" He gulped and reached for his coffee cup.

"It's all right to call me by my first name, you know," she said, the pink spots returning to her cheeks. "Anyway, they were eaten up by guilt, wouldn't you say? Strong stuff to remember for my mystery stories."

"Too real for me," Katherine said. "I thought they had killed you too. I was sick with fear. Mme Sabine came alive for me, ironically, because I felt the fact of her death deeply in that moment."

"I didn't help her though. I missed all the clues," Pippa said.

"Not really. You always said you suspected M. Sabine. You knew the missing wig would be important. Oh," Katherine said, "what about the c—"

Pippa made a face again. "It's okay. I told Philippe about the cross last night. Another stupid mistake on my part."

Katherine looked from one to the other.

"It had no bearing," Philippe said. "Mme Sabine's religious jewelry was still on her dresser in a little box. We called the *mairie* in L'Isle-sur-Serein and a resident there had posted a note saying she lost it."

"Last summer," Pippa said, sighing.

"The good news is, unlike me, you weren't holding back evidence. Philippe, I apologize. I kept meaning to turn that paper over but the longer I held on to it, the more embarrassed I was."

He looked at her with a stern expression he had probably practiced as a police cadet. "Any fingerprints are compromised. What is done is done and we have our man, or men, I should say."

"And well done, you," Pippa said to Katherine. "You came to find me and figured out something was wrong."

"The cats," Katherine said with a shrug. "I knew you wouldn't leave them out after dark."

No more, she thought as she buttered a piece of bread after the two had left. No more of this. I'm a painter, a middle-aged woman who wants nothing more than to lead a quiet life in a small town in Burgundy with my dear husband to take care of me. When the phone rang, she hesitated in case it was the reporter again, but picked it up on the third ring. *"Bonjour, Madame Goff ici."*

"Madame Goff, huh? Wife of the famous Mike Goff, the man of the year?"

It couldn't be. The voice shocked her. It was the same, but bolder if that was possible, as though he expected an audience was listening. She cleared her throat. "Eric?"

"Well, sure, baby, who else? How are you? As beautiful as ever, I'll bet. Mike is one lucky guy. Listen, I'd talk, but I'm meeting people in ten minutes. Is the man around?"

She had to work to keep her tone cool. "Eric. I'm sorry, he's out but he'll be back soon. Can he call you?"

"Milkin' the cows?" His laugh rattled over the distance and through the cell towers from one continent to the other.

"We don't have cows." She didn't think it would be a

great idea to tell him about the murder first thing after not talking to him for how many years was it?

"No? Well, I do, believe it or not. Small ranch in Idaho, beautiful spot I never get to see. Look, tell him to give me a buzz on the cell. I just want him to know my guys signed the contract and if he does, we're on, baby, for a helluva tour. Kisses to you, honey. See you next year."

She was sitting there, bread in one hand, phone in the other, when Michael came in and tossed the car keys on the top of the shelf. "That's that. Only one cop car there and they had no problem with me taking ours. Cats all accounted for, fed and back at their posts." He stopped. "Kay, what's up? Nothing new is wrong, is it?"

She shook herself, smiled weakly, and said, "Looks like you're in business. Eric called to say they've signed the contract. The tour's on."

CHAPTER 32

Of course the church was cold, but the clamminess had been offset by a space heater borrowed from old man Lacrois and lugged across the street by a much subdued Josephine Lacrois, whose face was puffy and who did not look at anyone directly. The extension cord snaked up the short center aisle to the side door. If she had followed the trail, Katherine would have found herself on the hard-packed ground, standing next to a small generator, lent by the mayor from one of his many businesses. It made some noise but the old people who made up most of the one-day congregation didn't mind.

Marie and Raoul were sitting as close to the heater as they could, baby Juliette swaddled and cozy in a knitted cap Mme Robilier had presented that morning. "Our Christmas present," she explained to Katherine as the two women stood smiling down at the tiny face. "I mean Juliette is the present. To us all."

Jeannette's brothers were fascinated, reaching out to touch the infant's cheeks. This morning, while she was scraping the baby Jesus's face paint off her palette, she had come up with an idea. Remembering those boys sitting in front of a blaring TV, she decided they could use a little attention. Maybe art lessons down by the river next summer? With lunch as an incentive? Surely, she could do that without taking on any responsibility for their welfare. After all, everyone should be exposed to art.

"Don't," Jeannette said, reaching out to slap her brothers' jacket sleeves. "You'll scratch her, and your hands are dirty."

"It's fine," Marie said, "really, she's not made of glass. You'll find that out when you start helping me care for her, *cherie*."

"She's almost four kilograms," Raoul said, beaming. "A strong *petite femme* already."

"You'd think he had the baby," Marie's mother said to Katherine, lowering her voice and chuckling. "Truth is, he thinks that baby is as delicate as the most fragile piece of porcelain ever produced. I don't think he's slept in two days. It's as if he thinks she'll vanish if he takes his eyes off her."

"Isn't that the way?" Mme Pomfort said. "Men, what do they know?"

Katherine had walked over to Château de Bellegarde to invite her old friend Adele, and Sophie and Yves, to join the carol singing and the potluck at the *mairie,* but they had gone. The housekeeper was locking up until New Year's Day, she explained, because the Bellegardes and M. Yves Saverin had decided to spend Christmas in Paris and then stop to pay their respects to Albert in the family's chapel in Nemours.

The sounds of two guitars began the melody of a favorite French carol, and people hurried to take their seats. Voices, some not too steady, some off-key, came together. *"Petit papa*

Noël," they sang. There was a sharp twang from one guitar and Katherine winced. Emile had convinced Michael to perform a duet.

"Heck, it's his town and it's only for one day. Life is too good for me to act like Scrooge," Michael had said, grinning at her, an unlit cigarillo rolling around between his teeth and his Stetson perched far back on his head.

It was too bad that Pippa wasn't here, but she was undoubtedly basking in the comfort of being with her father after her ordeal, eating Punjabi takeout and shepherd's pie. Basking, too, from the attentions of Philippe, which went far beyond what his boss required to clear up the last bits of the investigation. It was kind of cute that he was as charmed by her tendency to trip and knock over things in her orbit as he was impressed by her standing as a writer of crime fiction à la his favorite Maigret.

Katherine had been surprised and pleased to get a note from Cat, the American nurse who had helped during the moment of deepest crisis in the museum visit. The note came courtesy of Reigny's mayor, who walked over to the Goffs' house with an envelope one morning. *"Wasn't sure of your address, but knowing these small towns, I am betting your mairie will forward this to you. Sorry I couldn't get back down, but I hope I might visit the next time I'm in France. Maybe a day's wine tour? You live in the heart of great vintages. And I'll keep a lookout for your husband's tour. I did wonder how the mystery at the museum turned out. Do write and tell me. Happy new year!"* Yes, thought Katherine, she hoped so too. It would be fun to spend time with an American, someone her own age who loved Burgundy as much as Katherine had come to love it.

The newly painted Jesus looked in his mother's direction,

probably wondering why she looked so grouchy. Mme Pomfort had approved her repainting the faces so they looked less like figures from Grimms' Fairy Tales, and Katherine would get to work on that unhappy face in the new year, so that mother and child were in sync. As she gazed up, considering what color blue the virgin's dress should be, one voice in the church began to sing a different carol entirely. Katherine recognized it as the befuddled M. Robilier. His voice was unexpectedly sweet, joyful, and why not? Reigny-sur-Canne had a new life to celebrate, and the winter solstice had passed. The days would get longer, and spring would come again, hallelujah.